ALSO BY KATT ROSE

THE LOSS
A FATHER'S DAUGHTER
FORGET ME NOT (Coming Soon)

BUILDING IT *Up*

KATT ROSE

Country Roads Publishing
Vancouver Island

ISBN-13: 978-1-9993994-2-9
BUILDING IT UP
Copyright © 2019 by Katt Rose

This is a work of fiction. Names, characters, places and incidents are either the product of the author's imagination or are used fictitiously, and any resemblance to actual persons, living or dead, business establishments, events or locales is entirely coincidental.

Country Roads Publishing are trademarks used under license and registered in Nanaimo, Vancouver Island, Canada.
www.countryroadspublishing.net

Cover design by BespokeBookCovers.com
Formatting by Polgarus Studio
Author Photo taken by Kyle Trienke

Chapter 1

Autumn

Often times, it's the little scattered pieces in life that add up to lead to monumental changes. One small step can take you down a road you never would've seen coming. Autumn Miller was about to discover what may have seemed like such an insignificant decision was about to have a huge impact on her world. The balance would be forever shifted. They say people come into your life for a reason. Whether they choose to stay, or leave, they always leave a mark. Some more than others.

⌘

I held my breath as I punched in my pin number; I didn't want to see my balance, or lack thereof. I tapped my dark polished nails impatiently and waited for the overused machine to spit back my card with the statement. And there it was. I ripped it from the machine and gingerly looked down at the small print, $310. Not too bad, but it wasn't great either. Only three more days until my next paycheck.

I took my time ambling around the parking lot until my eyes landed upon my beat up '79 Bronco. It used to be a dark, steel blue, shiny and sleek as a polished sports car. The weather had taken its toll on the exterior, the paint had begun to fade and chip off into barely existent paper thin scraps. Rust spots were beginning to spread, but the engine was still good…if the weather agreed with it. My Bronco didn't like damp days, or the rain. It took a few good pumps of the gas pedal and lots of patience to get it started. Once up and running, I couldn't let it idle, not until it had at least one good run on the highway to really warm up, or else it would stall. I often found myself driving with two feet, one on the brake, the other lightly on the gas to give 'er some juice. My Bronco's moods suited me just fine; it was moody, temperamental, often unpredictable…just like me.

I reached for the door handle, wincing as the heat from the metal burned into my delicate skin. I pressed the knob and yanked as hard, and as fast, as I could. The door didn't budge. I braced my hand again against the burning sensation as I gripped harder onto the handle and yanked. Nothing. I jabbed my hip into the door with a solid force and pulled the handle in one swift, well practiced motion. I smiled in triumph as the door clicked open. I jumped onto the worn leather seat, and rolled down the window. I turned the key and smiled as the Bronco roared to life, knowing it wouldn't give me any trouble today. Summer was in full swing, the weather warm and dry, a perfect combination for the finicky beast.

I switched on the radio and focused on the soaring guitar and loud drums to keep my mind distracted as I drove to work. Today was finally my last day as a waitress. I would no longer have to wait on customers and smile through cheesy lines in hopes of a decent tip. All of that would end officially at 5:00 p.m. It hadn't been an easy choice, but I decided it was time to bite the bullet and go back to school. I had always been a bright student, learning things came easily; but I was also a free spirit. I didn't like to sit still very long and often had trouble settling on one particular idea. I wasn't entirely sure school was the right choice, but what else was there? I had been saving up the past few years, and school seemed like the natural next move. I pulled into a vacant spot and entered the small restaurant, tossing my wind tangled chocolate hair into a loose ponytail.

"Autumn! You're late!" Kendra tsked as she hustled past, balancing plates.

I stole a quick glance at the clock. "Only by five minutes."

Kendra tucked a lock red hair behind her ear. "We're swamped, can you please grab table six? I'm dying here."

"Sure thing." I gave one last secure tug of my apron and strode to the table to take their order. The day was chaos and we were short staffed. A few of the unreliable waitresses had called in sick, which was no surprise. When the weather turned warm and bright the staff seemed to drop like flies. I waited impatiently for my orders to be filled from the kitchen. I glanced at a section of my tables, sensing the impatience dripping off one table in particular.

"Orders up!"

I jumped in eagerness and filled my arms with the plates and hurried towards the restless table. "Here you are." I set the food in front of a couple and their two younger children. "Sorry about the wait, we're a little short staffed today."

A heavyset man grumbled. "That's not my problem."

A twinge of anger sparked at his demeaning tone. "No, sir, I guess it's not. Can I get you anything else?" My tone dripped in forced politeness.

"We will holler if we need you. I think you've done enough for now."

I clenched my fists together and smiled through gritted teeth. I twirled away and forced myself to take deep, calming breaths. *It's my last day. It's my last day. It's my last day.* I clung on to the thought for dear life.

I leaned against the counter and let out a frustrated sigh. Kendra came up beside me with a smirk. "Betcha you're glad it's your last day, huh?"

"You have no idea."

"Waitress! Waitress!" The heavyset man snapped his fingers impatiently.

I shot Kendra a look of despair as the heavyset man began to holler. "I'm being summoned," I muttered.

"Hang in there, you're almost there!" Kendra cheered.

I approached the lively table as the two children began fighting. Their mother tried with little success to quiet them. "Is there anything else I can get for you?"

The woman spoke this time. "My goodness the service here likes to take its time."

I forced a smile. "I'm sorry, ma'am, like I mentioned before we are short staffed today. We are all trying our best."

The two children shoved each other, and one of them squealed. The father tried his best to hush them before shooting an exasperated look at his wife. She threw her hands in the air. "Two chocolate milkshakes. Please, hurry."

I nodded wordlessly and wanted nothing more than to clack the children's heads together. If they wanted something to scream about, I would give it to them. I entered the kitchen and made the shakes.

"Here you go. Two chocolate milkshakes." I set them in front of the children. "Anything else?" *Please, for the love of God, say no.*

"No, that's all for now."

I nodded quickly and made my rounds to the other tables. The scream of a child tore through the restaurant. "Strawberry! I want strawberry!"

"Hush, keep your voice down."

"Strawberry!"

"Okay, okay. Fine. Waitress!"

You can do this. This is your last day. You have one more hour to go. Smile and it will all be over soon. I made my way to the table of dread once more. "Is there a problem?"

"We need a strawberry milkshake now!"

The young child picked up his glass, and heaved it at me. A shriek escaped my lips as I was met by a cold impact. The thick, chocolate liquid washed over me. Gasps echoed from around the room as I angrily wiped milkshake out of my eyes, and clenched my fists together. The rage had taken over now, there would be no containing the beast any longer.

"Oh god. Get her out of there." Kendra's voice floated across the room.

"That's it! I can't do this anymore!" I tore off my apron and glowered at the table. "Learn to control your children before you bring them in public, or put a muzzle on them!"

The parents gasped in horror. "How dare you!"

I glared darkly and stormed away. My boss, Ray, rushed out of his office and he looked concerned. "Autumn? Are you okay?"

"Ray, I know it's my last day and all but I-"

Ray held up his hands. "Go."

I gave Ray a nod in relief. "Thank you." I grabbed my purse from behind the counter and marched to the door that led to freedom. The last thing I saw before walking out was pure amusement written on customer's faces.

I found my faded Bronco in the parking lot. I gripped onto the metal handle and tugged swiftly at the door but it wouldn't budge. I tugged once more but the door remained shut. My emotions ran on overdrive and I lost it. My self-control spiraled down the drain. I hit the hood with my purse a few times before kicking at the driver side door.

"Open, you hunk of metal! Open!" I gave a frustrated yell, pressed my back against the stubborn door, and gently slid down onto the hot pavement, legs sprawled out in a straight line. My purse began to ring, snapping me momentarily out of my frustration. I leaned on to my side and dug through the contents of my bag until I found my phone.

"Hello?"

"Hello. Is this Autumn Miller?"

"Yes, it is."

"This is Westbridge College calling. I'm sorry to tell you this, but I have some news that's not going to make you very happy."

I hesitated before answering. I was already in a foul mood. "What's that?"

"I'm so sorry. We have had some students drop the course at the last moment and we have decided we won't be running the program until March."

"Are you freaking kidding me? That's eight months away!"

The voice on the other end paused before beginning hesitantly. "I'm so sorry but sometimes these things happen. We do hope you consider attending next spring."

I said nothing. I hung up the phone and tossed it into my purse. I lightly banged the back of my head against the stubborn door. This speed bump was not part of my life plan. What was I supposed to do for eight months? That was almost a whole year away. I quit my job for this. I glanced at the restaurant knowing I could probably talk my way back in. I considered it for a moment until I glanced down at the milkshake stained uniform. Just as quickly as the thought entered my mind, it was shot down with a violent defiance. And so, I sat on the hot pavement and stared up the sky wondering what my next move would be.

Chapter 2

Jensen

Jensen Owens awoke with a pounding head. He cursed softly under his breath and knew it was largely attributed to the large amounts of alcohol consumed the night before. He sat up and looked at the blonde lying next to him. For the life of him, he couldn't remember her name. Not that he cared. He had no plans of ever seeing her again. He slipped out of bed quietly and dressed swiftly. He gathered his things and left the apartment. He stepped into the early morning air, and fished his keys out of his jacket pocket. Jensen strode purposefully to his large, slick black truck. Hopping inside, he turned the engine on. It roared like a proud lion. The engine rumbled as he tried to get his bearings on where he was. He was slipping. This part of town looked old and worn. He could do better, he used to do better. Jensen stuck the truck in gear and pressed the gas pedal heading for home.

Half an hour later, Jensen found himself standing alone in his kitchen. He reached inside the fridge, pulled out a beer, popped the top, and took a long sip of the cool, smooth liquid. He wandered the kitchen aimlessly until his brown eyes landed on the notice he pinned to his fridge. His lease to the apartment was up at the end of the week. He had no intention of renewing it. He hated this town and the place was a hole. Jensen stepped out on the small deck and sat, waiting for the complex to wake up. He watched quietly as the tenants in the building began to get ready for work. Loved ones gave each other quick kisses goodbye and went their separate ways.

Jensen reached into his back pocket and took out a package of cigarettes. He lit the cigarette and took a long drag. He quit smoking cold turkey five years ago. Only recently had he picked up the habit again. He watched the cigarette burn before he put it out after three drags. His left shoulder began to ache again. He rolled it back carefully and cursed under his breath. The old ache would never go away; it would serve as a constant reminder of that day. He quickly tossed back a Tylenol followed by a cold swig. Jensen kicked the chair back and stepped inside the dim apartment. He went to his closet, pulled out a large duffel bag, and threw his clothing inside. He had no personal items, never did. Jensen liked to travel light; it made disappearing easy. He swung the large bag over one shoulder, and left his spare key on the counter. He planned to never return.

Jensen hauled the bag into the bed of his truck and headed for the highway. He drove from memory to the first place he lived as a child. He recognized the small farming community as soon as he took the exit. If memory served him correctly, a restaurant should be around the corner. He smiled as the familiar building came into view. A town like this didn't welcome change. *Don't fix what ain't broke.* He pulled into an empty spot and made his way inside. A pretty waitress with fiery red hair escorted him into a seat. He half heartily studied the menu while assessing the controlled chaos around him. Out of the corner of his eye, he saw someone who demanded his full attention, though she wasn't aware. *Autumn.* She was beautiful, but this he had remembered. They were merely kids when he last saw her. She had just celebrated her sixteenth birthday. Time had changed her from a gawky teenager into a woman. She had always been petite, topping in at 5'4" but she was now shapely. Her hair hadn't changed. She wore it long and untamed, almost as though she spent hours on the beach the way it tousled about.

Jensen continued to study her. She had grown up nicely indeed. She looked fragile yet somehow strong. Her skin was kissed by the sun, and her eyes were a startling blue. Jensen drew a small smile as he caught the faint trickle of freckles across the top of her nose.

The redhead came back to his table, drawing him away from his thoughts. "More coffee?"

"Sure."

"There you go. Anything else I can do for you?" The waitress smiled sweetly.

"Nope, that's all."

Her face fell slightly with disappoint. "Okay. Well, holler if you need me."

Jensen nodded and turned his attention back to Autumn. She looked lost in thought, somehow absent from the chaos in the room. He watched as she got the unfortunate hand at dealing with what looked to be a very trying table. He could see her unravel more each time she left the booth, her blue eyes sparking in an uncontainable fury. A part of him wanted to warn them to take it easy; they were playing with fire. Yet, he stayed put. He found himself strangely enchanted and amused by the pretty girl who tried so hard to follow the rules. Jensen looked away for a second. When he glanced up, she was covered in brown liquid and the rage flowed freely. All forms of pleasantries were officially off the table. Jensen watched her as she let the sparks fly, not caring what anyone thought. As she marched purposefully for the door he pitied anyone who dared cross her path. His eyes followed as she stormed through the parking lot. When he witnessed her beating her vehicle, he knew he would be going after her.

He swallowed hard as he felt a small fear for his own safety building within. As Jensen walked toward her, he heard her sob. Any fear he had felt quickly diminished. He stepped around the vehicle and saw her sitting helplessly on the hot pavement. She suddenly looked very small and harmless. He cleared his throat. She looked up at him. Her eyes were swollen with emotion and she looked exposed. As her eyes settled upon him, he wished he had left her alone. He didn't know what to do with himself when women cried. He tended to say the wrong thing which only made the situation worse.

She spoke first as she scrambled to her feet. "Look at me. I'm a mess." She gestured angrily to the chocolate stain. She studied him, almost accusingly. "What do you want?"

Jensen squirmed. "I, uh, I just wanted to see if you were okay. That looked pretty rough in there."

She let out a dry laugh. "Yeah, I bet. I'm sure I gave the whole town something to talk about for a few weeks."

Jensen shifted uncomfortably. "You're okay then?"

Autumn bit her lip, a new set of tears forming in her eyes. "I can't open my door." She began to cry as she lowered her face into her hands. Sobs racked her body as she let out a half hearted kick at her door once more.

Jensen fought a laugh. "Here," he stepped to the door, "let me see if I can get it for you." He gave the door a sharp tug and it creaked open. "There we go." He stepped past her and found her purse lying across an empty parking slot. He picked it up and held out his hand. "You've got a good arm on you."

Autumn let out a small, bright laugh then. She wiped at her eyes and smiled a little. "Thank you."

"You're welcome. Are you okay to drive?"

"I'll be fine, thanks again." She hesitated slightly. "I'm sorry you had to see me like that. I'm usually a lot more put together than this. I swear, I'm not crazy. Today in particular did not go as planned." She bit her lip. "I almost feel sorry for that family in there. I unleashed a lot of pent up emotions on them."

Before he could say another word, she raised an eyebrow and laughed. "But did you see the looks on their faces?" She leaned against the open door and sighed. "It was all kind of worth it." She looked toward him expectantly. Her blue eyes shone with pleasure.

Jensen felt a smile tug at his mouth. She was definitely a firecracker. "Yeah, I'd say it was all worth it. You gave me a good show."

She smiled and nodded. "You're welcome. I should go. Thanks, again." She hesitated a moment before hopping inside. "Do I know you? You seem familiar."

Jensen smiled. "Maybe. I'll see you around."

He walked back to the restaurant. Autumn hefted herself into the Bronco and fired it up. It took two tries to get the engine running and then she was gone. Jensen watched as she drove off, and couldn't help but let out a good, loud laugh, something he hadn't done in a very long time.

Chapter 3

Autumn

Today had not gone as planned. I did not plan to lose my temper, I did not plan on school backing out, and I most certainly did not plan to cry like a child in front of a stranger. Once I got home, I tore off my outfit and put on my running gear. I let my feet and the uneven country roads take me away. Lucy, my shepherd mix ran right by my side. Running was a daily ritual. It was the only activity that gave me clarity and a sense of peace. I had been running a lot over the past few years. I had gotten it into my head if I ran long and fast enough, I could forget that day. That terrible, unfortunate day.

After my run I showered, and crawled into bed. It was after midnight and my mind would not allow me to sleep. The simple question of "what now?" kept gnawing at me. How was I going to navigate this? Did I go back to waitressing until the program began? Or was this a sign? The thought of going back to college never truly thrilled me to begin with. But if I didn't go back, what was I going to do with my life? After my grandmother passed away, I dropped out of college. I had moved in with her on a permanent basis when I was eight years old. She was my best friend, and when she was no longer here, I fell off my path. My parents hadn't been thrilled with my choice but it was my life. I had to live it the way I wanted. My folks lived hours away from this small town. They traveled a lot for work and their lifestyle never suited me. I was content to stay in one place, and I had fallen in love with this town, even at a young age. This town and my grandmother were home. While my parents were straight laced, my grandmother was the complete opposite. She, like I, was a free spirit and a dreamer. We marched to our own beat, and we liked to create our own path in life. We had no desire to follow rules.

With a grumble, I knew sleep would not find me. I sat upright and an idea came to me. I began to gather my ingredients: a bottle of wine, scented candles, and bubble bath. I pulled my chocolate hair into a top knot and let the robe fall to the floor. I grabbed my glass of wine and stepped into the steaming tub. As the hot water caressed my skin, I sighed in contentment. This was exactly what I needed.

I settled against the bath pillow and my thoughts drifted to the stranger from earlier in the day. The one who had witnessed my momentarily lapse in judgment. Something about him seemed so familiar, but I couldn't place my finger on it. I closed my eyes and his image came into view. He stood 6'2" with broad shoulders and a lean frame. He had a country boy swagger and muscles that only hard, physical work could bring. He wore his dark blond hair a little longer and he was unshaven. His eyes were a warm brown, his smile teasing. *That smile. It's the smile. I know that smile. Could it be him? No. He would never come back here.*

"This looks nice. Can I join you?"

With a yelp, I nearly jumped out of my skin. I looked up in shock as Logan leaned carelessly against the doorframe. "You scared me half to death. I didn't even hear the front door."

Logan smiled and began to peel off his clothes. "I tried calling earlier to tell you I was on my way."

I glanced up at Logan's tall, fit frame. His dark blond hair matched his facial scruff. His bright blue eyes fell to mine and he grinned his carefree grin. Logan stepped into the claw foot tub and I scooted forward. Once he was settled, I leaned my back against him. His calloused hands fell gently around me.

"This feels so good," he said quietly.

"It sure does."

"Why are you up so late?"

"Rough day." I took another sip of wine.

"Yeah, I got your message earlier. It's why I came over tonight, I figured you might want some company."

I let out a breath. "Thanks."

"I really am sorry, Autumn, that sucks. I guess you'll be going back to the restaurant?"

I wrinkled my nose. "What makes you think that?"

Logan shrugged. "Well, you have to do something until school starts."

"Maybe I don't want to go back to school."

"You should. What else are you going to do?"

I didn't like the tone Logan had taken. "I'm not sure yet. I'll be okay for a bit. I have a nest egg set aside from when Grandma passed away, and with the money I have saved up for school, well, maybe I'll put it toward something else."

"I think that's the wine talking."

I leaned back into Logan's chest and pressed my lips together tightly, ignoring the jab. I wasn't in the mood to argue. Logan and I had been together just shy of a year. He owned his own house while I rented a small apartment in town. We led separate lives in so many ways, only seeing each other a few times a month. Logan was a good, hardworking man. I knew he cared for me, and I cared for him. But lately I was beginning to have my doubts. While I enjoyed his company, more often than not, something about him left me feeling a little empty. I felt as though I was always left waiting for him, everything was on his schedule: when we saw each other, when we spoke. I wasn't sure he would ever take time out of his world to be with me if I actually needed him. I began to doubt if a future would ever be possible between us. Logan tended to shy away from personal matters, he was so hard to read. For the most part, we just kept each other warm at night.

Logan whispered in my ear. "You ready for bed?"

I adjusted in the water which began to cool. "Yes."

"Good, let's go." Logan stepped out, and took me by the hand. He threw a large towel around us and brought me to his chest. He pressed his lips against mine and moved slowly down my neck. He dropped the towel and I pulled away, taking him by the hand. I led him across the hall into the bedroom. I got lost in the motions, forgetting my earlier doubts about him. At least for now, he offered some comfort.

⌘

The next morning, Logan and I had our morning coffee together before he left for work. I watched him drive away, simply ignoring his advice to get my old job back. I changed into my workout clothes and began my morning jog with Lucy bounding behind me. After a quick shower, I slipped into fresh clothes and grabbed the Bronco's keys. "C'mon, Luce. Let's go for a drive."

Lucy hopped into the passenger seat, riding shotgun. I leaned past her to open the window. Lucy immediately stuck her head outside; tongue flopped to the side as she enjoyed the summer breeze. I followed the paved roads until the cement ran out, replaced by dirt. The Bronco bounced unevenly side to side as the tires sunk into potholes. I rolled my window down farther, allowing the warm wind to kiss my skin. I slowed to admire the view. I was now firmly planted on the quiet farming end of town where the fields went on for miles, and the old dirt road ran straight.

The air had a sweet smell wafting gently on the breeze; it was hay season. I sucked in a deeper breath and could faintly make out the smell of the wildflowers that shone brightly amongst the tall grass. As I turned down a country lane, I slowed the Bronco to a stop. A 'For Sale' sign was plunked into the ground under a large maple tree. On a hunch, I turned down the long drive and parked in front of the old house. I stepped outside and glanced at the home. It was love at first sight. It was an old Cape Cod style with a steeply pitched roof complimented by three large gables and a chimney. The deck ran the entire perimeter of the home completed by a porch swing bolted to the ceiling of the low lying roof. There was a lot of work that needed to be done. The house had good bones, but it definitely needed a fresh coat of paint. The white had faded over the years and was chipped and peeling. The dark blue trim around the window frames and doorways had faded with time, making it appear washed out. The neglected exterior matched that of my truck, but unlike the truck, I knew I could give the house some much needed TLC.

To the right was an older building that matched the color scheme of the house. It looked to have been used as a garage at one point in time. To the left of the house lay a well traveled dirt path. I followed the trail to a hip roof barn that had clearly received much more attention than the home. The barn stood tall and sturdy, the walls painted in a fresh coat of a deep oak brown. Above the main entrance, hung a large black decorative star. The barn was tidy and functional with four large stalls, a wide alleyway, and a tack and feed room. The east side was designated for hay storage. On the west side hung an old tire swing secured by a large beam on the ceiling. Lucy trotted eagerly through the barn as her nose took her on an intriguing journey.

I leaned against a large wooden beam and studied the tire swing. It was a sign. I smiled slowly. *Thanks, Grandma.* As a child, my grandmother had an old tire swing in the front of her house. An old apple tree housed it. I spent many hours on the swing as she pushed me back and forth, filling my head with wondrous stories and dreams. She was the sole person who allowed me to believe I could do anything I wanted. Nobody else had to agree. As long as it made me happy, it was enough.

"What do you think, Luce? Does this feel like home?" Lucy stopped long enough to look up at the sound of my voice before she caught another intriguing scent. I twirled around in the alleyway. "Because it feels like home to me."

I made my way to the house and stepped on the covered deck. I tried the door but it was locked. I pressed against the window and peeked inside. I clasped my hands on the bottom of the windowsill and pulled up with all my might. As luck would have it, it opened. I climbed through the window and coaxed Lucy to jump inside.

"Wow," I muttered in wonder as I looked around my surroundings. "This is it, girl, this is what I've been looking for."

I stepped into a large living room that featured a wood burning stove. The room held large windows, allowing natural light to shine through. The ceiling was arched and high. I stepped around the corner which led into a functionally designed kitchen. Hardwood flooring ran throughout the house and it seemed to be in good shape. The colors on the walls however would need to be changed. A dull brown was splashed onto them; they needed to be revived in color. Across from the kitchen was a small bedroom and washroom. I found my way to the front door and it housed a little mud room and a feature staircase. I took the stairs two at a time which led to three large bedrooms. I stepped into each one with stars in my eyes. Even though the house was bare and cobwebs hung in the corners, the house welcomed me. It held a strong character and unique look. Great care had gone into the detailing of the woodwork and structure. It wasn't like the houses so common these days, they went up at an alarming rate, and they all looked the same.

I sat cross legged in the upstairs hall lost in thought. I wasn't in love with my tiny apartment. I would have no problem leaving. At the moment, my life was an unwritten book. I loved a good challenge, and this would be something I could call my very own. Every nail I slammed into wood, every layer of paint I spread on these walls would represent my own journey of being restored. The past few years had been a whirlwind. The first event was an unexpected tragedy, one that had led me to running in the first place. Afterwards, I lost my grandmother, and it started a chain reaction. I dropped out of college shortly after, only to find myself stuck in a job I hated for the last three years. I had been lost for so long, and looking back, I hadn't even known it at the time. Until I had absolute freedom could I see how much I'd boxed myself in. It was time to find myself once again.

When my grandmother passed, she left me a large sum of money. The money had been accompanied with a letter from her. The contents of the letter contained a very simple message.

Don't hold on to this, my darling girl. Your heart will know when the time is right. Listen to it. While others stand on the ledge of safety, you have always been the one who jumps, and you will fly. Remember, my child, nothing great comes from what is safe. Greatness is found within the unknown and it's a force that dared not be reckoned with. Love always, your grandmother.

I memorized that letter. I read it whenever I felt I was loosing myself in the day to day hustles of life, the days when I forgot who I was, or where I was going. My grandmother and I were so similar; we didn't quite fit the mold, and we had no desire too. We made our own rules to live by and it set us free. I toyed with the phone in my pocket. The phone number from the 'For Sale' sign was fresh in my memory. I pulled out the phone and dialed.

"Hello?"

"Hi. My name is Autumn Miller and I'm interested in the house you have for sale at the end of Ridge Road. And when I say I'm interested, what I actually mean to say is I want to buy it."

Chapter 4

Jensen

Jensen pulled into the long gravel drive and cut the engine. In his stomach, butterflies grew at an alarming rate. He hated putting himself in unpleasant situations if he could help it. He sat in the truck for what felt like a very long time. He tried to remember the last time he had been here. He couldn't. It had been years and he had no intention of ever coming back, yet, here he was. Movement caught his eye. He had been spotted.

"Shit," he mumbled as he stepped out of his truck.

"Holy hell. Jensen? Jensen Owens is that really you?"

Jensen watched as his old friend, Derik, cracked a smile. He instantly felt at ease. "Derik. It's been a long time."

"It sure has. Ten years now?"

"Along those lines."

"Wow, time sure flies. I haven't seen you since…" Derik's face fell but he quickly composed himself. "Jesus, we were just kids back then. You'll never believe it but I'm a married man these days."

"Who would have that you would settle down?"

"Ah, the single days are long gone. Come inside and meet my wife."

"Sure, why not."

Jensen walked in step with Derik as he listened to him chatter on about life. Jensen noticed in slight jealousy Derik hadn't changed much, he still had a youthful face and was always the optimist in the group. Jensen followed Derik inside the cozy farm house and sat at the kitchen table.

"Can I get you some coffee?" Derik asked.

"Sure, thanks. Black."

"All right. The wife's just on the phone. She'll be down in a minute."

"No worries."

Derik took a sip. "So, what brings you back to these parts? Visiting for the summer?"

Jensen ran his thumb around the rim of the mug. "To be honest, I'm not sure. I just wanted a change of pace, I guess. This was the last place that felt like a home to me. Just felt the need to come back."

Derik nodded, scrutinizing him. "I get it. How has life been? Last I heard you were having a bit of a rough go."

Jensen hardened slightly. "I'm fine."

"And the shoulder?"

"Good as gold."

"Just askin'. So, now that you're here, what are your plans? Where are going to stay? What are you going to do for work?"

"I checked in at the Hilltop Motel for a few nights. Haven't thought much about anything else to be honest."

"I see. Well, the garage is always looking for people. From what I remember, you were always getting lost under the hood of a vehicle."

Jensen smiled. "Thanks, I appreciate that."

Derik got up. "Good, consider it done."

Jensen sat up in surprise as a pretty redhead entered the kitchen. He recognized her as the waitress who served him earlier. Her green eyes took him in with surprise.

Derik brightened. "Jensen, I'd like you to meet my wife, Kendra."

Jensen stood to shake her hand. "Hi. Nice to formally meet you."

Kendra studied him with interest. "And how do you boys know each other?"

"From childhood. Jensen used to live down here."

Kendra smirked. "Oh," she began teasingly. "So you're the famous Jensen?"

Jensen turned pale in surprise. "Famous? I don't know if I like the sound of that."

Kendra waved her hands in the air. "Oh, sure you are! You and Autumn used to always get the group in trouble. The stories are famous. Speaking of Autumn, does she know you're in town? You must have run into each other at the restaurant?"

"I saw her actually. She didn't quite recognize me though. It's been a long time." Kendra beamed. "Well, you can come with us tomorrow tonight. We're going to the Tailgate, the local pub. We'll be celebrating Autumn's latest venture. You will never believe what she did. She bought the Henderson's old farm."

Derik set down his mug in shock. "Are you kidding?"

Jensen smiled to himself. That sounded like the Autumn he remembered. She was always the one who jumped into situations, both feet forward, never thinking about what could go wrong.

"Where are you staying?"

The question caught Jensen off guard as Kendra waited rather impatiently for an answer. "The Hilltop."

"Wrong. You can stay here with us until you decide how long you're going to be in town."

"I already paid for the night."

"Fine. Stay the night, get your money's worth, but tomorrow you better be here. We have a guest room that will suit you just fine."

"That's really kind of you but—"

Derik held up his hands. "Don't bother arguing with her, Jensen, you will never win."

Jensen left Derik's place once the details were worked out. He hadn't been given much of a say in the matter; Kendra was a very strong willed girl. Jensen found himself chuckling at the thought of Derik being second in the household. As teenagers, Derik was bullheaded and had a mind of his own.

Jensen's good mood dissipated in a matter of seconds. Derik had grown up. He changed…they all had after the incident. As a last minute thought, he pulled into the liquor store and hopped out of his truck. He wandered the beer aisle and grabbed whatever was on sale. He didn't have a preference to a particular brand. They all tasted the same after awhile. He made his way to the check-out and placed the box on the counter.

A pretty blonde rang in his order and smiled at him. Her eyes took him in appreciatively. She tucked her hair behind her ear. "That'll be $22."

He smiled at her, a habit that had grown to become almost second nature to him. "Here you go. Keep the tip."

She smiled coyly. "Thank you, stranger. Hope to see you around?"

There was a question in her voice and he knew it. "I'll be sticking around for a bit."

The blonde's eyes lit with hope. "There's a local bar around, I hope to see you soon."

He smiled at her and left the store. Time was on his side for once. He didn't think many people would recognize him these days. The last time he had been in this town he was eighteen years old. Ten years definitely changed a person.

As he headed back to the motel, he was almost sure he'd take the liquor store clerk up on her offer at some point. Nights were long. They had never bothered him before but a lot had changed over the years. Nothing felt the same anymore. He liked the comfort of someone next to him, simply for the companionship. He'd be happy to lie next to someone all night but they always wanted more, and he would give them what they wanted, if only for the night. He stepped into the empty motel room and sat on the edge of the bed. He twisted a beer open and tossed the lid into the trash. He took a long swig and for a brief moment he wondered why in the hell he had come here in the first place. He scratched mindlessly at his cheek. At least he had a job. He needed to work just to keep sane. And thanks to Derik's wife, he would have a place to stay for the meantime. It would be nice to catch up with Derik. It would be like old times. Well, almost like old times.

Jensen sighed heavily and reached for his phone. He dialed his folks' number and waited for a familiar voice to fill his ear. "Hello?"

"Hi, Mom."

"Jensen," relief poured through the soft voice. "Where are you? Are you okay?"

Jensen stood slowly and leaned against the doorframe. "Yeah, I'm all right. I'm in Pritchett."

Silence was heavy on the other end. "Pritchett? Why are you back there?"

"Visiting old friends. I wanted to make sure everyone was okay, I suppose."

"You're a good man, Jensen."

Jensen wasn't so sure. He used to be, but as of lately those lines had blurred for him. "I have to go. I'll call soon."

⌘

Jensen stared at the ceiling fan and watched as the blades made their never ending circle. He glanced impatiently at the blonde from the liquor store, who slept soundly. She was tangled amongst the sheets. Jensen let out a sigh and hoped she would get up soon. He needed to go on with his day, his horrible day. Today marked the anniversary of a memory he couldn't outrun. He got up and made his way to the washroom. He stared into the mirror for a moment before he turned away in disgust. He nodded to himself; at least he was here to make sure she was okay. She didn't need to be alone, not today.

Chapter 5
Autumn

The only room in the house I had set up was my bedroom. I placed my bed across from the large window. I wanted the fields and barn to fill my sight first thing in the morning. I set up my dresser in the far corner by the closet, and placed the nightstand next to my side of the bed. Lucy's dog pillow was nested in a cozy nook of the room. I hung a few select pictures on the only freshly painted wall in the house; I wanted to keep some memories very close.

A lot of work needed to be done, not only to the exterior. All the basics worked, much to my relief. The plumbing, electrical, even the flooring for the most part was good. The floors in the main rooms, such as the living room, bedrooms, and hallways consisted of oak hardwood. However, I would have to replace the tile floor in the kitchen and two bathrooms. All the walls needed a fresh coat of paint, as well as updating certain appliances. All that would come over a period of time, as my wallet had its limits.

Today marked the tenth anniversary of a horrible memory. An old wound over my heart began to throb as the images flashed through my mind. *We were just kids. Stupid kids. I'm so sorry.* I decided to start the day with a morning run, Lucy was right by my side. Running quieted my mind. The faster I ran, the darkness faded into light, and while it never lasted long, it offered me a glimmer of hope, redemption. As we ran along the quiet dirt roads, the sounds from the outside world simply stopped; everything did. I found comfort in the solace. I welcomed it like an old friend. The only forms of life around were cattle and horses grazing in the faraway fields.

Once we were home, Lucy lapped heavily at her water dish. I ruffled her ears and took a quick shower. I scooped my damp hair in a topknot and knew there was much work to be done. I threw on a pair of torn jeans, and a dark blue sleeveless shirt. I rolled up the hem of my jeans and slipped into a pair of comfy flats. I wandered the house from room to room, deciding what colors would look good. I wanted the place to be warm and cheery, something its current state severely lacked. The knot in my heart reappeared and I willed it to go away.

"All right, Lucy ready for a truck ride?"

Lucy trotted over happily, tail wagging heavily. I knelt and placed her head in my hands. "You are such a good girl, do you know that?" Lucy wagged her tail in response and followed me out the door. She hopped into the back of the Bronco with ease. I closed the back and struggled to open my door. With a quick hip jab it popped open and I slid inside, rubbing my hands together in anticipation.

"Come on, baby, start for me!" I turned the key expectantly and the Bronco came to life. "Good girl." I patted the dashboard in approval and placed one foot on the gas, the other hovered over the brakes in case it stalled.

The drive to town was short, only ten minutes via back roads. I pulled into town and drove slowly through the heart of it, making my way to the hardware store. There was a time I seriously considered leaving this place, for it harboured a terrible loss to the community. Initially, after the funeral, I left for six months but as time passed and the initial ache started to fade, and the memories I ran from began to hold a strong comfort. I needed to keep them close. I pulled into the hardware store and told Lucy to stay put. I knew she would, she was a good dog. I was greeted warmly by the staff, most of them I'd known all my life. A lot of the people who grew up here never left, and those who did most often came back. I was no exception. I chose my paint colors and handed them to the clerk. I browsed the store while the colors were being mixed, picking up odds and ends I needed. I wandered the home décor section and a man caught my eye. He could be no more than late twenties, maybe early thirties. Recognition hit me; he was the man from the restaurant. He must have felt me staring for he looked up and his brown eyes met mine.

"Autumn, your colors are ready to go!"

I turned to the cheery voice. "Thanks, Donna." I smiled warmly and wheeled the cart over.

She helped me load the cans. "You're going to be a busy girl by the looks of things."

I wrinkled my nose. "You bet. All I have to do is think of the end product, and it will all be worth it."

"It always is. If you need any help, you just let us know."

"I will, thanks."

I wheeled the cart to the register, made a dent in my bank account, and headed for the Bronco. I placed the new brushes in the front seat and focused my attention on unloading the paint cans in the back. Lucy began to wiggle uncontrollably, and a smooth male voice appeared behind me. "Do you need some help?"

I turned curiously at the voice. The attractive stranger stood behind me. He looked friendly enough, almost eager to help. "Umm…sure."

He nodded swiftly and leaned past me and grabbed a can, one for each hand. He swung them easily into the back. A smile broke out on his face, warming his features. "Nice dog." As his eyes met Lucy's the happy wiggle once again took over her body.

"Thank you. Her name is Lucy."

"Hello, Lucy." He ruffled her ears and gave her a hearty pat.

I placed a hand on my hip and tilted my head to the side and studied the man before me. His eyes met mine and he smiled again. "Oh, you are driving me insane!" I blurted.

He smirked once more. "You don't recognize me, do you?"

My eyes widened. "Ah-ha! So, I do know you, don't I? It's been driving me nuts!"

Jensen grinned from ear to ear. "Maybe I can give you a hint. I used to call you Tiny."

"Tiny? That's a cheap shot," I muttered. *Tiny. His smile. Could it be…* I stepped forward and grabbed his face between my hands, studying him. I ignored the fact that his eyes grew large in surprise and continued on with my assessment.

My jaw dropped and my hands fell to my sides. "Jensen? Is it you?"

He grinned a lopsided grin. "It's been awhile."

His smile hadn't changed. But his facial features sure had. The boy I remembered, was just that, a boy. His face had been rounder back then, his features were now well defined. There was however, something different in his eyes. The eyes I remembered were bright and happy. His eyes before me now, while still warm, held a vacancy to them.

I launched my arms around his neck into a bear hug. He returned the embrace. "You've grown up rather nicely. What brings you back to these parts?"

Jensen's smile faded from his lips. "To be honest, I'm not sure. Lately I've felt the need to be here; god knows why."

A sad smile fell over my lips. "It's today, you know."

"How could I forget?"

I fidgeted as the silence fell heavy. "How long are you here for?"

"I don't know, but I'm sure we'll see each other around. We should catch up. I'm really sorry to do this, but I need to head to work."

"Oh, okay. Where are you working, and where can I get a hold of you?"

Jensen winked and strode off. "We'll talk later." He turned on his heel and I watched him climb into a shiny restored old Chevy pickup. I admired the smooth finish of the black paint and chrome from the grill. It had a slight lift, complete with big, aggressive mud tires. The engine let out a nice rumble. I leaned against my beat up old Bronco and patted the hood softly. "You do good, old girl." I watched him drive away and felt a twinge of jealousy as another paint chip peeled off my vehicle to be taken by the breeze.

⌘

I needed to keep busy, to fill up the day with a task. I decided it was time to paint the fading walls. I flicked on the radio and cranked it up. I gathered paint brushes, rollers, tape, and finally popped off the tin lid of a paint can. I poured a deep blue liquid into an empty tray and spread it on the walls. I painted for a long time, letting the music and the repetitive task numb my thoughts. Finally when my shoulders began to ache, I stepped back to admire my work. Pride washed over me as I assessed my progress. The living room was now a deep ocean blue, the hallway a gray blue. For the sitting room, I painted three of the walls in a lavender/mauve but reserved the last wall in the room for a rich purple.

I opened up the large windows to let the fresh summer air circulate throughout. I still had to paint the kitchen, washroom, and the last two bedrooms. I rolled my stiffening shoulders and decided to call it a day. The rest would have to wait for another time. Silence filled the house and it was heavy. My movements were echoed by the bare walls, reminding me just how vacant the place was. I slipped on a pair of shoes and stepped outside. I leaned against the pillar on the porch, and crossed my arms. My eyes took in the still beauty around me. I owned ten acres of rolling fields. The mountain range lay in the distance under the open sky. This part of the world was untouched by big city buildings and never ending pavement. This was a place where the stars shone brightly, and the wildflowers bloomed. Tall trees were left to grow, offering shade to those who stopped under the twisted limbs.

Dusk was coming. I could feel the heat of the day slowly dissipating. The bright sky slowly turned a rich shade of fluorescent pink in anticipation of the sunset.

"Come on, Lucy."

Lucy trotted after me as I made my way to the empty barn. I rolled the sliding door open and stepped inside. One day I hoped to fill the empty stalls with horses. I had grown up riding and missed it sorely. One day. For tonight, I would settle for my tire swing. I stepped inside the hay barn and sat on the old tire. I leaned my head back and lifted my feet off the security of the floor. I closed my eyes and let the swinging motion take me away. It felt like I was flying. There was no noise, besides Lucy panting in the corner, and the gentle creak as the rope stretched left to right, right to left.

"Autumn?"

My eyes flew open and the tire continued to sway side to side rapidly. I knew the voice but could not slow the swing enough to turn around to face her.

"Kendra? Hold on, I'm trying to slow down."

Two strong hands grabbed my waist from behind and the world stood still. I glanced up as Derik steadied me. I slid off the tire and smiled sheepishly. "Thanks."

Derik grinned. "No problem."

A smile pulled at Kendra's lips. "How are you doing?"

"I'm okay," I said quietly.

Kendra studied me. "Go wash that paint off. We're all going out tonight. The groups expecting us at Tailgates, in case you forgot."

I raised a brow. Tailgates was one of the best country bars in town, one of the only bars in town, but the atmosphere was lively and upbeat. It always promised for a fun night. Kendra gave me a light shove toward the door. "Come on, chickie, let's get moving. Tonight you need to have fun."

"All right. I'm going."

We followed the path from the barn to the house and stepped inside. Kendra and Derik admired the progress I had made. "It looks good." Kendra beamed with pride.

I smiled softly. Kendra had been a very close friend after the incident. She had taken me in during one of the darkest points of my life and helped me find my way once more.

"I'll hop in the shower and get ready. Give me fifteen minutes."

I clipped my hair up and stepped into the shower. After a quick rinse, I stepped into a white lace summer dress, and shook my hair free from the clip. I thought about pulling my hair back to tame it, but I decided to let the waves fall free. I reached for a pair of ankle boots and slid my feet into them. For the final touch, I completed the look with a faded denim jacket. I was ready to go. My eyes fell to a picture on the nightstand and I gravitated toward the photo. I picked up the precious frame and traced my finger over the image. *Me and my boys.* The three of us laughed from within the frame; almost everyone knew us as the three musketeers back then. I set it down and wiped the tears that began to fall. A trickle of loneliness spread throughout my bones, and I stood abruptly. I left the room quickly and met my friends downstairs.

"Well, look at you. Ready to go?"

"Yep." I gave Lucy a quick hug and told her I'd be back soon. I followed my friends into the warm evening air, and slid into the backseat of Derik's Jeep.

"Here we go!" Derik started the engine and away we went, back to the old stomping grounds. The parking lot was full and the music trickled out of the building into the parking lot.

Kendra cleared her throat, and she and Derik exchanged a glance. "Autumn, we have a surprise for you."

"Oh? And what's that?"

Kendra bit her lip unsurely. "It's more of a who than a what."

"Would this certain someone be Jensen Owens?"

Derik's eyebrows rose. "How did you know?"

"I ran into him in town." I studied their concerned faces and added in a more cheerful tone. "It was really nice to see him. It took me a minute to recognize him. He's changed so much."

"It's been a long time," Derik began. "You should know he's working with me down at the garage, and he's staying in our spare bedroom until he figures out if he'll be sticking around or not."

I nodded my head quickly. "Okay." *Jensen stick around, here? Not likely.* "So," I continued. "Is he coming tonight?"

Kendra flipped her hair over her shoulder. "He is. Actually, it's just going to be the four of us. We thought you two would have a lot to catch up on. We invited Logan to come along but he had plans already."

I nodded and got out of the Jeep. *Of course, Logan couldn't be here. Today is a day I actually need him. He knows what today represents.* I followed Derik and Kendra inside the lively bar and we found Jensen sitting at an empty table. His face lit up in recognition as he saw us. I couldn't help but notice the lingering glances women sent his way. I sat beside him and he smiled warmly. Conversation flowed easily between us. It was nice to hear his laughter again. After what happened to Jake, Jensen left town, and I was certain I would never see him again. I had tried to contact him but his phone was disconnected. Rumors floated he had fallen apart. I couldn't blame him if they were true. After that day, I, too had stepped away from reality.

Out of the corner of my eye, I watched Jensen closely. His smile didn't seem forced but there was an unmistakable hint of loneliness in his eyes. I listened quietly as Jensen spoke. I studied him and wondered just how much of my childhood friend still lived within him.

Chapter 6

Jensen

For the most part Jensen found himself enjoying his company tonight. He had been caught off guard to see Autumn sit beside him, but it was a pleasant surprise. He was relieved to see that she looked almost happy. He hadn't been able to shake the image of her crying on the hot summer pavement. It was an odd feeling, being back in town, it left him feeling rather un-nerved. Jensen felt skittish amongst the crowd. He wondered if anyone would figure out he was the boy who ruined a life. Jensen watched Autumn closely. He knew she was doing the same as he; they were each judging just how broken each of them were.

Next to him, Autumn shifted uncomfortably and excused herself from the table. A short while later, Jensen watched Autumn make her way through the crowd, balancing a full tray of shot glasses. She set the tray carefully on the table and picked up a glass, holding it high. "Here's to Jake," she said.

Jensen felt the surprise around him. Her friend's mouths gaped and their eyes widened slightly. They recovered quickly and grabbed a glass. Autumn settled her serious eyes toward Jensen. "Well? Go on, there's one for you too."

Jensen set down his beer and grabbed one of the shots. He held up his hand cautiously, watching her. "To Jake."

With that, everyone tipped their heads back and swallowed the strong liquid. Autumn set her glass down loudly and looked lost in thought. She tossed her hair over to the side and found her way to the bar once more. She came back holding a fresh drink. She took a long sip and focused her gaze on the dance floor.

Kendra looked concerned. "Are you okay?"

Autumn nodded and took another long sip. "I'm fine." She took a shaky breath and continued. "Look, we all know what today represents. I don't think we should beat around the bush…we should be able to say his name."

Autumn smoothed out her dress and a small smile played on her lips as she took another sip. "I feel like dancing."

Jensen watched her leave in amusement. He didn't know what was going to come out of her mouth next, he couldn't predict her next move. Jensen watched Autumn on the dance floor. Though she didn't try to demand any attention, he couldn't look away. He was mesmerized as her hips swayed to the rhythm; her feet gracefully took her across the room. She wasn't alone for very long, a man came and joined her. She let him.

"I can't remember the last time I've seen Autumn dance," Kendra exclaimed.

Jensen's interest perked. "You mean she doesn't always do this? From what I remember, she was always the first on the dance floor."

Derik spoke. "Things change."

"Jensen! Is that you?"

Jensen turned as a dolled-up blonde stood next to him. "Uh, yes. And you are?"

The blonde pouted. "You don't remember me? It's Anna Lawson."

Anna Lawson. Jensen fought the urge to run. She always caused trouble and judging by the looks of her now, he doubted that had changed.

Jensen forced a smile. "Anna, how have you been?"

Anna twirled her hair and flashed a charming grin. "I've been wonderful. I must say, I am very, very surprised to see you round these parts. I thought you were run out of town eons ago."

Jensen swallowed hard. He opened his mouth for a witty comeback but nothing came out. The heavy, hot feeling of shame began to eat at his flesh. Autumn came up behind him and placed a hand on his shoulder. "Let me handle her."

Jensen watched in incredulity. Autumn pressed her lips tight, and her face took over a pained look that bore close to discontent. She took a step closer and held her small frame with the fierceness of a warrior. "I'd watch what you say, Anna."

Anna's painted face fell into a scowl. "Oh? I was merely stating a fact."

Autumn took another step closer. Jensen rubbed the back of his neck. He was uncomfortable. It made him nervous when women fought, he wasn't sure what to do. He had no problem stepping in between angry men; he could easily throw a hit their way without being penalized. But with women, that was a delicate matter, and from everything he had witnessed through his life, they fought dirty.

Thankfully for Jensen, Anna backed down. She sent a grimace toward Autumn and tossed her shimmering hair over her shoulder. "Forget it."

Kendra yanked Autumn into her. "Autumn, you have to learn to rein yourself in, girl!"

Autumn sighed. "Sorry, but she was quick to pass judgment. She wasn't there. She doesn't know all the details." She paused and met Jensen's gaze. "Only Jensen and I know what really happened."

Jensen shook his head. This is why he stayed away for so long. A lot of time had passed but the stories hadn't changed. He kept his voice quiet. "How is Jake's family doing? I wanted to see them but I'm not sure that's the best idea…"

Autumn shook her head. "They left town after the funeral. They didn't want to stay here."

The color from Jensen's face left. "Oh."

Derik cleared his throat. "You know what? I think Jake would want us to celebrate. I think we need another round of drinks."

Derik and Kendra came back with a loaded tray. "Oh my." Autumn whispered.

Kendra gave her a playful shove. "Tonight, Autumn, it's your turn to have fun for a change. You're not driving."

The conversation turned light and the drinks flowed freely. Autumn moved a step closer and brought her face within inches of Jensen's. She raised a brow, and teased him with a smile. "Do you want to dance?"

"Uh, sure. Why not."

Her smile turned coy as she reached out and took his hand. He allowed himself to be dragged through the crowd, and soon they stood among the bustling dance floor. She let go of his hand and threw her arms in the air, moving softly. She turned to him, chocolate hair bouncing. Jensen was hypnotized; her blue eyes shone bright under the lights. He was being drawn in. In this moment, Autumn reminded him of the girl he long left behind. By all rights he should walk away, but he couldn't. He took a purposeful step toward her filling the empty space between them. He pulled her close and twirled her across the dance floor. Her eyes went wide in surprise and she laughed brightly. They danced to a few more songs before he noticed Autumn's color had paled considerably.

He stepped closer, eyeing her carefully. "You all right?"

She closed her eyes and held a hand to her forehead. "I'm a little dizzy," she confessed.

"You've had a lot to drink. We should head back."

She nodded. "I think that's a good idea."

He stepped to her and placed his arm securely around her waist. She leaned against him heavily and groaned. "What you must think of me," she muttered.

He smiled. "That you're a bit of a lightweight. Always were."

She stopped and looked up at him, amusement flitted in her eyes. "Huh," was all she said.

"Up we go for the stairs." Jensen leaned into her, shifted his weight and plucked her off the ground ever so slightly. Her grip around him tightened and he lowered her as soon as they were up the steps. Jensen navigated through the sea of people until they reached the safety of her friends.

Derik saw them first and he let out a laugh. "Uh-oh, what do we have here?"

Kendra stumbled to Autumn, seeming a little intoxicated herself. "Oh, how are you feeling? I haven't seen you like this in ages!"

Autumn muttered something inaudible and placed her hand against her forehead. "I think I'll be feeling this tomorrow."

"Oh, you sure will. I guess we should get her home…" Kendra's voice trailed off and she looked dubiously at Derik. Her gaze settled on her grinning husband and she threw her hands in the air. "You're drunk! You were supposed to be the designated driver."

Derik's face fell. "I'm sorry, babe. I got carried away. We'll have to take a taxi home."

Kendra placed her hands on her hips. "Well, isn't this just lovely."

Jensen cleared his throat. "I've only had two beers. I can drive her home."

Kendra stared at him with an intense look. He shifted uncomfortably. Derik stepped beside him and placed a hand over his shoulder. "That's a nice offer, thanks man. This is almost like old times again, eh?"

Kendra pursed her lips. "I don't know…"

"He's been looking out for her for most of the night, babe," Derik gently reminded.

Jensen spoke. "If it makes you uncomfortable, I can leave her with you. I just think she's going to need to lie down, sooner rather than later." He glanced at Autumn with a concerned look. "I just want to see her get home safely."

Kendra studied Jensen and let out a heavy sigh of defeat. "Okay, thank you."

Jensen leaned down to Autumn. "Let's get you home. Can you walk?"

"Mmm." She mumbled and opened her eyes. "Oh, the world won't stay still."

He laughed quietly. "Let's try this." He began to walk slowly and was pleased she kept up with his pace. She drew both arms around his torso and held on tightly, her eyes squeezed shut. They stepped into the warm evening air and he found his truck easily. He fidgeted in his pocket, pulled out the keys, and unlocked the door. In a single motion he scooped her up and gently placed her inside the truck. Closing the door quickly behind her, Jensen ran to the driver's side and hopped in next to her. "Let's get you sitting up shall we?"

Autumn opened her eyes and pushed herself upright. She let her head fall onto the window and clumsily buckled up her seatbelt. "Good to go," she whispered.

Jensen chuckled. "All right. Where abouts is your place?" He turned the ignition and his truck rumbled amongst the still night.

"You know the four way stop by the market?"

"Yes."

"Turn right and follow the road for awhile. The road will bend, and you will see the mailboxes on your side of the road. My place will be the next driveway on the left."

"Sounds fairly simple."

Autumn let out a yawn. "It is. Everything is simple out here."

Jensen edged the truck out the lot and turned the radio down low. Jensen's mind began to wander. This was something he was not used to; being the semi-responsible one of the group. He had been worried when Derik suggested he meet up with them at the pub. It was a weakness that grew worse with each passing day.

But tonight, Jensen surprised himself. His thirst was not for the drink, at least not tonight. Jensen followed her directions, and soon enough they were out of the glow from town's lights. The back country roads were dark and uneven. He slowed his speed as he didn't want to jostle his woozy friend. He kept his eyes peeled for landmarks and turned down the nearest driveway he could find. He pulled into the long drive and followed it as it rounded to a bend. He came to a gentle stop in front of a large colonial home. He placed the truck into park and killed the engine. He recognized the place immediately from childhood visits. He unbuckled his seatbelt and carefully did the same for Autumn.

His touch stirred her. She sat up slowly, blinking as she gazed out the window. "You found it."

"I did. Stay put, I'll help you out."

He jumped out and ran to her door, opening it carefully. She hugged her arm around his neck for support and slid out herself. She rummaged through her purse until she found a set of keys and handed them to him.

"I don't think I'll be able to do this one myself."

He took the keys gently and led her to the door. He unlocked and opened it. The smell of fresh paint greeted him before Lucy bounded over. She whined in excitement, happily running from one human to the other as though she'd been alone all her life. Jensen gave her a quick pat and Autumn clumsily reached down to her dog.

"Hello, Lucy," she said tiredly.

Once they stepped inside, Jensen felt unsure of his next move. He should walk away now; she was home safe. However, curiosity can be a strong lure. His eyes took in the large foyer. He took a step farther into the house, and began to study an old childhood memory. To the left he saw the entrance to the living room. To the right in the distance was the kitchen. A large stairway was before him, where he assumed the bedrooms were situated. Autumn took a few unsteady steps as she tossed off her shoes.

"Thank you for bringing me home."

"It was my pleasure."

She looked up at him through sleepy eyes. "I hate to be a pain, but do you mind helping me with something?"

He stepped forward, curious. "Not at all."

Autumn looked around the corner. "My kitchen is just down the hall, do you think you can grab me a glass of water?"

"Of course. I'll be right back."

He followed the short hallway to the kitchen. He flicked on the light and searched through the cupboards until he found a glass. He noticed the laminate floors peeled up in the corners and the walls were faded, but the room still managed to hang on to its charm. He quickly filled the glass and found Autumn where he left her, sitting on the bottom stair. Jensen offered her the glass and she took it gladly. She took a long sip and smiled softly. She stood and when she started to sway, Jensen moved in quickly to steady her. He looked up the flight of stairs and knew she would need help.

"Hold on to me, I'll help you up," Jensen spoke softly.

She nodded silently and did as asked. Once they were up the stairs Autumn directed him to her bedroom. Lucy trotted alongside, glancing up curiously at the stranger in their home. He stepped inside and flicked on the light. The bedroom was large and tidy. It welcomed him as soon as he entered its embrace. He noticed this room, unlike the rest of the house, had a personal touch.

The walls were soft and soothing. He studied the color and wasn't entirely sure if it was mauve or a gentle blue, perhaps a mixture of both. The bed stood on a sturdy oak frame, the hardwood floor rich. He noticed pictures on the wall; pictures of them as children. The old aching emptiness formed in the pit of his stomach. He studied the photos silently and he envied the carefree stance they all took. It was a ridiculous notion, he knew how things had ended. Jensen stole a glance as Autumn fell to her bed. After all this time, she chose to display their friendship within frames on her walls.

Lucy curled on her dog bed and contently fell asleep, knowing her human was once again home. Jensen watched Autumn climb under the covers and she let her head fall heavily against the pillow, completely unaware he still stood amongst her. He smiled a little and once she was safe in her bed he flicked off the light and stepped quietly out of the house. An unsettled feeling washed over him. He was used to leaving women sleeping in their beds, he looked forward to the relief the front door always brought. Tonight, however, a part of him wished he could stay.

Chapter 7

Autumn

I awoke in a tangle of sheets, head copiously pounding. I let my body lie limp as last nights events played through my head. My eyes rolled heavily toward the nightstand to stare at a familiar photo. Jake, Jensen, and my own smiling face looked back from within the frame. In the image, we were twelve years old. It was summer time, and we were dressed in next to nothing, lying stomach first on a round bale. Per usual, we each had a large smile plastered against our lips. The ache in my heart began to throb weakly. I doubted it would ever go away entirely, but the spasm wasn't enough to make me keel over in agony anymore. The picture represented another lifetime; the days where Jake's laughter rang through the air, letting the world know he was here.

My thoughts then drifted to Jensen and I sat up quickly. Too quickly. The world slightly wobbled and I slowed. I briefly remembered him hauling my sorry self to his truck and helping me up the stairs to my bedroom. A flush crept into my cheeks and I glanced down at my clothing nervously. I let out a sigh of relief once I realized my clothes were still in tact. I hadn't done anything too reckless.

Lucy sat at the edge of my bed, chin resting against the mattress in anticipation for some affection. "Good morning, Lucy."

Lucy's head snapped upwards and she bounded on me in a single leap. "Ooof! Lucy!" My face was met by a warm tongue. I pushed her head away gently. "I know. I love you, too. What do you think? Shall we get up?"

I moved at a tortoise pace. The first stop was a warm shower. I hoped the water would wash some of my stupidity away. Afterwards, I dressed into my painting clothes and fed Lucy breakfast. I had a slice of toast followed by Advil. I blew a strand of hair out of my eye and decided to throw what little energy I possessed into painting. I made a small goal to at least complete the washroom.

With a flat head screwdriver, I popped open the paint can lid and gave it a quick stir before pouring the liquid into an empty tray. I dipped my roller and placed it against the wall. My arms extended up and down with precision as I put forth effort into making this house feel like a home. Once I started, I couldn't stop. I felt an urgency to finish. A quiet dare entered my mind, doubting I would be able to set my heart into this house.

I would prove it wrong. I set my hands upon my hips and stood back feeling satisfied. I had finished the washroom, kitchen, and the two empty rooms. My arms ached in protest and my head hurt. After I gathered up the mess I had made, I stretched out across the living room floor in a poor attempt to loosen my tight back. Lucy laid down beside me, stretching out. I patted her head and let myself drift off.

A knock at the door broke the stillness. I sat up, startled at the unexpected noise. I rolled over onto my stomach and glanced out the living room window that viewed the front porch. "Hello?" I called out tiredly.

The sound of footsteps on the porch filled the room and a familiar face peeked into the large window. Curiosity faded and turned into amusement once he saw me. Jensen lifted an eyebrow and gave me a small smile. My stomach flopped over; the man had terrible timing when it came to my stellar moments. Here I was, severely hung over, passed out upon my living room floor. I forced a small grin and knew I did not have enough energy within me to pick myself up off the floor. I let my head fall back down and raised a hand weakly. "Come in!" I yelled.

The door squeaked and a set of footsteps filled the room. Lucy leapt toward her new friend begging for a pat. He filled the dogs wishes. I kept my eyes closed until I felt his presence was near. I opened them slowly and Jensen crouched beside me smiling.

"Oh, what you must think of me," I mumbled.

He took a minute to answer. "I'm not quite sure at this point. I've been seeing a lot of colorful sides to you in such a short amount of time."

I managed a small smile. "Ha ha. Funny guy."

"Come on. Let's get you up." Jensen stood tall and held out his hands. I turned onto my back and placed my hands within his. He pulled me up easily. His eyes looked around the house and whistled quietly. "Looks like you've been busy. It looks nice."

I stretched tiredly. "Thank you…at least the inside of the house looks good. I still have to paint the exterior and that's going to take me awhile."

Jensen studied the surroundings. "By yourself?"

"Yes. I can do it."

"I admire your gumption. That's a big project."

"It is, but I don't have anything else going on at the moment."

"Ah," he said quietly. "Kendra told me what happened. I'm sorry."

"I think it's for the best…if I'm being honest with myself, I didn't really want to go back to school."

Jensen smiled. "You were never one to sit still very long. Your attention span has always been quite limited."

I tossed a playful punch his way. "Hardy har har. Aren't you a funny one." I motioned for Jensen to follow and plunked onto the porch swing.

"This is a really beautiful place you have here, Autumn. It suits you, it's got no limits." He paused and faced me. "What are you going to do when the place is done?"

I frowned. It was a question I had been asking myself over and over. What was I going to do? As great as it was to fix up the house, I knew it couldn't last forever. At some point, the money would run out. "You know…for years I have lived my life according to what others thought was best. I took all the right classes, got the good grades but it never truly felt fulfilling. I don't remember much of it. I was on autopilot."

Jensen nodded. "I get that. Well, I think it's time you do something for you, for once."

I studied him. "You love working on cars, don't you?"

"I do. It's always been an escape for me."

"I'm glad you didn't lose your happy place after…what happened."

Jensen dipped his head. "On the contrary. I lost myself there."

I calculated his handsome features, and there was no mistaking the great wave of sadness and guilt that ran heavy. I slipped my hand around his. "I'm glad you had some place to go."

Jensen tilted his head and sighed. "I know that look, Autumn. Something's on the tip of your tongue, just say it."

I bored my gaze into Jensen and ripped off the Band Aid. "I could have used you here with me. I was so lost after Jake died. I lost one of my best friends and then you disappeared too. In a matter of days, both of my best friends were no longer there." I let out a heavy sigh and squeezed his hand tightly. "I am glad to have you back. It sure took you long enough."

Jensen smiled weakly. "I'm so sorry, Autumn. I was just a kid; my parents took me away and I didn't argue. I *couldn't* be here. I am sorry for leaving you behind; I always wondered how you were doing. I tried to come back, honestly I did. But I never could. I ran so far away and somewhere along the way, I lost who I once was. It got easier and easier to stay away."

"Have you ever spoken to anyone about what happened?"

"No. Have you?"

"Yes. I was in counseling for almost two years."

Jensen focused his gaze on the ground. "I never knew that."

I nodded. "The nightmares wouldn't stop. They haunted me all the time. What about you? Do you still see it?"

Jensen turned away. "Not if I drink enough."

I examined Jensen's face for awhile. It was clear to see time had not healed much for him. "You're broken. No matter how much you drink, how many pills you swallow, it won't help you. It's a temporary mask. You need to accept what happened and forgive yourself. We were just a bunch of dumb kids. Jake wouldn't want you to torture yourself."

Jensen stood and leaned against the porch pillar. He turned to me harshly. "Have *you* forgiven yourself?"

I stood and looked at him defiantly. "Yes, I have. After a long, long road of self discovery and forgiveness, I have. It wasn't easy, but I had a solid support of people by my side." I paused. "What about you? Who's been standing next to you?"

Jensen sighed loudly. "It's been just me. I don't stay in one place for very long."

"Something brought you back here. Your subconscious is trying to tell you something, Jensen, and you better listen to it. Right now, I need you to pay attention to what I am about to say. Can you do that?"

Jensen gave a curt nod. "Sure."

"You are not alone. I am and have always been here. That's all I'm going to say. You may have forgotten, but I haven't. I know you. I have always known you. Forcing you into something will do nobody any good. So, when you're ready to talk, or fall apart, I will be waiting."

Jensen rubbed the back of his neck. I watched him, knowing he would soon be leaving. Jensen was careful with his emotions, especially when it came to Jake. What happened that night changed us all forever, but it was an accident. A horrible, horrible accident. A very small part of me resented Jensen for leaving me alone to mourn. He had been one of my best friends. I thought we would stand side by side to keep each other from falling into the darkness. But he let go of my hand and the blackness found me. I was left to face my demons alone, but in time, I slayed them, and was finally at a place where I could feel peace. Looking at Jensen now, I knew he was nowhere near. He had fallen into the shadows and he let them swallow him whole.

"I should go," Jensen said quietly. "I wanted to make sure you were okay."

"I'll walk you to your truck."

We walked side by side in silence. The wheels in his head were turning, his eyes were no longer present. "Thank you," I began. "For last night and checking on me today."

"You're welcome."

Jensen opened up his gleaming door and hopped inside. With a nod, he started up his beast and drove away. I watched him go, sadness gnawing at me. Never had I seen a person look so lonely before. I hoped he would help me let the light in.

Chapter 8
Jensen

Damn girl. Jensen pressed the gas pedal harder heading for work. He needed to get lost under the hood of something, anything. The world made sense there. Tighten this, loosen that, check the fluids. Every move was calculated, and most of all he knew what he was doing. He had a purpose, every problem had a solution. It was one of the only things in his life he was good at. He felt safe there. Everything had an order..

Jensen pulled into his spot and shrugged into his coveralls. He grabbed his trucker hat, slammed it over his tousled hair and set to work. His first project of the day was a 2001 Ford F150 that was having trouble starting. *Another Ford with its hood up.* He got busy to the task ahead as he tested this and that. He replaced the starter solenoid which fixed the issue at hand. He got lost in another vehicle but hard as he tried, he couldn't get Autumn's voice out of his head. He knew she was right. Not once had he spoken about that night, nor had he even considered forgiving himself.

He was taken aback by how much effort Autumn had put into herself to move forward. He admired the strength and determination that surely would have taken. While he had never tried to move on from what happened, he had also never revisited the events that led to his downfall either. He was stuck somewhere in between. Jensen had become a master at stuffing the monster in the closet and throwing away the key. It wasn't healthy, but it kept the worst of it at bay, or so he had convinced himself.

"Hey, Jensen. I'm heading out for a parts run. Some lady is here to get her car, can you deal with it?"

Jensen wiped his hands on a rag and tossed it aside. "Sure."

Jensen entered the main office and his blood ran cold as he recognized the woman standing there. A tidy brunette in her late forties. She hadn't changed much. Doe-like brown eyes darted around the room impatiently. It was JoAnne, Jake's aunt. Jensen slowed his stride as he rounded the corner. He hoped she wouldn't recognize him. The last time she had seen him he was eighteen years old, a child. He was now chasing thirty.

"Your car's all ready to go. The total will be $628."

JoAnne shook her head. "My these things aren't cheap, are they?"

Jensen forced a smile. "No, ma'am." He reached behind the counter and grabbed a set of keys. "These are for you. Will that be cash or credit?"

JoAnne took the keys. "Visa."

Jensen placed the card in the reader and handed her the machine. She punched in her numbers, and while she waited for it to process JoAnne had begun to study Jensen. He tried to keep himself busy by fussing with paperwork, but he knew there was no escaping her stare. JoAnne's sharp eyes took in his name tag. *J Owens.* She let out a sharp gasp and her hand flew to her chest.

"Jensen Owens?" She nearly cried.

Jensen slumped forward; he knew there was no escaping this one. "Yes, ma'am."

"You have a lot of nerve showing your face around these parts. You certainly left this town at lightning speed. Why are you back?"

Jensen stood, staring at JoAnne wordless. He had no answer for her, not a single one. The printer spit out her receipt and he grabbed it, and stapled it together with her paperwork. He handed it to her and forced himself to meet her gaze. "I'm sorry."

JoAnne grabbed the receipt, her eyes darkening. "You don't belong here." She turned on her heel and hurried out.

The ticking of the clock seemed deafening to Jensen's ears. The familiar coldness crept down his spine. His mouth went dangerously dry. He needed to get out of here, quickly. He set out at a fast pace for his truck and hopped inside quickly. He spun the tires in the gravel parking lot and flew out. He had every intention of hopping onto the highway and leaving here once and for all. But something stopped him. He cursed and slammed his steering wheel and began back tracking. Instead, he pulled into a liquor store and stocked up on some old comfort. He ignored the cashier's flirtatious attempts and silently paid for his poison.

At Derik and Kendra's, he kicked off his boots and went to his temporary room.

"I'm sorry," he whispered to himself as he sat alone in the dark. Jensen reached for a bottle of whiskey and unscrewed the cap. He took a long sip and closed his eyes. He let out a sigh of relief as the liquid burned his insides, the only warmth he had felt in years. Jensen clutched the bottle to his chest and contemplated dumping the contents down the sink. He should, but he couldn't bring himself to do it.

The liquid was an old friend, a close friend, one who tended to his deep wounds and masked the pain. It never judged him; it always promised to provide him with much needed comfort. The alcohol called to him seductively, softly. *I can take the hurt away, I can take you to a place where no one will find you. I am always here. I will always be here.*

For just a moment, Jensen held onto his sobriety and thought of Autumn. *I will always be here for you.* Her sweet words floated in his mind and lingered before he shoved them aside. He was no longer the friend she knew. Years of self loathing and self destruction had killed him. The hope he had once searched for was forever lost. Autumn had been through enough. She had found the strength somewhere inside and fought off the despair. He would not drag her down with him. She had come much too far. He took another long swig and began chasing the numbness he knew he would find.

⌘

"Jesus Christ. Get up! Jensen, get up!"

Jensen groaned and remained where he was, face first on his bedroom floor. The annoyed male voice kept speaking. "Get your ass up!"

A bright light lit the room. Jensen moaned. "Turn the damn light off. It's too bright."

A soft voice spoke. "Only for those who don't want to see it."

Autumn. Jensen made an attempt to rise then. He tried to open his eyes, but the best he could manage was a squint. In his hazy daze, he barely made out Autumn's delicate build next to Derik's tall one.

"How long has he been like this?" Autumn whispered.

"A damn week. He's been an angry son of a bitch, too."

Autumn knelt in front of Jensen. "Can you see me?"

"Yes," Jensen croaked.

"Good. Will you be able to comprehend what I'm about to tell you?"

"Yes."

"Okay. Derik has packed up all of your belongings, which from what I understand is only a bag of clothing. You with me so far?"

"Yes."

Derik cut in. "Autumn, I'm not so sure how I feel about this. He's not the same person we grew up with."

Autumn's voice went hard. "Hush. He's in there somewhere."

Jensen stiffened in surprise as Autumn placed her hands on the side of his face. "Jensen Owens, you are a mess. I told you before if you needed me, I would be there and since you've chosen to ignore my offer, I am now forcing it upon you. You officially have no say in the matter." She paused to make sure Jensen watched her. "You are staying with me."

"I-I don't understand. Why? Why would you want to help *me?*"

"I will not lose another friend, do you understand me? I think you're forgetting I have been where you are; well, not quite. Alcohol wasn't my choice, but I do know what you're running from. Besides, the house needs a lot of work. I could use the help."

Autumn stood upright and nodded to Derik. "Well, let's get him up."

Derik sighed, knowing he couldn't win. "Fine. Come on, you drunken fool. On your feet."

Derik helped Autumn get Jensen into her Bronco. He stumbled and uttered colorful phrases under his breath. Jensen was vaguely aware of what transpired around him. All he wanted was to crawl back into the darkness and stay there. Why would nobody let him?

Once they had him in the front seat, Autumn buckled him in and she glared up at him. "Do you see what I'm doing? I am buckling you in like a child and Jensen, you are no child."

Jensen stammered over his words and let his head fall against the cool window. He closed his eyes and heard Autumn curse for her vehicle to start. He smiled slightly. Once the engine turned over, his body swayed side to side from the rocking motion of the vehicle.

"Don't you dare throw up in my truck, do you understand? I can't be held responsible for my actions if you do."

Jensen didn't hear a word. He was fast asleep.

Chapter 9

Autumn

I pulled into the driveway, cursing. I glanced at Jensen, he was fast asleep. I decided to leave him sleeping in the seat. There was simply no way I could carry him out myself. I slammed the door shut and watched Jensen, waiting to see if the sound would cause him to stir. It didn't. As soon as I unlocked the door, Lucy plowed into me, wiggling in excitement.

"Hey, pretty girl," I mumbled. "It's time to get to work."

I entered the house and tossed on work clothes. I needed a job to occupy my mind and calm my nerves. I had never taken anyone in with a dependency issue before. I was blindly walking into very unfamiliar terrain. I looked around the house and wondered what task to tackle next. My eyes settled on the kitchen. It was time to give the kitchen counters TLC.

There was a new paint on the market that mimicked the look of marbled stone. It promised to make any surface look brand new. I started off by sanding the counters and applied the primer. While I waited for it to dry, every now and then I'd steal a peek to see if Jensen had moved. He hadn't. With a frustrated sigh, I tested the counter. It was dry. I mixed the thick, grainy paint and applied the first coat. Stepping back, I admired my work. I nodded with satisfaction. The product held up its promise. The slate gray paint looked like stone. It accented the hardwood floor and the cabinets very nicely. Another check off the list. The kitchen was now near completion.

A male voice cut through the silence. "Who is that sleeping in your car?"

I jumped in surprise, and Logan stood in the entrance. "Jeez, Logan, you nearly gave me a heart attack! Don't you ever knock?"

Logan shrugged and stepped closer. "Who's the guy in the car, Autumn?"

"An old friend. He's having some…issues."

"An old friend?"

"Yes. Jensen."

Logan raised an eyebrow. "As in *the* Jensen?"

"*The* Jensen?" I rinsed the paintbrushes in the sink, and tried to remain calm. I hated that Jensen had such a bad rap. He had done everything he could that day. "He's my friend, Logan, tread lightly."

Logan's tone darkened. "Your friend? I thought he hightailed it out of here after Jake's death. How can you call him your friend?"

I threw the towel in the sink and turned to Logan, fuming. "We were kids, Logan. It was an accident and we did the best we could." I took a breath to steady myself and met Logan's eyes. "Where were *you?* You know how hard it is for me around the anniversary of Jake's death and you weren't there. You're never here when I need you. I've been calling for days and all I ever get is your voicemail."

Logan shook his head. "I was busy."

"Clearly." I let out an exasperated breath. "Why are you here now?"

"I wanted to see you."

"Ah, I see. Glad you could fit me in with your busy schedule."

"Come on, Autumn, don't be like that."

I studied Logan quietly and my eyes fell to the window. "Can you help me bring Jensen inside?"

Logan widened his eyes. "Are you serious?"

"Dead serious. I can't move him myself. You two are about the same size."

Logan raised a brow. "Fine. Where are we putting him?"

"Down here in the guest bedroom. He'll be close to a washroom where he can have privacy."

Logan twisted his lips and stepped closer. "Do you know what you're doing with him?"

"Not a clue. But I can't just leave him alone, he's my friend. Out of all the people in the world, I know what he's going through. I was there too."

Logan softened his voice and clasped my hands. "I know you were, but you chose to get help. It's different. You've made your peace with what happened. I'm not sure revisiting the issue will help you any."

"Some people don't know how to ask for help. Some people need help forced upon them. I know Jensen…he just needs someone to take him by the hand and help him find the trees amongst the forest."

"All right, let's get this over with."

I fell into step with Logan and ignored his disapproving glances. I opened the door and lightly shoved Jensen. "Wake up, Jensen. It's time for you to move."

We were met with inaudible mumbles. Logan threw another look of displeasure my way. "That's not how you get through to these people, Autumn. Let me try."

I stepped back and Logan leaned forward. I watched him closely as he shuffled Jensen and tossed one of his arms around his neck. Logan proceeded to drag Jensen out of the vehicle until he had him somewhat upright.

Logan wore a painful expression on his face. "Autumn, can you balance the other side of him? Otherwise he's going to topple over."

"Sure." I moved quickly and propped up Jensen as best as I could.

"Okay," Logan began. "Let's move him in."

We guided Jensen into the bedroom and sat him on the edge of the bed. Logan held him upright while I took off his boots. Jensen managed to open his eyes for a few moments but he didn't seem to take in anything.

"Autumn, grab a large glass of water, a cool cloth, a bucket, and some Advil."

Logan laid Jensen onto his side. I was surprised at how gently Logan handled him, seeing at how angry he was earlier with the situation at hand. I ran to the kitchen to gather the requests. I set them on the nightstand next to the bed.

Logan nodded. "Hey, buddy. Can you hear me? Jensen? Can you hear me?"

Jensen spoke, his voice hoarse. "Yes."

"Good. You have water here if you're thirsty and a bucket by your bedside. Trust me, you're going to need that. There's a cool cloth here as well. It'll feel good on your head. When the pounding gets to be too much, the Advil will help."

"Mmph."

Logan nodded and stood. He took me by the hand, led me out, and shut the door quietly behind him. Logan let go of my hand and leaned against the wall. He looked rather pale.

I stepped toward him cautiously. "Logan? Are you okay?"

He shook his head slowly and let out a shaky breath. "Jesus, Autumn. He's bad. Do you have any idea what you're getting yourself into?"

"No." I studied him closely and placed my hands gently against his face. "But I have a feeling you do."

Logan's blue eyes fell to mine. "Yes."

"Who was it?"

"My mom," he whispered.

"Oh, Logan. I'm so sorry. If I had known I would have never asked for your help."

"It's fine. I don't talk about it much."

"I know. You never talk about anything personal."

Logan straightened up. "No, I don't." He glanced at the door and looked weary. "I'm guessing he's been dry for awhile. Looks like a binge to me. Something must have set him off. I'm warning you, the next little bit is going to get ugly. He's not going to be happy."

"Okay. What do I do?"

"Don't let him drink. Force him to eat things like dry toast, lots of water. Do you

have any alcohol in the house?"

"No. I don't really drink, as you know."

Logan smiled a little then. "That's right. Well, that's good. He's going to be a pain in your ass."

I studied the closed door, and wondered what obstacles lay before me. Jensen and I had been best friends as children, but that was so long ago. The man laying in the bedroom was not my friend. I had no idea who he was. A knot formed in the pit of my stomach. What was I doing? Could I handle this? Surely, the boy I once knew still existed in him, somewhere? Time couldn't have destroyed him completely…could it? There were so many unanswered questions, but the one thing I was sure of, I could not, would not, turn away a friend in need. Especially one who looked so entirely damaged. I owed him a chance to find his way.

"Logan?"

"Yes?"

"Thank you for being here."

Logan took a step closer and wrapped me in a tight hug. "You're welcome, kid."

I fought back a grin at the horrendous nickname he had given me over the years. I looked up, and though he was smiling, it didn't reach his eyes. "How are you doing?" I asked softly.

"I'm fine. I'm just worried about you. Do you mind if I stay the night?"

"Not at all."

"Good. I'm going to run home and grab some things then. I'll be back within the hour."

"Okay, I'll start dinner."

Logan took my hand and we walked together to the front door. "Thanks. By the way, the kitchen looks great. The facelift for the house is going well, kid. I'm proud of you."

I swelled at his complement. "Thank you, things are clicking along nicely. I just need to tackle the exterior of the house."

Logan nodded and gave me a quick kiss. "Okay, I'm going to gather my things. I'll be back soon."

"Drive safe." I shut the door behind me and crossed my arms. An uneasy coldness fell heavy around me. I recognized it as fear. What had I gotten myself into?

⌘

I placed the last of the vegetables into the pot and stuck the casserole in the oven. I walked down the hall to the guest bedroom then paused. My feet seemed to have a mind of their own; they were frozen in place. I craned my neck as far as I could, staring at the closed door. *This is ridiculous. He's your friend and this is your house. Move, girl, move!* I grumbled to myself and forced my stubborn feet forward. Without hesitation, I managed to grab the door handle and twist it open. I peeked inside hesitantly. I froze in place again. Jensen was awake. He sat on the edge of the bed, hunched over. The cool cloth was pressed firmly against his forehead and he moaned slightly.

"Jensen?"

He looked up, his handsome face haggard. "Autumn? Where am I?"

I stepped inside. "You're at my home, with me. You…had a lot to drink, it would seem." I bent over to flick on the lamp.

Jensen's hand clasped around my arm. "Please, leave it off."

"Oh…sure."

"Thank you. Is there a washroom close by?"

"Yes, right across the hall. Do you need help?"

"I might need help getting up. Let me try."

I stepped back and let Jensen find his feet. It was shocking to see how little control he seemed to have over his own body. His skin was covered with a light layer of sweat and he swayed. I came to his side and did my best to keep him stable.

"We better hurry. I think I'm going to be sick."

I let out a groan. "Walk fast, let's go!"

We made it to the washroom and he fell to his knees, and hugged the toilet bowl. I stood in the corner and danced uneasily. Jensen came up for air briefly before tipping his face downwards once more. I let out a small dry heave myself, yet I walked toward him. I placed my hands on his back and rubbed soothingly.

"Are you okay, Jensen? Do you want some water?"

"I want a drink," he moaned.

"That's not what I offered you. Water, that's all you get. Yes or no?"

"Fine. Water it is."

"I'll be right back."

I came back to find Jensen sitting against the wall, his head in his hands. "Here's your water."

"Thanks." He took a long sip, all the while staring at me. He placed the cup down gently and let out a disgusted laugh. "Well, what do you think of your old friend?"

I pressed my lips together and walked past him. I opened a drawer and pulled out a cloth and ran it under the tap. I sat in front of him and dabbed the cloth against his face. I didn't say a word, couldn't, my brain was empty. I didn't feel words would do much to soothe him at this point anyway. I hoped a kind gesture could do the talking for me.

However, I wasn't one to stay silent for long. "Derik said you've been at this for a week. Is that true?"

"Yes."

I stood and threw the cloth at him. "Dammit, Jensen! I told you if you needed to talk to someone to come and find me! But no! You chose damn liquid over me; a human being!"

Jensen pressed his hands over his ears. "Please, not so loud."

"Get up."

Jensen looked toward me at my harsh tone. He puffed in a defiant manner. "No, leave me alone."

"I will not. Get up."

"No."

"You need a shower. You reek of stale alcohol and puke."

"I don't feel good. Please, just leave me here."

"Fine, if you won't get up, I'll help you."

I marched past him and shoved open the shower curtain and reached inside. I grabbed a bottle of body wash, opened the lid and squirted its contents onto Jensen. I grabbed the extendable nozzle and pulled it out as far as it would allow.

"You wouldn't dare," he taunted.

"Oh, but I would." And I did. I turned on the water and pointed the nozzle onto Jensen.

"Hey! Dammit. Stop, I said stop!"

"Are you going to get up and clean yourself up?" I yelled over the spray of the water.

Jensen sprang to his feet and tried to wrestle the nozzle out of my hand. He managed to turn it on me a few times, soaking me in an instant. But he was still clumsy and slow. I had the upper hand. I wriggled out of his grasp and pointed the nozzle directly onto his face. Lucy stood barking in the doorway.

"Autumn, what are you doing?" Logan ran inside, nearly slipping on the wet floor. He reached inside the shower and turned the water off.

Jensen was furious, and so was I. "I was trying to get him clean!" I propped my hands on my hips. "You better take those clothes off and get clean ones on or I'll do it for you!"

Jensen wiped the soap out of his face and swore. "You damn crazy girl."

I let out an angry muffle and stormed toward him, reaching for his shirt. Logan let out a curse and swooped his arms around my waist, hauling me out of the bathroom.

"Logan, put me down! What are you doing?"

"What are you doing? I leave you alone for half an hour and the place turns to chaos."

Jensen opened the door angrily. "Well, do you have my clothes here or not?"

"I do."

"Can you grab me a clean pair then?" Jensen glared. "Now that I'm covered in soap, and soaking wet I might as well have a shower."

I beamed. "Great! I'll bring you your clothes."

Logan grinned and looked at Jensen. "Well, you have to admit, for a small girl she puts up a helluva good fight."

Jensen's eyes narrowed. "Damn crazy, that's what she is."

Chapter 10
Jensen

Jensen hated to admit it, but the steaming water felt good; he almost felt alive. His stomach was raw, his head pounded, and his eyes felt scratched to hell. He stepped out of the shower and tossed on the clean clothes that Autumn had laid out for him. Every inch of him hurt. All he wanted to do was go back to bed. As he stepped into the hall, he almost expected to be pounced on by Autumn. He heard her and Logan's voice off in the distance. He just about slumped to the floor in relief.

He had never wanted Autumn to see him like this. So weak, so broken, so completely exposed. He had to give her credit, she was a determined thing. She hadn't lost that quality over the years. She always tried to fix things, always tried to find the good in whatever was thrown her way. Jensen looked around his surroundings; like this house for instance. She was fixing something that was long left to rot, but piece by piece she was turning it into gold. She never did see the obvious, she always looked past that and saw what could be.

Jensen set himself on the bed and curled up into a tight ball. He felt nauseous and the room spun. He hated withdrawals. He knew what would come next; the awful tremors that would take over his body followed by a cool sweat. His mind began to wander to Autumn and Logan. Jensen wasn't aware she had someone by her side. He hoped she was happy. She deserved someone good. At the same time, the thought bothered him. A sound at the door caused him to stir. He looked up, waiting for Autumn to burst in the room and get him up. The door creaked open and in came Lucy. The dog entered politely and hopped up beside Jensen. Lucy whined softly and stretched out beside Jensen.

He let out a sigh and ran his hand over her soft coat. "All right, you can stay. No judging me." Lucy answered by wagging her tail.

⌘

The water was dark and murky. Jensen sank below the surface, and though he swam desperately to the top, he could never break for air. The water had a mind of its own, and it held him down gladly. Under the hazy view of the water, Jensen saw a dock. The current slammed him into the dock's pillars, deeply rooted beneath the lake. The impact knocked what little breath he had out of him.

The water toyed with him now as it tossed him this way and that. The temperature began to drop, and he felt chilled to the bone. Panic built within him as he knew this was it, he was dying. His heartbeat slowed in his ears and he sank lower and lower toward the sandy depths. He let his body go limp and he stared out amongst the black depth.

A few feet in front of him, something came closer. He tried to open his eyes a little wider to make out the image before him. The object came forward slowly with bits of lake weeds intertwined. Jensen closed his eyes for a brief moment. When he reopened them, he stared into a mangled, lifeless face.

Jensen let out a cry and sprang out of bed. He was soaked in a cold sweat and his heart raced. He ran to the window, opened it and gasped for air. His hands trembled violently and his head began to swirl. A sound came behind him and he jumped to face the intruder. He stopped mid tracks as Autumn stared back at him, her eyes wide.

"Jensen? Are you okay? I heard you scream and—"

"A drink. I need a drink."

Autumn studied him and her eyes fell to his trembling hands. Jensen noticed she looked frightened; she had every right to. He knew he looked like a wild animal on the verge of pouncing its prey. Autumn straightened her shoulders and tried to appear tall. "No, Jensen. You cannot have a drink."

Jensen cursed and stepped toward her. "Move out of my way."

Autumn barricaded herself in the doorway. "No."

"If you don't move, I will move you."

Autumn narrowed her eyes. "Try it."

Jensen came forward and shoved her aside, heading for the front door. To his sheer surprise, he felt something hard hit him in the back. He turned and saw Autumn holding a shoe. "Did you just throw a shoe at me?" he asked incredulously.

"I did and I have a good arm on me. You are not leaving this house, and besides your truck is still at Derik's. I guarantee you will not get very far."

Jensen opened his mouth in surprise and then he got angry. He took a menacing step to Autumn. She stepped back and her eyes flew to the stairs. "Logan! Logan, I need you down here!"

Logan raced downstairs and took in the situation immediately. He stepped in front of Autumn and glared. "Look at her, Jensen. You're scaring her."

Jensen glanced at Autumn and guilt coursed through him immediately. He knew she was only trying to help, but he needed a drink. He needed one so badly. Logan cleared his throat and took a step forward. "The tremors are kicking in. It's going to get worse before it gets better, but you need to hang in there. Do you think you can do that?"

Jensen stared at Logan but didn't say a word. Logan shook his head. "That's not a good enough answer. I won't have you in here scaring Autumn. You either abide by the rules or you get out."

Autumn let out a gasp to protest. "Logan, we can't just—"

Logan squeezed her arm reassuringly. "It's up to you, Jensen."

Jensen knew how far out of town he was, and he was in no condition for a hike. He ran his hands through his hair and sank to the floor. "I just want a drink. You don't understand, I saw him. He's always there."

Autumn ran past Logan and crouched in front of Jensen. She held out her hands for his, hesitating slightly. Jensen watched as she had a silent conversation with herself before she grasped his trembling hands. "He's not here anymore. It's okay. I used to see him, too."

Jensen looked up at Autumn, his eyes haunted. "How do I make it stop?"

Autumn glanced at Logan and nodded reassuringly. "It's okay, I've got this."

Logan hesitated and Autumn prompted him again. "I promise, it's okay."

Logan rubbed the back of his neck. "Call me if you need me." He stepped past Jensen and gave him a hard glare. "If you so much as lay a hand on her, I will drag you out of here myself."

Autumn cleared her throat. "Come on, you're burning up. Let's get you back to bed."

"I can't."

"Yes, you can, come on. I've got you."

Jensen rose and they walked in step to the bedroom. He stood aimlessly in the doorway and Autumn sat on the edge of the bed. "C'mon, make yourself comfy."

Jensen hesitated and then sat next to her. He could feel her eyes taking in his ragged appearance and he hated himself in the moment. He should have stayed away. Autumn scooted closer to him and pulled her knees to her chest, and rested her head upon his shoulder. Jensen stiffened in surprise at her touch.

"How does it work for you, Jensen?"

"How does what work?"

"Is this how you numb the loneliness, the guilt, the pain?"

"Yes."

"I see. And how is that working out for you so far? Because from where I'm standing, I think your method needs some restructuring."

Jensen forced himself to look at Autumn. She stared back at him, no judgement within her soft eyes.

A pained expression overtook his face. "I don't know what's happened to me. I lost myself somewhere along the way. When I first started drinking, everything felt so good. It was just enough to take away the guilt and I could sleep. But then things escalated and I couldn't control myself anymore. I couldn't stop."

Autumn bit her lip, looking lost in thought. "Jensen?"

"Yes?"

"Have you ever spoken to *anyone* about what happened?"

"No."

Autumn nodded. "You need to face it. You can't move past this unless you do. And I'll be here for you when you're ready."

Self-loathing crept into his mind. It was always the same battle in his head, he hated himself for what he had done. He hated himself for being such a coward and trying to out run something he knew was a loosing battle. He was slowly destroying the man he once was. But this time, it felt even worse than before, for this time was different.

An old friend sat beside him, she was witnessing his ugly side and yet, she wasn't running away. She was here, willing to help him. And he hated that. Jensen wasn't so sure he could be helped anymore. He had given up on himself so long ago, he wasn't sure where to begin, or if he would have the strength to face his demons. Jensen stared into Autumn's kind features and quickly looked away. He didn't know if he could stand to see the disappointment on her face he would surely put there.

"Are you going to be okay for the night?" Autumn asked quietly.

Jensen nodded silently. "Yes, thank you."

"You're welcome. Have a good night." Autumn stood and made her way to the door.

Jensen spoke quickly. "Autumn? I'm not worth this."

Autumn froze and turned to him. "You are. Don't you forget, I remember you. I *know* who you are. The person I once knew is still in there. I see flickers of him in your eyes every once in awhile. I won't deny you are beaten down right now, and this is going to be hard, very hard. But dammit, Jensen, I will help you find yourself. I won't lose another friend, especially like this."

"Why would you help me, after everything?"

Autumn sighed. "Because I was there that day too. I saw it." Autumn closed her eyes briefly. "I had people holding my hand along the way, navigating me through the aftermath. You clearly did not. I can't leave you where you have left yourself. I won't do it."

Jensen stared back, wordless. He watched her leave, shutting the door quietly behind her. He stared into the darkness and for the first time in a long time, he felt the promise of change. Maybe, just maybe, the force Autumn provided would be enough to get him out of the hole he'd dug for himself. Jensen curled into a ball, and moaned softly. His mouth felt as though it was full of cotton balls, his head hurt, and his body trembled beyond control. This was going to be a long, hard road. He hoped to hell he could survive the climb.

⌘

In the dim room, a loud rumble awoke Jensen. He sat upright, his heart beat rapidly. He knew that sound. It was his truck. Jensen sprang out of bed and ran down the hall. He skidded to a stop when Derik entered the kitchen, holding the keys. Autumn held a mug of coffee in her hands and looked towards Jensen with a new interest.

"Good morning." Autumn's voice held a smile. "Feeling a bit better today? Want some coffee?"

Jensen tore his eyes away from the keys and nodded curtly to Derik. "Thanks for bringing my truck over."

Derik's eyes slowly evaluated Jensen. He nodded. "Nice to see you're still alive. Come, sit with us and have a coffee."

Jensen protested in his head. He hated being treated like an invalid but did as told. The smell of the freshly brewed coffee helped awaken his spirts, as much as he hated to admit it. Derik and Autumn kept the conversation light, but he couldn't help but notice the way Derik scrutinized him. He searched for any signs of progress he could find amongst Jensen's features. Judging from the grimaces here and there, Jensen was pretty sure he was in the exact state Derik anticipated.

Jensen looked around the room for Logan. There was no sign of him. "Where's Logan?"

Autumn stiffened as though the question caught her off guard. "He's not here right now."

Something in her tone told Jensen not to prod any further in the moment. "Okay."

Derik stood. "I guess I'd better be going. It was nice to see you moving about, Jensen."

Autumn sent Jensen an apologetic look and shrugged her shoulders. She mouthed the words "I'm sorry" as she walked Derik to the front door. Jensen stayed where he was and waited for Autumn to return. She entered the room clutching his keys in her hand. She looked at him with one eyebrow raised. Her stance told him she was ready for an encounter.

"Where would you go if you took these from me?" she asked.

Jensen set down his cup of coffee and stood carefully. He noted she wore clothes with paint stains. He sighed in defeat. "I'm not going anywhere. I have nowhere to go at this point. Do you have Advil by chance?"

Autumn grinned. "I sure do. I'll be right back." A moment later she placed two capsules in his hand. "There you go."

"Thank you."

"On a scale of one to ten, how bad are you feeling right now?"

"Eleven."

"Then, you're no good to me right now. Tell you what we're going to do. Today, you're going to sleep and take it easy because tomorrow I'm putting you to work. Deal?" Jensen let out a dry laugh. "You're not giving me much of a choice are you?"

"Not really, no. So I strongly suggest you go back to bed and rest up. There's a lot of work that needs to be done."

Jensen watched Autumn turn on her heel. With a wink, she left the room. Jensen chuckled to himself. She certainly was relentless, and he didn't have the energy in him to argue.

Chapter 11

Autumn

Every muscle in my body hurt. My arms were scratched to high heaven from cutting down all the blackberry bushes around the house. Once I had them chopped down, I lit a small fire to burn their remains. Between cutting the bramble and weeding, I checked in on Jensen from time to time. He slept the majority of the day, and for this, I was glad. The house would remain quiet and peaceful. I didn't think he would give me much trouble, unlike the night before. His hands had quieted, his presence was almost calm today. I stepped into the kitchen and made myself a light dinner. I toyed with the soup before pouring most of it down the sink; my appetite evaded me.

I hopped in the shower for a quick rinse, threw on a pair of shorts and a light shirt. Lucy trotted after me as I walked slowly to the barn, barefoot. I slid open the door and settled onto the tire swing. I leaned my head back and closed my eyes, getting lost in the motion. A small surge of childhood pleasure flowed through me. I leaned into the swinging rope eagerly, and enjoyed the feeling of simply having no control.

I worried about Jensen and if I could guide him in the right direction. Being around him had stirred up old feelings from many years ago. I wasn't sure I was ready for them to resurface. I tried to ignore the knot that had taken over my stomach. Not only was being around Jensen an old comfort, but it also gave life to the hurt and devastation of losing one of our best friends all over again. I had mourned Jake's loss years ago. I was left here, front and center, to see the aftermath. Jensen was not. His family hightailed it out of town, and judging from the state Jensen was in these days, he had not properly dealt with the loss. He tried his best to ignore the incident by shoving it in the dark corners of his mind but it was coming out to haunt him. I knew there was an element of danger in staying close to Jensen; there was a very good chance I could get lost in this all over again. And I couldn't go do it again.

"I knew I would find you here."

Logan's voice snapped me out of my somber thoughts. I turned toward him, still at the mercy of the tire swing. "I'm surprised to see you back here after last night," I choked out.

After Jensen went to bed, Logan and I had a heated argument. Logan wanted Jensen gone, and I couldn't ask him to leave, not now, not when he had finally come back after all these years.

Logan stepped forward and steadied the swing to a stop. He took me by the hands and helped me onto my feet. "Thank you," I said quietly.

Logan set back his shoulders and took a step back. "He's still here."

"Yes, he is. I'm not asking him to leave. I can't. We've been over this."

Logan slammed the wall with an open palm. "Autumn, I don't think he should be your problem. Just tell him to go."

"No."

"Dammit. What is it that ties you to him? He's been gone since you were sixteen. A lot has changed since then. He's not the same person he used to be, is he?"

"You wouldn't understand, Logan. You didn't grow up here. He was my best friend…I still see him beneath the rubble. He's still in there." I bit my lip and continued carefully. "I know your mother was an alcoholic, if this is bringing up bad memories for you—"

Logan held up his hands and his voice went hard. "Stop right there. No. Do not bring her into this. This is not the same thing."

"I'm sorry," I whispered. I raised my eyes to his. "What do you want me to say? What do you want from me?"

Logan ran a hand through his hair. "I don't know. I don't even know why I'm wasting my time with this conversation. It's not like we're a couple, right? This was always just a fun, casual thing."

I sucked in a sharp breath. Even though I had always known Logan wasn't the type to commit, his words hurt. The truth left no room for imagining otherwise. I had been holding on to the hope for over a year now that he would see me standing in front of him and he would make the jump, for me, and meet me in the middle. All I ever wanted from him was to feel secure in where I stood.

I nodded quickly. "I guess you're right. I was always more of a convenience than anything." I marched past him, holding back tears. The ache that tore through my chest caught me off guard. I didn't think he could have that kind of effect on me.

"Autumn, wait!"

I ignored Logan and continued up the path to the house at a swift pace. Logan caught up and grabbed me by the arm. "Just tell him to go."

"I'm not about to kick him out, he needs help." I placed my hands on my hips. "Why do you care anyway? You just said we're a casual thing, nothing serious."

Logan glowered. "But you're *my* casual thing. We always have a good time together. What more do you want?"

I threw my hands in the air in exasperation. "I want to know the person I'm with will be there for me, during the good times and the bad." I softened my voice. "Last night you were a huge help, but I won't be asking him to leave. I'm sorry, I just can't."

Logan looked at the house and cursed. "He's going to eat you alive."

Anger rose within me. "Thanks for the words of encouragement."

"If he stays, I'm gone."

I held my head high. "Then I guess this is goodbye. Find another *casual* thing."

Logan's voice turned cold. "Unbelievable." He turned away and stormed to his truck. He slammed the door and sped out of the driveway.

I jumped back as his tires spit gravel my way. I wrapped myself in a hug as I watched him speed away. A heavy emptiness settled into my stomach, and I let the tears fall quietly. I sat on the porch steps, quietly petting Lucy until the tears came to a halt. I had known for sometime this was the inevitable course for Logan and me. The event that triggered it, however, I did not see coming. The smell of cigarette smoke caught me off guard. The porch squeaked behind me as Jensen sat next to me.

"Are you okay?" Concern filled Jensen's features.

"I'm fine. I had always known we were heading down different roads."

Jensen nodded slowly and took a drag. He sucked in a deep breath and blew a cloud of white smoke. "I'm sorry to hear that. The guys an idiot, though."

Despite the moment, a smile found my lips. "He was my idiot," I muttered. I wiped at the last of my tears and took a sidelong glance toward him. "Since when do you smoke?"

He shrugged. "It's an off and on habit."

I wrinkled my nose. "I see. Normally I would grab that thing out of your mouth and put it out, but I suppose it would be cruel to take away both of your dependencies at once. We'll work on this one later."

Jensen's face turned in surprise as he let out a laugh. "Sure, if you say so. One day at a time it is."

I smiled slowly and stood, trying to work a kink out of my back. "I'm going to go to bed. Are you going to be okay by yourself?"

"I'm not a child. Yeah, I'll keep myself outta trouble."

"Okay. Goodnight, Jensen."

"Autumn?"

I stopped and turned around. "Yes?"

"Please hide the keys from me. I don't trust myself yet."

"Okay, I will."

Jensen's shoulders sagged in relief. "Thank you. Goodnight."

⌘

The smell of coffee woke me. I followed the delightful scent into the kitchen. I watched in wonder as Jensen popped pieces of bread into the toaster.

"Good morning," he said brightly.

"Morning."

"Are you hungry? I scrambled eggs."

"Sure." I sat on a kitchen stool as Jensen placed a plate in front of me. He smiled and got back to his meal prep. I took in his appearance, his jeans were dirty and he had paint splatter on his arms. "Were you working on the house?" I asked in surprise.

Jensen shut off the stove and turned to face me. He leaned casually against the counter. "I was up at five-thirty this morning, I couldn't sleep. I found your tools and decided it was time to paint the outside of the house. I wanted to help. It's my way of thanking you."

My mouth gaped and I ran outside to see the progress. The grass was wet with morning dew as my feet met the cool earth. I looked up in excitement at my home. My hands flew over my mouth as I let out an excited squeal. The house was beginning to look alive. A fresh coat of white paint hid the dull, patchy base. The dark blue trim was vibrant once again as it carefully etched out the windows and doorframes. The house looked proud and new. Jensen followed me outside, stopping on the porch.

I met his eyes and he smiled. I ran to him, and bulldozed him with a hug. "Thank you, thank you, thank you!"

"You're welcome. I like having a project. It feels good to keep busy."

With my arms still around his waist I looked up. "Oh? What other talents do you have?"

"I'm a man of many talents. What else needs doing?"

I tapped a finger against the side of my cheek. "The upstairs shower is leaking. I'm not sure what to do about that one."

"Okay, I'll check it out once I'm done with the painting. I figure it should take me about two days to get it done."

I beamed in reply. "Excellent."

Jensen studied me curiously and sighed. "Make me a list, Autumn. Put me to good use."

I grinned and ran inside, doing just that.

⌘

The afternoon sun was hot. I wiped a bead of sweat on my forehead. Jensen and I were outside painting the house. He took the ladder while I stayed along the base. I stepped back to stretch, and turned at the sight of a familiar car pulling up the drive. An elderly woman stepped outside wearing a bright floral dress. Her graying hair was wrapped up in a tidy bun. She climbed out of her car carefully and shielded her eyes from the sun as she looked at the house.

A smile grew on her plump face. "My, the house looks wonderful," she breathed.

I smiled in return and tugged my ponytail tighter. "Thank you. It's been a labor of love."

The woman's eyes watched Jensen on the ladder. His back was bare under the sun, his muscles worked in unison as he moved the paintbrush back and forth in smooth strokes. Her lips twitched once more. "It looks like you have some good help."

I smiled knowingly. "I can't complain too much."

The woman locked her eyes with mine and held out her hand. "Where are my manners? I'm Anna, I work at the town's small museum."

I wiped my paint blotted hand against the leg of my shorts before grasping her fragile one. "I thought you looked familiar. I'm Autumn."

"I know who you are. I've actually come here to see you."

"Oh?" I raised an eyebrow in question. "Sure, do you want a glass of iced tea?"

"That would be lovely."

I motioned Anna to follow. Her quick eyes took in every detail of the house and she noticed, admiringly, the work put in. We sat at the kitchen table with cool glasses of refreshments before us. Anna folded her hands neatly onto her lap as she studied me curiously. "I remember you as a child. You were always full of questions. You often came into the museum and got lost in the artwork. Do you remember?"

I nodded. I had always been drawn to history. Like a good book, every piece told a story; I had always been enchanted by it. "Of course, I remember. When I went to college I took art history."

Anna nodded. "I heard through the grapevine. I was rather disappointed you never came to see me once you were done. I must admit, I was shocked when I heard you were working at the restaurant."

I bit my lip, I felt I was being scolded by my grandmother. "After my grandma passed, I will admit I lost my way a bit."

Anna nodded fiercely. "I was good friends with your grandmother. She spoke of you often and fondly. Actually, I am here to offer you a small push in the right direction."

"Oh?"

Anna nodded proudly. "I would like to offer you a job at the museum. I'm getting older and having trouble keeping up with all the duties. I need help organizing events, paperwork, tidying displays and what not. A little bit of everything really. Are you interested?"

My eyes flew wide. I placed a hand over my now racing heart. Excitement coursed through my veins. It had been a long time since life had excited me this way. "I don't know what to say!"

Anna took a sip of iced tea. She set the glass down carefully and smirked. "Well, honey, I do hope you will say yes."

"Yes! Yes, of course, I will!"

Anna stood and shook my hand. "I will see you tomorrow morning at eight."

I walked Anna back to her car and helped her inside. I waited until her car was out of sight before I let out a very happy squeal.

Chapter 12
Jensen

Jensen climbed down the ladder to towel off. The sun grew hot and his shoulders had begun to burn. A squeal spilt the silence and he ran toward the noise not quite knowing what he would find. A part of him expected to see that fool hardy girl hanging from a window sill. He stopped in his tracks as Autumn bounced up and down in place. She turned to him and her face lit up like a thousand stars.

"I just got offered a job at the museum! Can you believe this?"

Jensen's heart returned to its usual rhythm. She was happy, not in danger. "Wow, congratulations. This is good news I take it?"

"It is," she breathed. Her blue eyes took on a faraway look as she glanced over the house once more. She shook her head slowly. "It's all coming together, Jensen."

"What is?"

"My life. I've been stuck in a rut for a few years and now that I'm out, I can't believe I stayed there for so long. I didn't realize how unhappy I was until this moment."

Jensen rubbed the back of his neck. He was happy for her, she looked radiant. He, on the other hand, began to feel even more out of place. His life was nowhere near where it should be. Autumn noticed his hesitation. She stepped forward and laid her hand on his arm. "You won't be stuck here forever."

Jensen nodded quickly and pulled his arm back. "Yup. I better get back to work."

"Oh, okay. Don't you want to take a break? You've been working for hours."

"No, I'm good. I like to work."

"Okay. I'm going to take Lucy for a run then. I'll see you later."

Jensen nodded and headed back up the ladder. He dipped the roller in the paint and left his stain on the wood. He tried to keep his mind quiet; he wanted a drink so badly. On a hot day like this, there was nothing more quenching than a cool, crisp beer. Jensen kept busy painting until the sun began to set. The entire front end of the house was completed by the time he called it a day. Autumn tried to get him to stop working earlier to eat dinner, but he had refused. He knew when his thoughts turned against him, it was best he kept himself busy. An image came into Jensen's mind, one that had played all afternoon; he would find his truck keys and drive to the nearest bar. It was there Jensen felt at home, in the dimly lit setting where the smell of stale alcohol greeted him.

Jensen nodded past Autumn as he entered the house. She was stretched out on the couch, a book in hand. He had a quick shower and realized he was hungry after all.

Autumn sat up from the couch lazily and tossed him a knowing smile. "Leftovers are in the fridge, enjoy."

Jensen heated his food and sat in the living room across from Autumn. She looked up from her book for a split second to smile before her attention was quickly drawn to the words on the page once more. Jensen watched her for a moment as a flashback unfolded before him. They were children once more. He and Jake ran in the tall grass of the fields trying to find snakes. Autumn stretched out on a rock, lazing under the hot sun with a book in hand. She had always loved to read and was full of tales to tell. Autumn ignored the boys as they jumped and hollered about. She tossed them a look of disbelief every now and then, and rolled her eyes. Jensen found a snake and tossed it at Autumn. She dropped her book and screamed. The boys laughed out loud, and once the snake slithered into safety, Autumn pouted. She was upset about losing her place in the book and she worried about the snake. Jensen began to chuckle out loud at the memory.

"What's so funny?" Autumn mused.

"Do you remember when Jake and I threw a snake at you?"

Autumn wrinkled her nose. "Yes, that was not pleasant. Poor snake."

Jensen laughed out loud then, Autumn joined in. They got to reminiscing and before Jensen realized it, the memories didn't stab him with regret. For once, revisiting something that caused him such pain was almost pleasant. They talked awhile more before Autumn set her book down.

"I better go to bed. I have work tomorrow." She stopped and tilted her head to one side. "Isn't that a great sentence?" She sighed.

"It is. I'm happy for you."

"Thank you." She bit her lip. "Are you going to be all right tomorrow?"

"Yes. There's a lot to keep me busy here."

"Okay. If you need anything, call my cell."

"Will do. Goodnight, Autumn."

Autumn paused before leaving. "This was fun, talking to you tonight." She leaned down and threw her arms around his neck. She pulled back and met his eyes. "I've missed my best friend. I'm glad to see he's still in there. Goodnight."

Jensen watched her leave the room, Lucy by her side. He sat back into the couch, and for once, he wasn't thinking about a drink.

⌘

"Dammit." Jensen tossed the drill onto the floor. It was officially dead. He looked at the dismantled bathtub before him and knew he needed more tools. He stepped back from the mess and went to look for Autumn. She would need to do a store run.

It was now the weekend. Jensen and Autumn had settled into a routine. While she was at work, he kept busy around the house and yard. When she came home, she would go for a run and then make dinner. Afterwards she would help Jensen finish whatever project he had been working on earlier in the day. He enjoyed his new routine. It made him feel useful and it was safe. No one could knock him down. No one but himself.

Jensen found Autumn downstairs, scraping off the old kitchen floor. "The drill bit the dust. We're going to need a new one."

Autumn looked up, and wiped away dust from her face. "Okay, I'm going to need some grout for the new tiles too, I don't think I'll have enough to finish. Are we taking your truck or mine?"

Jensen froze. He hadn't driven anywhere since he arrived over a week ago. He felt safe right where he was; he had a routine. He wasn't sure he trusted himself to venture out on his own yet. "Let's take yours."

Autumn dusted her hands together. "I think I should rephrase the question. I really want to ride in your truck." She stopped to watch his reaction. "Don't worry, I'm going with you. I'll keep us on a tight schedule." She softened her voice. "You have to get back out there, Jensen, baby steps."

He sighed with resignation. "Okay, let's do it."

"Great. Be right back."

Autumn came down the steps and tossed him the keys. He caught them with one hand. He clasped his grip around them tighter, these keys could take him down a good road, or a very dark one. It was up to him. They walked to his truck and he hopped inside.

Autumn hauled herself in and sat heavy in the passenger seat. "Wow. This is a beast."

Jensen laughed quietly. "Watch this, mine will start on the first try."

"Oh, ha ha. Aren't you a funny one."

Jensen turned the ignition, and sure enough it came to life on the first turn. Jensen pulled the gear into drive and made the journey to the hardware store. Jensen settled into the smooth rhythm of his truck and realized how much he missed this. He considered his truck to be a big part of who he was. He found it years ago in someone's yard, shortly after Jake's death. It was left to rot away. Jensen had been drawn to it. The man who used to own it let it go for free. Jensen spent months taking it apart and putting it back together. He buffed out the scratches, welded new panels, scrubbed out the rust, and lovingly replaced all the broken pieces. Once it was done, you would never know it had been left to decompose. Jensen felt a sense of accomplishment in the finished task; he had been able to bring something back to life.

They pulled into an empty parking spot and wandered the aisles. They were in and out. By the time Jensen parked the truck in front of Autumn's house, he felt like he was somewhat in control. His mind was tuned in to what needed to be done to the house; it had a focus.

Autumn hopped out and sidled up beside him. "How did it feel?"

Jensen smirked. "Really good." He gave Autumn a side long glance and laughed. "Your face expression just screams 'I told you so.'"

Autumn made a motion her lips were sealed. "I'm going to get back to tiling."

"Okay, I'll deal with the shower."

For the rest of the afternoon they kept busy with their separate tasks. Jensen found his mind wandered to Autumn frequently. She provided a sense of security for him. While the world looked down and judged him, she gave him hope he was worth more. Jensen had been with many women over the years, but they never meant anything to him. He couldn't even recall half their names. He used them as a filler for the guilt and loneliness that taunted him.

After Jake had passed, his parents whisked him away in the blink of an eye. He not only had to work through the grief of losing his best friend, but he had also left behind his first love, Autumn. Though they had never said the words to each other, her memory stayed with him through the years. When he closed his eyes at night, her image filled his thoughts. She had left a mark on him. He wanted to contact her over the years, but the more time passed, the harder it became to reach out. He hoped she was happy, and that her life was a pleasant one. To this day, he still didn't know what it was that made him come back. He wasn't sure it had been the right decision.

He never wanted Autumn to see how he had turned out. He didn't want to burden anyone with his faults, which was why he stayed gone in the first place. Jensen liked to keep moving, he didn't want to get attached to anything, or anyone, for he knew he would only end up hurting someone. But when Jensen had laid eyes on Autumn the day he returned, he knew he wouldn't be strong enough to walk away, not again.

⌘

Three weeks later Jensen and Autumn stood in the front yard and stared at the house. Autumn beamed from ear to ear and shook her head in amazement. "It's done, Jensen. Can you believe it? The house is officially finished."

Jensen nodded wordlessly. He was having a hard time finding pleasure in the situation. This was it, it was over. What was he going to do with his time now? He loved having projects, especially ones that occupied so much of his time, most importantly, his thoughts.

Autumn peeked at Jensen. "I'll be right back, I have a surprise."

Jensen watched her run into the house, and come back a moment later with two champagne glasses and a chilled bottle. His heart began to beat rapidly, and his mouth went dry.

"Sparkling apple juice," Autumn said proudly. "I thought we needed something to mark the special occasion. I couldn't have done all of this without you, thank you so much."

Jensen rubbed the back of his neck and smiled crookedly. "It was my pleasure. I enjoyed it."

Autumn handed him a glass and raised hers high. "To us, to the house. Cheers!" They clinked their glasses and took a sip. He savored the feeling of the bubbly liquid though it didn't hold the kick he had been longing for. Autumn sat cross legged in the grass and admired the house and its surroundings once again. Jensen sat beside her, feeling envious. She was the picture of content. She had a purpose in life. He felt like a fish out of water. He was left to flop on the beach, desperately trying to reach the safety of the sea. It was so close and yet he was so far. The ringing of the phone sent Autumn to her feet and she ran inside. She came back a moment later with a look of obligation.

"That was work, they need me to go in for a few hours."

"Okay. I can clean up the last of the tools for you."

"Thanks, Jensen. I'll try to be as quick as I can. I really want to celebrate with you."

"No worries. We can celebrate tonight."

"Deal. I should go. See ya later!"

Jensen heard Autumn's truck pull away as he gathered the last of the tools.

He locked them in the shed and stepped back. He looked at the yard then took a quick wander throughout the house. There was nothing left to do. Jensen sat outside on the porch swing as a silent argument played through his head. He stood quickly and hit the side of the house, cursing.

He grabbed his truck keys, hopped in and made his way for town. He circled the liquor store three times before he parked in front. Jensen sat in the drivers seat and begged himself to drive away. He knew his willpower was fading and so, he bargained with himself. He would only have one, just one lousy drink to celebrate.

Jensen purchased a bottle of whiskey and quickly drove to Autumn's. His mind was quiet as he set the bottle on the kitchen counter. He paced back and forth hating himself for what he knew he would ultimately do. With trembling hands he unscrewed the cap and raised the bottle to his lips. Familiarity and longing coursed through him with the first taste. He let out a deep sigh and had another sip, followed by another and another. The beast Jensen tried to contain for weeks was now released. And it felt good.

Chapter 13

Autumn

"Okay, I think that's the last of it. All the records are now up to date," I said tiredly. My eyes hurt from scanning the small print most of the afternoon.

"Thank you, Autumn, I really appreciate it. I don't know how I let things get so far behind," Anna mused.

"No worries, that's what I'm here for." I glanced at the time. "I should get going. See you on Monday."

"Have a good weekend."

I stepped into the late afternoon sunshine and headed for the grocery store. Tonight I would splurge on good food to celebrate the success of the renovation. I picked up T-bone steaks to barbeque and an assortment of vegetables to grill. On an impulse buy, I grabbed Jensen's favorite ice cream from childhood. As I drove home, I felt uplifted. It had been a long time since I actually felt like I belonged somewhere. I smiled broadly. I had a home. A real home. I hummed a happy tune as I unloaded the groceries. Lucy trotted into the kitchen for her greeting.

I crouched and ruffled her ears. "Do you want to go for a run, Luce? We have time before dinner."

I ran upstairs and changed into my running gear. Lucy followed at my heels. I took to the back roads and enjoyed the sounds nature provided. The birds chirped their happy songs and in the distance, and frogs croaked. Normally I enjoyed running to music, but today I welcomed the silence and the company of my thoughts. My mind drifted to Jensen. It felt surreal that he was in fact here. So much time had passed between us, yet, when I was around him, it felt like nothing had changed at all. Well, almost. Life had beaten him down but I had faith he would find his way. He just needed to find the right path.

I ran until my lungs burned and my legs ached. I stopped to catch my breath when Lucy tore ahead of me, barking loudly. She bounded into the bushes ahead. "Lucy! Lucy, come!" Lucy ignored my protests and continued barking. I stepped toward the commotion and called to her once more. "Lucy! Come here!"

Lucy pulled away and trotted over, her tongue hung lazily from her mouth. "You brat. What do you think you were doing?"

From the bushes came a rustle followed by a low moan. I backed away in surprise as Lucy pounced once more. The moan sounded again, this time louder. I took a hesitant step forward and craned my neck as far as it would go. "H-hello?"

The groan came again. I tiptoed forward and glanced at the blackberry bushes. My mouth gaped in surprise as there lay Jensen, sprawled out amongst the brambles. "Jensen!" I shrieked. "What are you doing in there?"

Jensen moaned and tried to look up. "I don't know."

I picked my way down the ditch carefully, evaluating the situation before me. Jensen was belly first in the thistles. He wore jeans, boots, and a T-shirt. His arms were scratched and bleeding as well as the left side of his cheek.

"Oh, Jensen. This is not going to be fun." I stepped closer and knelt in front of him, meeting his eyes. "Can you look at me?" Jensen raised his eyes and nodded. I shook my head in disappointment. "Have you been drinking?"

Jensen winced and let his head fall. I stood and studied his position. I could roll him out, but it was going to hurt. "Dammit," I muttered.

I looked around, no one would hear us if I called for help, we were in the middle of farm land. A barn sat in the distance on the hill, but there was no sign of a house anywhere. I bit my lip, thinking. There was no way I could walk Jensen all the way back to my house. It was too far. I let out a sigh of defeat. I placed my hands on my hips and studied Jensen. "Do you have your phone on you by any chance?"

"I don't know," he groaned.

"You better hope you do," I muttered. I stepped toward him carefully and felt his pockets. I smiled in triumph as my hands clasped around his cell. I pulled it out and dialed Derik and Kendra's number. I was going to need help.

"Hello?"

"Hi, Kendra, it's me."

"Autumn! I have been meaning to call you. How are things?"

I looked at Jensen's nearly lifeless body. "Could be better. I'm in a bit of a situation."

Kendra's easy voice turned serious. "What's wrong?"

"I need you or Derik to meet me by Johnston's field. I'll wait on the road so you can find me."

"What's wrong?"

"Jensen is drunk. I found him in a blackberry bush on my run. There is no way he will make the walk back."

"My god. We're on our way."

I slipped the cell phone into my pocket and made my way back to Jensen. I winced in sympathy as I grabbed his arm and hauled him towards me in one quick movement. He landed with a thump and another groan.

"Come on, Jensen, hold on to me. You're going to have to help me a little bit." I leaned down and placed his arm around my neck. Jensen looked up and grabbed on to me. Though his legs were clumsy, he straightened them until he stood. He clung on to me tighter.

"Autumn?" he moaned. "Is that you?"

"It is. Keep moving, place one foot in front of the other. We need to get up the hill to the roadside. Help is coming."

"Help?"

"Yes."

"Autumn? You're my savior," he whispered.

I didn't say a word. I held back tears that threatened to escape. We made it to the top of the hill and I set him into a seated position. I sat beside him, and held his hand. Jensen shifted his body until he lay down, his head in my lap. I ran my fingers through his hair and listened to him quietly as he mumbled sorry over and over again. His body trembled at my touch and realization hit me hard. I was out of my element with him. I wasn't sure what my next move would be, but I knew if I didn't do something for him, I would indeed lose him. Jensen was a confused, broken man. He looked to a bottle to heal a hurt he couldn't face himself. Time had changed him. He wasn't quite the boy I used to know. He carried with him a burden that weighed him down, one he shouldn't have had to carry alone. Despite everything time had taken from us, my heart still belonged to him. I would find a way to help him, I had too.

The sound of tires sounded before me. I looked up and Derik and Kendra hopped out of the Jeep. Kendra's eyes went wide in concern. Derik's face was an unreadable mask. "Let's get him up." Derik quickly assessed me. "Are you okay?"

I nodded as Derik helped haul Jensen up. Kendra wrapped her arms around my shoulders and squeezed reassuringly. Jensen followed Derik willingly until he suddenly broke away. He fell to his hands and knees, and got sick. I closed my eyes and turned away for a moment.

I stepped out of Kendra's grasp and made my way to Jensen. I brushed the hair out of his face and glanced up at my friends. "Did you guys bring a bucket by chance?"

They exchanged glances and nodded. "Derik brought one. He thought it would come in handy."

"Good thinking."

Derik kept his face hard. "Figured it was a good idea. When this guy drinks, he drinks to the point of black outs. That's not easy on the body. I'll get it."

Derik handed me the bucket and I placed it into Jensen's hands. "Keep it close. Let's get you home."

The drive home felt long. Derik helped Jensen out of the Jeep and we set him in the washroom. As Jensen wrapped his arms around the toilet, we disappeared into the kitchen.

"I don't understand. He was doing so well," I whispered.

Derik placed a hand on my shoulder. "He has an addiction, Autumn, it's not going away just like that."

I furrowed my brows. "But the night we all went to Tailgate's, he was good. I was the one who fell flat on my face."

Derik sighed. "Some days are better than others, I guess. I think something set him off and he fell hard." Kendra and he exchanged a glance. "Are you sure you want him here?"

Anger boiled in me. "Of course, I do. You can't expect me to kick him to the curb, not now! He has nowhere to go, nobody else to help him."

Kendra cleared her throat and spoke carefully. "I know you two used to be close, but are you sure you're up for this? Is he worth it?"

I met Kendra's eyes. "Yes. Time may have taken many things from us, but he's still my friend. We have a history, a bond formed a long time ago. He still has a piece of me."

Derik nodded matter-of-factly. "Okay, then. What do you want us to do?"

I looked at Derik quizzically. "Us?"

"Yes, us. You're part of our clan. If he means that much to you, then he means that much to us."

I slumped over in relief. "Thank you. I'm going to go check on him, clean him up a bit."

"Do you want us to stay here for the night?"

I thought about it for a moment. My last run in with Jensen while he was drunk had frightened me. There was a desperation in his eyes that resembled danger. But this time felt different. He looked different. He looked frail. "No, I can manage."

"Are you sure?"

"Positive. Thank you for everything. I don't know what I would have done if you guys hadn't found us."

"You're welcome. We'll call you in the morning."

"Okay, drive safely."

"We will."

I locked the front door behind me and made my way into the washroom. Déjà vu washed over me as Jensen sat against the bathroom wall, eyes closed, head in his hands. I rummaged through the medicine cabinet and pulled out antiseptic lotion and gauze. I knelt in front of him and took his arm gently.

His hands fell away from his face and he watched as I quietly tended his wounds. I kept my eyes glued to his cuts and worry fell heavy over me. Seeing him like this broke my heart.

I raised my eyes to his. The left side of his cheek bled. I placed my hands softly against his face and cleaned out the cuts. Jensen closed his eyes tightly. I pulled back my hands and noticed they trembled. I tightened them into fists but Jensen noticed.

"I'm so sorry," he whispered. "I don't even remember how I got there."

I placed the lid on the ointment and set it down. I looked at my disheveled friend. "This scares me, Jensen. The way you treat yourself is terrible. You don't deserve to be where you are." I fought back a cry. "I thought I finally had you back. I can't lose you, not again, not like this."

Jensen opened his eyes and met mine. "I never wanted you to see me like this. It just feels so good in the moment, everything fades away. Nothing hurts."

"What about now? Right now, in this moment. Look at yourself."

Jensen raised his arms and winced. "Ow. What happened?"

"You really have no recollection at all? I found you in a blackberry bush."

"I don't remember." His face twisted and he crawled to the toilet, and hugged it firmly.

I sat against the wall and pulled my knees toward my chest. Watching someone you cared about fall apart was hard and frustrating. I wanted so badly to put him back together, but ultimately, it would have to be up to him. You couldn't change someone who wasn't willing to change for themselves. I feared I would be left with a hard decision: knowing when to stay, and when it was time to finally walk away.

Jensen fought his way to his feet. He took an unsteady step forward and his legs gave out on him. I wasn't quick enough to catch him, and he hit the ground hard. "Jensen! Are you okay?"

"Ouch," he groaned.

"Come on, let's get you to bed where it's safe. Take my hands."

Jensen reached out and grasped me tightly. I hauled him up with all the strength I possessed. We stumbled into the bedroom and I laid him on his side. I dug out a bucket from under the sink and placed it next to him on the nightstand. I pushed the hair out of his eyes. He opened them to meet mine. The man I had loved so long ago wasn't looking back at me, not tonight. The eyes I remembered from childhood were full of life, mischief, humor, and affection. Tonight they remained dim, sad, so very lonely. An ache stabbed my heart and I wondered what he must be feeling. I took off his boots and pulled a blanket over top him. From the closet, I grabbed an extra pillow and placed it on the empty side of the bed. I kicked off my own shoes and laid beside him quietly. I didn't want him to be alone, and as much as I hated to admit it, neither did I.

We didn't speak, Jensen drifted asleep almost immediately. I shifted on my back and stared at the ceiling. How far a person could fall, and so quickly. It saddened me he had never reached out for help. I would have never turned him away. Never. I was also angry at him. He had always known where to find me, why didn't he come back sooner? How could he have left me all alone when he was the one person I desperately needed by my side after Jake's funeral.

So many regrets ran through my mind. So many things I would have done differently. I should have tried harder to find him, maybe then he wouldn't have lost himself. I should have never let his parents take him away. I should have held on to Jensen, fought for his voice to be heard. I let out a deep sigh. You can't go back; you can only move forward. I could no longer battle the heaviness of slumber. I drifted to sleep, listening to the deep breaths of the man who lay next to me.

Chapter 14

Jensen

Jensen awoke. He blinked slowly as his surroundings came into view. He looked to his left and was startled to see Autumn lying next to him. He watched her for a moment as she slept soundly. She looked so peaceful, so innocent. He tore his eyes away and focused on the ceiling. Jensen adjusted his body position and pain shot through him. His eyes opened in surprise as he saw his arms, it looked like he ran into an angry feline. The scratches throbbed and stung, his stomach felt uneasy.

Jensen placed a hand over his face and cursed. He always hated the day after he drank. It took a lot out of him. He wasn't as young as he used to be, he didn't recover as fast as he once did. Jensen let his eyes fall closed and images of last night played like a broken film. He briefly remembered hearing Autumn calling for him. He remembered hugging the toilet, and Autumn handling him like he was a child. He studied his arms once more and briefly recounted blackberry bushes. That would explain the scratches. He couldn't recall how he got there, but he sure as hell remembered the taste of whiskey burning his throat. It had felt so good.

Jensen opened his eyes once more. He couldn't keep living like this, it wasn't much of one. It would take him at least two days to feel human again. He hated the way he felt. He was humiliated. He was a grown man, for Christ's sake, he didn't need a full time babysitter, or at least he shouldn't.

He remembered the look of concern, hurt, and disappointment in Autumn's eyes. There was no one to blame but himself for putting it there. Next to him, Autumn blinked open her eyes. He turned to her and her startling blue eyes met his. He had been with his fair share of women, but none of them even came close to her. She wore an innocence that time couldn't age. Looking at her in the early morning light took him back to another lifetime, one he missed sorely.

Autumn wore a sleepy smile. "Morning. How do you feel?"

Jensen shifted on his side, facing her. "Sore, and like an ass."

Autumn's smile twitched. "Sounds about right." Her eyes fell to his torn arms and her smile faded. She lightly traced a fingertip over the marks. "Do you remember what happened last night?"

"Bits and pieces. I don't remember how I got there, or where I was going. Thank you for taking care of me last night…again."

"You're welcome." Her face grew serious. "Jensen…why did you drink?"

Jensen's face fell. "You have no idea how hard it is to fight something that no one can see. Hell, even I can't see what I'm up against. A feeling washes over me and I can't say no."

Autumn listened intently. He watched her features closely for signs of judgment. He saw none. She looked back at him, deep in thought. She pursed her lips for a moment before speaking. "I don't know what I can do for you, but I want to help. I'm not going to stand by and watch you destroy yourself. I can't lose another friend."

Jensen nodded. "I'm sorry you have to see me like this."

"So am I." Autumn sat up. "I'm going to make breakfast. Do you want anything?"

Jensen shook his head quickly. "No, thanks. The thought of food makes me feel nauseous."

"Okay. I'll get you some water then." Autumn studied him. "You look a little green."

Jensen rolled to his side and grabbed the bucket. Autumn winced and left the room, giving him privacy. He placed the bucket onto the nightstand and rolled onto his back. Every inch of him hurt. His head throbbed as though he got hit with a bat. Jensen held out his hands, trying to keep them steady. The tremors were starting already. He clasped his hands into a tight ball until his knuckles turned white.

He had nothing. No home of his own, no job, and he had lost most of his friends along the way. In a moment of desperation, he had made an unconscious decision to come back to a place he used to call home. He had been searching for something, anything that would help him feel alive, like he belonged. He wanted to know if he was worth saving. Jensen knew a big part of it was Autumn, he had been searching for her for a long, long time. Jensen hoped by coming back to the one place he remembered feeling happy would automatically heal him. But he knew strings would be attached. For it was here he also witnessed one of the very things that haunted him. Despite it all, a connection had been formed to this place and her.

No matter how much distant he created, his memory wouldn't let go. He ached to come home. He knew his time for running was coming to an end. It was time to make a decision, he could finally face the things he had been trying to forget and come to terms with what happened. It was the only way to move forward. He knew what the alternative would be; one of these days he would drown himself in alcohol until he could no longer recover.

Autumn came in with a tall glass of water. "Here you go. I imagine you're going to sleep most of the day?"

Jensen nodded wordlessly. Autumn crossed her arms. "Okay. I'm going to go out for a run then. I need to clear my head."

"Okay, I'll be here."

"I hope so." Autumn let out a deep breath. "Jensen, I won't be able to do this forever. You have to make me a promise."

"What is it?"

"You have to try. There's only so much I can do for you. A lot of this depends on you, and how much you're willing to fight." She took a step back. "I had to put myself back together once before, and then my grandmother passed away. I did that all on my own."

Autumn looked directly into Jensen's eyes. "You left me. You left me when I needed you the most and you never came back. I waited for you for so long. And now you're here…you damn well better fight. If you keep going down this road, there will come a day where you can't turn back, and I don't want to be there to see that's what you've chosen."

The words hit Jensen like a cold slap in the face. "Autumn?"

She stopped but didn't turn to face him. She straightened her shoulders and spoke very softly. "I hate missing you. If you don't have any intention of changing your life, than please leave. There's only so much my heart can take."

Jensen watched her walk away, quietly closing the door behind her. *Shit.* He sat up slowly, ignoring the fact his head screamed in protest and his stomach danced. Jensen had never stuck around long enough in one place to see the effect his behavior had on others. He had never formed any bonds with anyone who would even care. Maybe that's why he came back here, to her. Autumn was the only person he knew who still cared about him, she still made him feel like he was worth something. Jensen placed his feet on the ground and slowly stood. He tossed off his clothes and stepped into the shower. The hot water bit his scratches; he ignored them. His mind was too busy sorting out his next move.

Jensen threw on clean clothes and forced himself to sit outside. The air was sweet, the smell of honeysuckle was so strong in the air he could almost taste it. He looked at the stillness around him. He knew why he chose to hide in the noise of the city. He could never hear himself think, there were too many distractions, so much noise. Out here it was silent, there was nothing to muffle his thoughts. Jensen's eyes landed upon Autumn's worn Bronco. He smiled to himself as he walked over and lifted the hood. He began examining the engine, making a mental calculation of what needed to be done, and parts he would need.

"What are you doing?"

Jensen jumped as Autumn's voice sounded behind him. He turned to face her, smiling. "I'm going to give your vehicle some lovin'."

Autumn raised an eyebrow and wiped a bead of sweat from her forehead. "Are you serious?"

"Yep. I need something to do, and this heap of metal needs looking after."

Autumn's jaw dropped. "I-I don't know what to say."

"I think the words you're looking for are thank you."

She grinned. "Thank you."

"Leave it with me for a few days, you can borrow my truck to get to work. I should be able to start on it tomorrow."

Autumn looked toward his truck, and rubbed her hands together eagerly. "Really? I get to drive *that?*"

"Yes, just be careful. She's the only solid thing I have."

"Not the only thing, but I cross my heart, I will take good care of her."

⌘

The Bronco was a bigger project than he anticipated. It was now day four of working on the hunk of metal but he was finally beginning to see progress. Jensen stepped away from the hood once the new starter was in place. He slid into the driver's seat and turned the key. He smiled in satisfaction as the vehicle started on the first try. A familiar Jeep rolled into the driveway and Derik stepped out. Jensen slid out from behind the wheel, wiped his hands and went out to meet him.

Derik looked over his work in appreciation. "It looks good. That thing's needed work for as long as I can remember. I can't believe Autumn's kept it running for so long."

Jensen chuckled. "You and me both."

Derik nodded and began scrutinizing Jensen. "You're looking better."

"I have a project. I like to keep busy."

"That project looks about done. What's next?"

Jensen winced. The thought had crossed his mind earlier. "I'm not sure. One day at a time I guess."

"You know Jensen, my earlier offer still stands. You do good work and we could really use help at the garage."

"Really? I thought I blew that chance."

"Not yet. I should get going, I just wanted to check in on you. Think about my offer."

"Thanks, I will."

Jensen cleaned and put his tools away. A familiar anxiety followed him once he completed a project. He toyed with the keys in his hand and his eyes lingered over the Bronco. He should take it out for a test drive to make sure everything was working properly. A cold sweat formed on his brow and his body went tense. *No, not this time. Think of something else, anything else.* Jensen paced, but his mind thought of only one thing. Jensen slid into the Bronco and headed down the driveway. He sped into town toward the darkness he battled. He pulled into the liquor store parking lot and cut the engine. He locked his hands around the steering wheel and gripped with all his might.

He wanted whiskey with a chase of cold beer…so badly. Jensen began the fight with his sobriety and the drunken comfort he wanted to get lost in. He stepped outside and took a single step forward. His legs locked on him and he stopped. He balled one hand into a fist, and punched the side of the Bronco, letting out a yell in anger.

Jensen quickly sat in the drivers seat and closed the door. His breaths came out short and staggered. He didn't want to fall, he wasn't ready. Jensen slammed the key into the ignition and started the engine. He stuck it into gear, pressed down on the gas hard and headed toward the old part of town.

He didn't know where he was going until he got there. He pulled into the spot next to his truck, killed the engine and sat deeper into the seat. The demons in his mind taunted him, teased him. They did their best to lure him, tantalize him with memories of alcohol. The taste. The smell. The wonderful numbness he knew it would bring. Jensen gripped the wheel as his hands began to shake. He closed his eyes tightly and begged for a miracle.

Chapter 15

Autumn

Today had been a busy day and I relished in it. The museum was not large, but it held a wonderful assortment of historical artifacts. Today I was allowed to rearrange some of the displays. I was able to touch the things so few were allowed to handle, my eyes examined every square inch, every small detail. It was a real honor. For the moment, I felt as though I were special. Afterwards, I updated the website and posted local events coming up.

Anna had taken it easy for most of the day. She had put her absolute trust in me. Being surrounded by the ancient things in this world made me feel like I was home. Too many things these days were so generic, they all looked alike. Nothing was special anymore. I enjoyed being surrounded by history. Each piece had a story to tell, everything once had a meaning, and that purpose stood the test of time.

Erika, one of my coworkers leaned over the front desk. "Hey, Autumn, isn't that your truck parked out front?"

I leaned over the counter and glanced into the lot. Sure enough, my old beater was there. "Huh, that's odd."

Erika shrugged her shoulders. "You might want to check it out."

"I will. I'll be right back."

I stepped outside and approached my car. I was shocked to see Jensen inside. He didn't notice me coming. His eyes were shut tightly and he held onto the steering wheel for dear life. My heart caught in my throat, he looked distressed. I gripped the door handle and pulled it open. Jensen's eyes shot open and he looked at me in a wild frenzy.

"Jensen? What happened? What's wrong?"

He shook his head. "I want to drink, Autumn. I need a drink so badly."

"Have you had anything yet?"

"No. I went to the liquor store but I couldn't go in."

Relief tore through me. "You didn't go in? Jensen, that's huge!"

"No." Jensen closed his eyes once more. "Look at me, Autumn! I'm a mess."

I leaned in and peeled his hands off the steering wheel. They trembled and I took them in mine, squeezing tightly. "Jensen, look at me. Open your eyes."

He did. I nodded. "Good. Do you see me?"

"Yes."

"Do you feel my touch against yours?"

"Yes."

"This is real. You are not alone. I am standing right by your side. I won't let you go."

Jensen squeezed back tightly. "I didn't know where I was going until I got here."

"It's okay. I'm glad you found me." I glanced at the museum. "Will you be okay for a minute. I have to take care of something, but I'll be right back."

Jensen nodded. "Yeah, I'll be right here."

I let go of his hands and ran inside. I found Anna in her office and knocked on the door gently. She looked up from her paperwork and motioned me inside. "Autumn, are you all right? You look a little shaken."

"I'm okay. I'm wondering if I can leave early today?"

"Oh? Well, I suppose we can manage the rest of the afternoon. I'm very pleased with the progress we all made today."

"Thank you, I really appreciate this."

I stood to leave but she stopped me. "How bad is he?"

I stopped in mid tracks and turned to face her. "Excuse me?"

Anna's face softened. "I saw you through the window. This is a small town. Rumors run rampant."

My face fell and I sat back down. "I don't know. He wanted a drink but he came to me."

"That's a solid first step. I'm afraid both of you will have a hard climb. But it won't be impossible. He's going to need strong people he can lean on when the world gets too heavy."

"How do you know all this?"

Anna's face took on a faraway look. "My husband. God rest his soul."

"I'm sorry, I didn't know."

"It was a long time ago."

"How did you get through it?"

"With more patience then I ever could imagine. I had to be strong when he wasn't. He had to find the strength to carry on. It's a tough fight, Autumn. You both have to hold on to the things that fuel you to keep going. If he can find it within himself to carry on, I promise you, it will be okay."

"I don't know what to do for him."

"Just be there. Listen to him. You can't force someone to change, they simply need to be ready. If you think he is, stand by him. Sometimes all it takes is knowing we're not alone in this world."

I let out a shuddery breath. "Thank you, Anna. Thank you so much."

"Go to him."

I jumped out of my chair and took off running. Jensen was where I left him. He looked up and smiled weakly. I grabbed his hands and pulled him out. He leaned against my car wearily. I linked my arm in his and dragged him to his truck.

"What are you doing?" he asked.

"We're taking a trip down memory lane."

"And we're taking my truck?"

"We sure are. Do you mind if I drive?"

Jensen looked down at his hands and shook his head. "Not at all."

"Good. Get inside."

Jensen climbed into the passenger seat and I hauled myself in. I turned the key and the sound of the engine cut through the silence. I popped it into gear and took the street that led to the edge of town. The uneven road bounced us this way and that. I slowed the truck down a steep hill, took a sharp left and drove into the middle of a vacant field. The tall grass was brown under the midday sun. A single oak tree stood, offering the only shade to be found.

I cut the engine and looked at Jensen. His features lit up in recognition. "I remember this place. We used to come here and watch the stars at night."

I nodded. "I come here often when I need to think. Come on, let's go outside."

I walked to the great oak and sat, resting my back against its gnarled trunk. Jensen sat beside me and chuckled.

"What's so funny?" I mused.

"Do you remember the summer, I think you were fifteen at the time. I climbed to your bedroom window and we snuck out here for the night. I thought your grandma was going to kill me the next morning."

I laughed at the memory. "You had just got your license that summer. That was a good night."

"It sure was." Jensen looked down at his arms and his smile faded. "I was a different person then. Everything has changed."

"Not everything. I'm still here."

"But I'm not."

I scooted closer and rested my head against his shoulder. "Parts of you are. I still see you."

"Why do you do this, Autumn?"

"Do what?"

"Put up with all of my crap."

"Because I care about you. Most of my fondest memories include you. What am I supposed to do? Let you figure this out by yourself? Because from where I'm standing, you need help." I looked up to meet his eyes. "Jensen? Why did you come back?"

Jensen focused on the sky. "Because I didn't know where else to go. I have been running from this place for so long, yet it's the only place that feels like home."

I let his words sink in. A question burned the tip of my tongue and I released it. "How could you leave me here?"

Jensen stiffened in surprise. His eyes met mine and he looked remorseful. "I thought you never wanted to see me again. Once I hit the self destruction mode, I figured it was best if I stayed away." Jensen ran a hand through his hair and stood. "Autumn, you should know not a single day went by where you didn't enter my mind. Leaving you behind was one of the hardest things I have ever done."

Jensen began to pace. "I toyed with the idea of coming back to find you, but I wasn't sure how you would react. I let myself go. Every day I would look into that mirror and I had no idea who the man staring back at me was. As the years passed, it got easier to stay away. Until one day it no longer made sense and that's when I found you again."

Jensen sat beside me. "A part of me hoped you would tell me to leave. It would have made things so much easier."

"Easier?" I shook my head fiercely. "No, it wouldn't have. I grew up with you, we talked almost every single day. You were a big part of my world. One day I woke up and you were gone. We had lost one of our best friends forever and then I lost you. That didn't make anything easier."

I blinked back tears and looked at him. "Do you realize when you came back, I didn't recognize you? That's how long you were gone for. That's how much you let the world beat you down. I could have helped you. You could have helped me. We should have been able to lean on each other."

I stood and began to walk away. Anger and hurt brewed beneath the surface. When my emotions got the best of me, whether that be happiness, anger, or sadness, I tended to cry. It was something I carried from my childhood, I had always hoped to outgrow the inconvenience, but it stuck with me like a bad habit.

"Autumn?"

I waved a hand back. "Just give me a minute, Jensen."

I marched down the field and climbed through the wire fence. I stomped my way through the tall grass and came to an old tree stump. I sat atop, crossing my legs together. I hadn't meant to unload on Jensen, he was going through enough right now. He had taken his first step down the right road and what did I do? I bit his head off about the past. As badly as I felt, it also felt good. I had years of pent up emotions toward him, and he needed to hear it. I had carried the thoughts with me long enough, I had every right to get them off of my chest. If he was going to heal, well, then so was I.

I stayed in my secluded spot for awhile. The sun began to set, lighting the sky on fire as the colors began to fade. I left the truck keys under the tree with Jensen, but I felt pretty confident if he decided to take off and leave me, I would hear his truck. Behind me, the sound of music pulled my attention. I climbed to the top of the hill and Jensen leaned against his truck. Music poured through the open windows.

He saw me and smiled. Jensen stepped forward and extended his hand. "Want to dance?"

My earlier anger faded away in an instance. *Damn, boy. He's good.* I placed my hand in his and he pulled me in close. We settled into a rhythm that matched the beat. I relaxed into his hold and rested my head against his chest. The music sped up but we didn't. We swayed side to side so very slowly. I felt like I was a teenager again as I danced under the stars in the comfort of once familiar arms.

Jensen looked back at me softly. His lips pulled into a smile. "This brings back memories."

"Very good ones."

His hands fell around my waist and he pulled me in closer. I stole a glance at him once more and studied his face. He gazed back curiously. "What?"

I smiled warmly. "You're here."

Jensen looked confused. "I've been here for awhile."

"No, you haven't. But right now, I see you. You've been gone for awhile." I let out a sigh. "I've missed you." I settled in closer and closed my eyes. I hoped this marked the promise of Jensen beginning to find his way back home.

Chapter 16

Jensen

Jensen couldn't believe how good it felt to have Autumn in his arms once again. Though they had changed, she still fit neatly against him. Of all the women he had held over the years, no one even came close. He had been distant and uninterested. Deep down he only wanted one person. Jensen was thankful he could be present in the moment. It was hard to believe only hours earlier he had begun to unravel. From the very bottom of his soul, he was so glad he didn't drown himself in momentary comfort.

The feeling it provided was temporary and the after-effects cruel. What he was feeling now was so very real. Jensen held her tighter and rested his jaw on top of her head. He pondered the effect a single person could have on another, whether it be positive or negative. Jensen considered Autumn his miracle. She had been the push to keep him going when he was to weak to carry on.

Jensen cleared his throat and pulled away. He linked his fingers within Autumn's and met her eyes. "Can you promise me something?"

"Anything."

"No matter what happens, promise me you won't forget me."

Autumn looked puzzled. "Forget you? Why would you ask that?"

Jensen shook his head. "Life is tricky and unpredictable. Please, just promise me."

"Of course. I will never forget you." Autumn's gaze softened as she looked around. "After all, it was here in this very spot that we promised to be best friends forever. Do you remember?"

Jensen looked around and smiled. "How could I forget?"

Autumn's grin grew teasing. "Do you promise to never forget me?"

Jensen laughed. "I think that's been proven already, don't you?"

Autumn let her hands fall and she stepped away. "Mmm, but a girl likes to hear these things out loud."

"Ah. I see. Well then, Autumn. I promise to never, ever, forget you."

Autumn clapped her hands together. "That's better."

Jensen looked her up and down and a smile grew. He could feel a new life stirring within, one he hadn't felt since he was young. He felt light hearted and free.

Autumn's face fell as she recognized the mischief that spread to his eyes. She held up her hands and backed away. "Oh no, you don't. Don't even think about it, mister."

Jensen rubbed his hands together eagerly. "You better run."

"No!" she squealed and took off as fast as her feet could carry her.

Jensen sprinted after her, surprised at how fast she had gotten over the years. He remembered it used to be easier to catch her. They ran through the tall grass, Autumn squealed with childlike joy. Jensen put one last effort into his speed and in an instant his arms wrapped around her, and he tossed her over his shoulder.

"Jensen! Put me down! I am not a football!"

"What are you going to do about it?" Jensen broke into a slow jog, Autumn groaned in defeat. A few feet ahead, he stopped and set her down. Autumn launched toward him with a playful shove. Jensen side stepped out of her way and she tumbled into the grass with a surprised gasp.

Jensen bent over with laughter. Autumn stood, dusting herself off. "My, my don't we have fancy feet?" she grumbled, but her eyes remained bright.

"Sorry, I couldn't resist." Jensen studied her and crouched. "Hop on."

Autumn beamed and launched herself onto his back. Jensen carried her to the tailgate and set her down. He hopped up beside her, smiling. Autumn lay back in the bed of the truck and pulled Jensen with her. She rested her head against his chest and looked at the stars.

For a moment, Jensen felt the pieces of his life click together. Somewhere deep inside his head, a switch clicked and lit up the dark places in his soul. *There is beauty in the broken. We just have to be patient and soon the world will see.* Autumn's voice went through his head. She once spoke those words, the last summer he spent with her. A smile found his lips as he remembered the memory. Autumn was in the midst of restoring a painting. To Jensen it looked like a mess of colors, but her eyes had seen so much more. She dared to look beyond what others simply threw away.

Autumn shifted onto her stomach. She placed her hands on his chest and gazed up at him. "How are you feeling?"

"I'm lying in the bed of my truck, staring at the night sky with a beautiful woman by my side. I could stay here forever."

Jensen was surprised at the honesty of his words. For once, he wasn't lying to a woman, he wasn't saying something just to please her. He truly meant them. But then again, Autumn had always brought out his better half. He took great comfort in her presence, he always had. Her kindness overwhelmed his darkness, and soothed his wounds. The moment of comfort came to an abrupt halt as an unpleasant thought crept into his mind. He couldn't use Autumn as a patch forever. He would have to find a way to stand on his own two feet. He couldn't lean on her at every given moment of weakness. The thought dampened his mood momentarily. He still had a long way to go before he could consider himself to be okay.

Autumn sensed the change in him. She stood and held out her hands. "Come dance with me, Jensen."

He sat up and grinned. "In the back of the truck?"

"I can't think of a better place, can you?"

Jensen stood and drew her to him. "No, I can't."

Autumn settled against him and began to hum along to the song on the radio.

Jensen sang along quietly. Autumn joined him. "Jensen?"

"Yes."

"Don't ever let me go, okay?"

"I won't let you go." A pain tore through his chest. It was such a simple question but one filled with uncertainty. He wasn't sure what he would face with each day that found him. He hoped to hell he could keep his promise, not only to her, but to himself.

⌘

It was after midnight when Jensen pulled into Autumn's driveway. Jensen was able to drive this round. Autumn sat sleepily in the passenger seat and blinked. "We're home already? I'm ready for bed, I'm beat."

Jensen nodded. "Me, too."

They walked into the house together. Autumn stopped in the hallway, and gave him a warm hug. "Thank you for tonight."

"You're welcome."

Autumn pulled back. "Goodnight, Jensen."

"Night."

He watched her walk upstairs toward her bedroom. He walked slowly to his room and sat on the corner of the bed. Something inside was slowly awakening. Tonight, he felt a part of something very real. Remnants of the man he once was made an appearance. Perhaps Autumn had been right all along, maybe he wasn't completely gone, not entirely. Jensen lay down and stared at the ceiling. He felt restless. He got up and paced the room. He tried so hard to fight the old feeling that began to taunt him.

Jensen cursed himself and headed up the stairs. He knew he needed to learn to face uncertainties on his own. He couldn't depend on something to fill the void forever. But it was too much in one night. He would need to take small steps until the day came when he could finally look back and realize he was free. Jensen paused in front of Autumn's door. He raised his hand to knock but froze. He took a step backward until his back met the wall. He stared at her door, scrambled up some courage and tried again. His knuckles hovered inches over the door, but couldn't find it within him to connect. He dropped his hand once more and lightly pressed his forehead to the door.

He jumped in surprise as the door swung open. Autumn stared back at him with an amused expression. "Were you going to stand out here all night? Or were you planning on coming in?"

Jensen felt his face flush. "How did you know I was out here?"

"I heard you pacing."

"Ah, I see."

Autumn softened her tone. "Is everything okay?"

Jensen pulled himself together. "Yes. You know what, I'm sorry to wake you. I'm going to head to bed."

"Jensen?"

Jensen paused at the top of the stairs. "Yes?"

"I don't mind the company."

Jensen froze and turned to her. "Are you sure?"

"Positive." Autumn leaned against her door and motioned Jensen inside.

He followed her lead and stood uneasily at the bed. He was thrown off by how unsure of himself he was. He never fumbled around women in the past; it was one of the things he had always been good at, sober or not. It was the one act where nerves or hesitation ceased to exist for him. He was able to keep emotions at bay, simple really. He never got to know them, never wanted too. He let out a sigh. It all boiled down to Autumn. Autumn pulled the covers to her chest and waited for him to lie beside her. He felt a little more at ease when he saw flickers of uncertainty in her own eyes. Jensen found his place beside her and pulled her against him. She cradled herself beside him and Jensen let his body relax into her comfort.

He cleared his throat. "I don't know how this is going to sound."

"Say it anyway."

"You have always been mine." Jensen held his breath as soon as the words were out. He did not care to be vulnerable, but when he considered recent events she had seen him at his absolute worst, and she was still here.

Autumn stiffened next to him and sat up. She bit her lip and locked her eyes in his. "Jensen, I-"

He sat up, looking at her, trying to read her. She looked lost in thought, almost nervous. Her blue eyes fell to him once more and he was done. Autumn locked her eyes in his, searching. She nodded to herself and spoke carefully. "I have waited a very long time for you to come back. You need to understand when you left, I did not see it coming. I never thought you would leave. I counted on you."

She took a deep breath and continued. "If you say these things, please mean them. Please promise me you won't up and leave, not again."

Jensen widened his eyes in surprise. He hadn't expected that response. The last thing in the world he wanted was to hurt her, but he couldn't make that promise. He didn't know what he would be facing amongst himself with each day that came. He was scared half the time, trying with what little strength he possessed to keep himself together. He decided to be honest.

"Things aren't going to be easy with me. I can't promise I won't hurt you, but what I can promise is this. I don't intentionally mean to cause you any pain. Autumn, look at me. I am pretty close to a wreck. You are the only speck of light I see most days. I don't want to ruin that, I don't want to disappoint you."

Autumn listened quietly. She thought to herself before speaking. "That might be part of the problem."

Jensen pulled back, confused. "What is?"

"You put so much emphasis on *me*. You don't want to hurt *me*, disappoint *me*. I am fully aware of the risks involved by getting close to you again, but you need to have more faith in yourself. Hold yourself to a higher standard. You are worth more than you know."

Jensen opened his mouth to speak but nothing came out. He pressed his lips together as her words rang loud in his ears. No one had ever forced himself to take a good hard look at himself, not really. So much emphasis from others forced him to pay attention to the consequences he left everyone else to face, but never himself.

Autumn placed her hands against his face. "Please, don't lose yourself. You're just beginning to step out of the shadows. Keep moving forward."

Jensen slowly met her gaze. Her words tugged at his heart in a way that almost felt good. The loneliness that was forever with him began to lighten. He knew she wouldn't leave him. She would always be there reaching out to him. She wasn't going to give up. If she was willing to fight that hard for someone who caused her so much pain, he owed himself to put up a fight, a damn good one.

"You still with me?" she whispered.

Jensen nodded. He brushed a lock of hair out of her eyes and moved in closer. He kept his eyes locked with hers, waiting to see if she would pull back. She didn't. He lowered his gaze to her lips and brushed his against hers. Autumn sighed and wrapped her arms around his neck. Jensen's hands fell to her waist and pulled her closer before gently lying her down. Autumn ran her fingers through his hair as their lips met eagerly.

Autumn pulled away, breathless. "Jensen? I don't know if I'm ready for this."

Jensen backed off quickly but she locked her arms around him, anchoring him down. "That didn't come out right. I'm just not ready for things to go there, not yet. It means a lot more with you than anyone else." She bit her lip and looked uncomfortable.

Jensen found himself smiling, despite it all. He pressed his lips to hers once more. "So what you're saying is I'm special? Say, more special than that Logan guy."

Autumn laughed in surprise. "You could say that."

"Good." Jensen went in for one more kiss before he pulled her to his chest. He linked his fingers within hers and she brought his hand to her lips. He stroked her hair, and hummed their favorite song. Autumn began to drift off, he felt her head grow heavy against him.

"Autumn?" he waited for a response but none came. He continued speaking as though she could hear him. "Not a day went by that I didn't love you."

Chapter 17

Autumn

I awoke in the middle of the night wrapped up in Jensen's arms. I blinked twice to make sure it wasn't a dream. The last time we had spent the night together, Jake was with us. We camped in a farmer's field, daydreaming about the day we would be done with high school and moving on with our lives. What I wouldn't do to get those moments back. It was such a common mistake people made, counting down the days in anticipation for something big, that you end up missing all the little moments in between.

I missed Jake. He was like an older brother to me. More than anything I wished I could hear his laugh again. It was so contagious and he laughed with everything he had in him. Jake was always so full of life, he never missed a moment. He truly lived for every second. He was also the instigator of the group. He would often set me up as the distraction, he claimed because I was a girl, and a small one at that, people would label me as the innocent one. I could do no wrong. While I was busy pouring my sweet talk on someone, Jensen and Jake would slip past and do whatever it was they found invigorating in the moment. Often times it was as simple as stealing extra sodas from someone's fridge. The memory made me chuckle. They were such boys.

Jensen stirred beside me and I noticed he was awake. I smiled. "Hi."

"Mornin'. What are you laughing at?"

I hesitated and proceeded carefully. "I was thinking about Jake actually. Do you remember the time you two snuck me out of the house and dragged me into an R rated movie?"

Jensen laughed. "Oh that was a fun night."

"Hardly. I couldn't sleep for a week!"

Jensen chuckled. "Baby. What about that time we got those dirt bikes? We took turns hauling you around on the back. Jake let you drive his for what, a minute? You bailed as it went down the hill and you nearly totaled it. He was so mad at you."

"Oh, I forgot about that one! He didn't even ask if I was okay. All he cared about was that stupid bike."

Jensen grew quiet. "I miss him."

I leaned onto my stomach to face him. "I know. Me, too."

"Do you ever think about that day?"

"Almost every day."

"Me, too."

I sat up. "Oh! I have something." I leaned over the side of my bed and grabbed an old shoebox. I blew the dust off the top and sat cross legged in the middle of the bed.

Jensen flicked on the lamp and sat next to me. "What is that?"

I smiled at him coyly and lifted the top off. "Photos of all us and our adventures."

Jensen leaned forward eagerly and grinned. "Wow, I can't believe you still have these."

I grinned. "Of course, I do."

We flicked through the photos, and relived cherished memories. I watched Jensen from the corner of my eye and was relieved to see he looked relaxed, almost happy as he studied the images. The photos were nothing special, probably like any other childhood friends collection. There were photos of us barefoot tearing across open fields, at the lake, eating ice-cream, riding our bikes, endless summer nights, camping trips and from school.

In every photo, we wore a smile. We were always laughing. In most of the pictures, it wasn't uncommon that I stood sandwiched between Jake and Jensen. During our younger years when we were at the age where we didn't quite understand the 'girlfriend' 'boyfriend' concept, we thought it was only natural that I was their 'girlfriend' since I was a girl. I studied the photos closer and peeked at Jensen. It was clear from the pictures when we began to figure out the world of dating, Jensen began to look at me in a different way. He still looked at me in the same way.

Jensen held up a photo. I laughed when I saw it. Jake gave me a piggy back, and we were both soaked from head to toe, and I didn't look happy. Jensen smirked. "Remember this day?"

"How could I forget. I was so mad at you. That was one of my first dresses and I loved it. You pushed me in the creek. I broke my heel and ruined my dress. At least Jake was kind enough to help me out."

"He was a good guy," Jensen placed the photos down carefully. Sadness overtook his features. "It wasn't my fault."

I set the box aside and scooted closer. "Nobody said it was."

"Are you kidding me? Half the town blamed me."

"That's not true. People were upset. They needed to take their anger out on someone. It wasn't fair of them to pin it on you. I was there too you know."

"You were the girl and younger than us. Nobody would have blamed you."

"That's not true. I blamed myself."

Jensen looked at me in surprise. "You did?"

I leaned against the headboard. "Of course, I did. Just like I know you blame yourself. It was neither of our faults. It was an accident, a horrible, stupid accident. It could have been any one of us."

"You don't understand, Autumn. I saw it. I saw the life slip out of him. That image will haunt me for the rest of my life." Jensen stopped for a moment. "It's ironic, isn't it? That I turned to alcohol, the very thing that killed him."

I winced at his words. Our conversation had been so light just moments before. Now it had taken a very somber turn, one I did not want to venture down. After Jake's death I closed myself off from the world. I didn't speak for a good two months. There was no point, I had nothing to say. All I did was cry and sleep. I had watched one of my best friends be lowered into the ground, and the other took off without so much as a goodbye. In an instant, my life was empty. My grandmother was the one who convinced me to go to a counselor. At first I fought the notion, I had no desire to talk about anything. What was the point? It wouldn't bring anyone back.

Once I let my defenses fall, something shifted within me. Nothing I did would ever bring Jake back, whether that was to curl up in a ball on the floor, or pick myself up and keep going. Jake would have hated to see what I had become. It was through talking I realized a part of him would always be with me. I had to keep him alive in any way I could. Jensen never had that opportunity. He locked the memory away and threw away the key.

Jensen looked at me. "I need a smoke."

It was hard to read his features. I followed and sat across from him on the porch. Jensen looked lost in thought as he took a long drag of his cigarette. I shifted away from the smell of the smoke.

Jensen spoke. "How much do you want me to put this out right now?"

"Quite a bit actually."

"Figured as much. It's either this or drink."

I recoiled at the harshness of his tone. I knew he was going to be irritable, he was fighting back an urge he had given in to for so long. Jensen looked away. "I'm sorry, I don't mean to snap at you."

"I know."

Jensen put out the cigarette. "Can I ask you something?"

"Anything."

"What was it like for you after he died?"

I sat up straighter, the question caught me off guard. Jensen stared back at me with a pleading look. I bit my lip and looked at the fields. "I felt as though a part of me had died. An emptiness settled over my heart and spread through every fiber of my being."

"I was so lost. The people I had surrounded myself with were suddenly no longer there. I didn't know what to do myself. I wanted to hide away forever." I glanced toward Jensen, his body remained tense. I continued on sadly. "I remember crying all the time until one day, the tears stopped. They didn't stop because I felt better. I honestly think I had cried until there was nothing left."

Jensen placed his arms around me. "I'm so sorry. I should have never left."

"No, you shouldn't have." I stole a peek. "What was it like for you?"

He let out a harsh laugh. "Clearly you can see I didn't deal with things well."

I remained quiet until he sighed and forced himself to continue. "I couldn't get the image out of my mind. It haunted me every single day. I couldn't look at you, couldn't talk to you, it made it all the more real. I know what I've done, Autumn. I shut myself off from everyone. I chose the easy way out. Once I figured out that if I drank enough, the realization disappeared. It didn't last forever, but it lasted long enough that for awhile I didn't think about it."

"That sounds so lonely. Is that why you came back?"

"It was time. I began to notice I felt nothing, absolutely nothing all of the time." Jensen stood abruptly and kept his back to me. "I got scared. The last time I remembered feeling anything at all was here."

"For what it's worth, I'm glad you came back."

Jensen turned to me, his eyes stayed low to the ground. "I don't know what I'm doing half the time."

"You're starting to put your life together. It won't happen overnight, but if you keep going, one day I promise you will be okay. The hurt won't weigh you down, your breaths will come freely. One day, Jensen, you will find what you've been looking for." I took a step closer and grabbed his hands. "I saw you tonight while you were chasing me in the field. While we were dancing. I saw the boy I used to know. Hang on."

Jensen pressed his forehead to mine. His brown eyes fell heavy with tiredness. "I think I'm ready for bed. You?"

"Yes, I'm exhausted." Jensen placed his hand in mine and we crawled under the covers. I pressed my back next to his chest and he held me until the morning light.

⌘

I awoke the next morning before Jensen. I slipped out of his arms, grabbed my workout clothes, and tiptoed out of the room. Lucy trotted after me eagerly; she knew the routine well. I wrote Jensen a note and pinned it to the fridge. I laced up my running shoes, grabbed my Ipod, and stuck the headphones into my ears. It was just after seven. The morning air already held the promise of heat sure to come. I took to the quiet roads and got lost in the music. The trees were full and bright green. I kept a steady pace and followed the curve in the road which led me to a long straight stretch. I sucked in a sweet breath, hay bales lay in the morning fields waiting to be picked up and stored for the season. I crossed the bridge that stood over the creek and made my way back home.

Lucy trotted past me to her water bowl. She lapped up the water and plopped down against the cool floor. I had a quick rinse and got dressed for the day. Jensen was still fast asleep. As tempted as I was to wake him, I chose to let him sleep. I knew it was not an easy thing for him to come by. I went to the kitchen to make breakfast. I turned the coffee on, and gathered ingredients for pancakes.

From the corner of the room, Lucy hopped to life. In a single bound she took off full tilt toward me. I balanced the eggs and milk as I watched her in confusion. She let out a high pitch yipe and her eyes were glued to her prize. My eyes widened in horror as I realized what had caught her attention. A small mouse ran for its life, and headed directly for me. I could not move, though I wanted too. I remained frozen in place as the small creature ran across my barefeet. I let out a yell that could have woken the dead. The eggs and milk fell from my hands. I jumped back, shuddering and climbed onto a kitchen stool.

"Lucy, get it!" I wailed.

Clumsy footsteps sounded from upstairs. "Autumn! Autumn! I'm coming! Are you okay?"

"No!"

Jensen tore around the corner, his hair was tousled and his eyes wild in confusion. He stopped and took in the scene around him. Eggs and milk were splattered on the floor, and I clung to the stool for dear life, eyes wide in panic. I pointed as Lucy tore through the room once more. "There it is!"

Jensen jumped back. "What? What's going on?"

"A mouse!"

Jensen's jaw dropped and he rolled his eyes. "Are you kidding me? All of this commotion was over a mouse? I thought you were being murdered."

My voice rose an octave higher than normal. "I do not care for rodents. Don't you dare mock my fears!"

Jensen burst out laughing. "Sit tight, I'll take care of it."

"Thank you!"

"That better be coffee I smell," he called over his shoulder.

Ten minutes later Jensen strutted in with Lucy by his side. I was still atop the stool. I looked at my team, eyes wide. "Is it done?"

Jensen came over and gave me a kiss. "Morning and yes, it's done. It's safe to come down now."

I scanned the room uneasily and hesitantly stepped onto the floor. "I did not plan to be scared out of my wits this morning."

"It's an old farmhouse. I hate to tell you this, but it could happen again."

"No," I groaned. I bent over to clean up the mess. "I was going to make us pancakes."

Jensen poured coffee into mugs and set them on the counter. He crawled onto his hands and knees, helping me clean up the mess. "There's a few eggs still intact. We can make something edible."

"Not pancakes," I grumbled.

Jensen smiled. "Tell you what, how about you sit, I'll make us eggs and toast."

"Fine. But just so you know, I can still see you're eyes mocking me."

We both stood. I sat at the table, and gripped my mug closer to my chest. He winked. "I'll be teasing you about this one for awhile."

Chapter 18

Jensen

It was Monday morning. Today would be the day Jensen joined the working world once more. He was dressed and ready to go. He sat on the edge of the bed and watched Autumn as she dressed. She slipped into her dress and pulled back her long hair. She noticed him watching from the reflection of the mirror and she sent him a teasing grin.

Autumn smoothed the front of her dress and made her way to him for a morning kiss. "Good luck today. Keep those hands busy."

Jensen wrapped his arms around her. "I can think of another way to keep them busy."

Autumn swatted him away, laughing. "You're bad. I have to go to work. I'll see you tonight. Have a good day."

Jensen rose with a reluctant sigh. It was time to get a move on and get this day over with. He was glad for the opportunity to work, he needed to occupy his time. The weekend had passed quickly and he couldn't remember the last time he had laughed so much. But there was also a very large part of him that lingered in the shadows, waiting to make its move. He had wanted a drink so badly, on more than one occasion. He did his best to hide it from Autumn. She had seemed so relaxed and happy. If she saw the longing, she said nothing. For that he was grateful. Jensen waved goodbye as Autumn drove away. She smiled brightly as her car started on the first try. It was the little things that pleased her to no end. Jensen unlocked his truck as a familiar Jeep pulled next to him.

Derik stopped and rolled the window down. "Ready to go?"

Jensen walked over to the open window. "Yeah, I was just getting ready to leave."

"I thought you might want a ride."

Jensen did his best to keep his calm. He knew Derik meant well, but he wasn't thrilled with the idea of having a chauffer. Derik watched him closely and held up his hands in surrender. "I just thought it might make the day a little easier on you."

Jensen slid into the passenger seat. "Was this Autumn's idea?"

"Nope, it was mine. We need all the help we can get. I can't afford to lose anyone."

Jensen forced a smile. "Fine."

Derik stuck the gear in drive and headed out. "You're looking good. Kendra ran into Autumn over the weekend. She said she looks really happy these days. We think you might have something to do with that."

Jensen smiled. He wasn't used to inflicting happiness in someone's life, he tended to have the opposite effect. "She's good for me."

"She's a great girl. You should know we're all rooting for you. Don't mess it up."

Jensen looked out the window and watched as the fields rolled by. He said nothing.

⌘

Derik pulled into the garage and hopped out. Jensen followed and slipped into his old jumpsuit. He settled into the routine quickly. The aromas of oil and grease filled his lungs. They put him at ease. He was in his happy place. None of the guys were bothered by his return. They seemed eager to have him back. The one place Jensen rose above the rest was fixing things that were broken, in a mechanical sense. He knew what needed to be done and he welcomed a challenge. He hoped he could transfer the same skills to his personal life.

A familiar voice sounded behind him. "Hello? The guy in the office told me to come out here and talk to you."

Jensen slid out from under the hood and turned to the voice. He found some pleasure in seeing the surprise in the other mans face. "Surprised to see me back in the real world?" Jensen said dryly.

"Jensen?"

Jensen wiped his hands on the oil stained cloth. "Yep. It's Logan, right?"

"Yeah." Logan studied him, his voice grew flat. "You look better."

"I should hope so. The last time you saw me I was on my ass."

Logan looked around wearily. "Yeah. So about my truck, do you think you'll have time to squeeze it in?"

Jensen strode passed and nodded to a blue pickup. "That yours?"

"Yep."

"What's the problem?"

"It's been driving rough and over revving. My check engine light came on but I'm clueless when it comes to this kind of stuff."

"Can you start it for me?"

"Sure."

Jensen lifted the hood and waited for it to start. Logan turned the key and Jensen leaned in to investigate. The engine began to rev and Logan held up his hands. "I'm not doing that." The engine returned to normal, over revving every once in awhile.

"It might be your vacuum seal. I should be able to get to it in an hour or so. Leave the keys up front and tell them to book you in."

"Thanks, I appreciate it."

"No problem."

Jensen got back to his previous project but Logan remained. He cleared his throat and spoke. "Are you still at Autumn's place?"

"Sure am."

Logan waited for a more elaborate answer, when none came he continued. "How is she doing?"

"She's doing good. She seems happy. She got a gig working at the museum."

"She did? Huh, good for her."

Jensen smiled, her smiling image lit his memory. "She's something else."

"Yeah, she is." Logan's voice turned hard. "So, how long are you staying at her place for?"

A protectiveness came over Jensen. He stiffened and looked up from his work. "Look, I'm really busy here. They'll give you a call when your truck's done."

"So, I'm going to take that response as awhile then. Must be nice."

Jensen gripped the tools at hand harder than necessary. His eyes bore into Logan's. "You shouldn't be back here. I've got a lot of work to do."

Logan backed off. "Fine. I'll drop off my keys."

Jensen watched him walk away and muttered in frustration. He focused his attention back to the task at hand. Jensen got lost in the motions of the tools. When he glanced back at the clock his shift was almost over. Relief washed over him. Today had been a good day. He closed the hood as he finished tightening the last bolt. Jensen walked behind the garage and pulled out a cigarette.

He wished he had driven himself after all. He was eager to get home. The thought startled him, *home.* He wasn't sure what the future plans were, whether Autumn wanted him to stay forever or not. They had never discussed things like that, everything seemed to be heading down its own course. He didn't sense he was outstaying a welcome, in fact, it felt like the opposite. To him, he got a strong impression they were working towards something, together.

"There you are."

Jensen turned as Autumn appeared around the corner. "Hey, you. What are you doing here?" he asked in surprise.

Autumn smiled as she made her way to him. "I had lunch with Kendra today. She mentioned Derik may have picked you up."

Jensen flicked his cigarette. "Yep, he did."

"I'm sorry, I didn't know they had planned that. They're only trying to help."

"I know."

"So, how did today go?"

"Good. Busy. One of my customers asked about you."

"Oh?"

Jensen watched her closely. "Logan."

Autumn's face fell. "Ah, I see."

Jensen put out his cigarette and draped an arm around her neck. "I think he misses you."

Autumn kept her tone level. "That's nice. Come on, let's go home. I need to get out of these heels. My feet are killing me."

Jensen gave a lazy wave to the guys as they walked toward the Bronco. Autumn unlocked the doors and kicked off her heels, tossing them in the backseat. She let out a content sigh as she wiggled her toes. "That's better."

The engine started, first try, Jensen smiled in pride. That was his doing. They rolled down the windows and sang along to the radio. Once they were home, Autumn let Lucy out of the house. She bounded over and let out an excited whimper.

Jensen watched as Autumn shook her hair loose, the tousled waves bounced under the late daylight. He walked toward her and took her by the hand, and led her to the barn. He slid open the door and she ran barefoot down the alley to the tire swing. She climbed onto the tire and he pushed her gently, watching her sway back and forth.

She sent him a teasing grin. "You can fit on here too, you know."

He steadied the old tire as she stepped off. Jensen sat and Autumn sat across from him, wrapping her legs around his waist. She grinned as he rocked them into a steady flow.

"Isn't this relaxing?" she sighed. Jensen stared at the ceiling, judging how sturdy they were rigged up. Autumn gently kicked him with her foot. "Sit back and enjoy the moment."

Jensen focused his eyes back on her. Her blue eyes twinkled in the dim barn. "You're beautiful, do you know that?"

A warm flush crossed her cheeks. Jensen grinned. She was still very much the same girl he carried with him all these years. He was genuinely glad the hardships of life hadn't dampened her spirit. He watched her admiringly, she was so much stronger than him. She had overcome just as much as he had, if not more, and she still managed to carry a sense of peace with her. Being around her was good for his soul and his heart. She brought a sense of warmth and hope to his life.

Autumn tucked a strand of hair behind her ear. "Thank you."

Jensen pulled the rope to a stop. Autumn looked around unsurely and smiled crookedly. Jensen stood and took her by the hand, bringing her close. "For the first time in a long time, Autumn, I feel…safe."

She swallowed and pushed the hair out of his eyes. "I'm glad." Autumn stood onto her tiptoes and gave him a soft kiss. She pulled back and gave a small nod. "Okay."

He stared down at her in interest. She looked vulnerable and delicate in the moment. She kept her eyes on his and smiled softly. Jensen's hand traced down her back and found her zipper. He slid it down and the dress fell to the floor. Autumn kept her eyes locked to his as she slid the T-shirt over his head. Autumn stepped back and let out a shuddery breath. "You and I have never gone this far."

Jensen pulled her by the waist. "No. Are you sure you want too?"

Autumn's eyes lingered over his body. "Very much so."

Jensen stepped forward and Autumn pressed herself into him. He treated her differently than all the others, and for once, lovemaking actually meant something to him. Autumn's grip tightened as she brought him closer. He found her hands and clasped them over her head. Any hesitations either of them had were tossed out the window.

⌘

Jensen held Autumn gently in his arms. She looked up at him with a wondering smile. After a night with a woman, Jensen felt empty and unattached. This was different. His stomach twisted into knots, his heart raced, he realized it was fulfillment.

"So, that's what it's like," he mused.

"What?"

Jensen kissed the top of her head. "I haven't been present in the moment for awhile. I forgot what it felt like."

Autumn shifted onto his chest. "And? Did I meet your expectations?"

"Above and beyond."

Autumn beamed and pressed her lips to his neck. "Good answer."

The sound of tires on gravel outside caused them to jump. Autumn slid into her dress and Jensen jumped into his clothes. Outside, Lucy barked in recognition. Jensen and Autumn walked hand in hand to see Derik and Kendra knocking at the front door. Autumn placed her fingers in her mouth and let out an ear splitting whistle. The noise caught their attention and they turned. Autumn waved and towed Jensen along with her.

"The place looks incredible," Kendra gasped.

Autumn beamed and nudged Jensen in the ribs. "He painted the outside."

"It looks amazing."

Derik nodded to Jensen. "We just got back from dinner and wanted to stop in to say hi. By the way, you did great work today. We're glad to have you back."

"It's good to be back."

Autumn grabbed Kendra by the arm and led her inside. "Come on, you have to see inside!"

Autumn led Kendra and Derik to every corner of the house. Jensen watched in delight at the amount of pride Autumn displayed. And she should, she had every right to be proud of the work she accomplished. She brought life into something that had withered. They walked down the downstairs hall and a cold shiver tore through Jensen as he passed the room that once acted as his temporary bedroom. That room held nothing but regrets and humiliation for him.

Autumn and Jensen stood at ease in each others company. Jensen tried to ignore Kendra's eagle bearing eyes as they shifted between him and Autumn. It was as though she knew the act that transpired between then moments before. Kendra met his eyes and the smile she gave him said everything he needed to know.

Kendra flicked her red hair over her shoulder. "Well, we better get going. We're having a barbeque this Friday. You two better be there!"

Autumn looked at Jensen and he nodded. "We'll be there."

Kendra clapped her hands together. "Excellent. Be there by four." Her eyes glanced over the two of them once more and she smiled coyly. "Enjoy your night."

Jensen smiled broadly and gazed at Autumn. "I intend too."

Chapter 19

Autumn

The week passed quickly. It was Friday afternoon and I helped Anna update insurance claims for pieces in the museum. A bubble of excitement danced in my stomach as I glanced at the time, only two more hours and my workday would be over. Tonight was the barbeque at Kendra and Derick's. I was excited to see everyone and Jensen would be by my side.

Things seemed to be going very well for him lately, his eyes had a new spark and he carried himself with more self worth. I noticed the battle he fought, though I didn't say anything. It made a daily appearance, but it didn't seem to break him like it used to. He was beginning to find a balance of walking the line without crumbling.

Jensen had done something to me. He had given me something I wasn't even aware I was missing. Despite it all, he added a sense of security to my world, a completeness. When Jensen let himself relax and enjoy the moment, it took me back to the days before we knew the sting of destruction or loss. I hoped more of those days would be in our future.

Anna clucked to herself. "My dear girl, you just can't sit still today."

I glanced up from the stack of papers. "Oh? I didn't realize."

"Things are going good at home?"

I smiled. "Yes, knock on wood."

Anna grinned. "Good, I had high hopes for you two. I still remember Jensen as a tiny thing. He was a cheeky one."

I smirked. "Some things never change."

Anna looked at the clock. "I can handle things from here. How about you get going."

I set down a stack of papers. "Are you sure?"

Anna waved her hand. "Yes, go on get out of here. I'll see you on Monday."

I beamed and gathered my things. "Thank you! Have a good weekend."

Half an hour later I parked in front of my house. I ran to the front door, ruffled Lucy behind the ears and took the stairs two at a time. I laid out three dresses on the bed, trying to decide what to wear for the evening. I settled on a deep blue sundress, knowing it would make my eyes pop. I unraveled my messy bun, and pulled back a section into a loose braid.

I hummed myself a familiar tune when my phone rang. "Hello?"

Kendra spoke on the other end. "Hey, Autumn. I'm sorry, I have bad news."

I held my breath, my thoughts immediately went to Jensen. "Oh? What is it?"

"We're going to have to cancel the barbeque tonight. I came home early, I'm not feeling good."

Relief hit me. "No worries, feel better. Do you need anything?"

"I already called Derik with a list."

I let out a laugh. "Good! Feel better."

I placed my cell on the counter and plopped down on the couch. I looked down at my dress and sighed. *All dressed up but nowhere to go.* I flicked off my flip flops, grabbed a book and settled deeper into the couch. Two hours later Jensen strode through the front door.

He kicked off his boots and came into the living room. "Sorry I'm late. Let me just shower and we can head out." His brown eyes gazed over me. "You look nice."

I peeked up from my book. "Thank you, but there's no hurry. The party was canceled."

"Oh, okay. I'm still going to hop in the shower." Jensen tilted his head. "You okay?"

"Yeah, I was looking forward to going out is all."

"Oh." He turned and left the room.

I watched him go and went back to my book. Fifteen minutes later Jensen trotted down the stairs. He gave me a quick nod, grabbed his keys and headed out the front door. "I'll be back in half an hour," he called. Before I could respond he was already in his truck and driving away. *That's odd.* Concern washed over me and I did my best to let it slide. Things had been going so well between us lately I had no reason to worry. A small part of me was waiting for things, for him, to unravel. I hated the part of my self conscious that went there. I willed it to go away and never return.

Thirty-five minutes later headlights came through the window, followed by the rumble of Jensen's truck. A knock sounded at the door. I set my book down, confused. Why didn't he just walk inside?

"Come in," I yelled. Again the knock sounded. Lucy ran to the front door, tail wagging. She scratched at the door and let out a single bark. I reached for the handle to pull it open. My eyes widened at the view before me, and I placed a hand over my mouth.

Jensen stood on the other side, smile wide. He extended a hand with a bouquet of purple lilacs. "These are for you. Are you ready to go?"

I grabbed the flowers and the sweet, floral smell filled my lungs. "These are my favorite." I wrapped an arm around his neck and gave him a kiss. "What are these for?"

Jensen grinned. "I think it's high time I took you out on a date."

"A date?" I asked in surprise.

"Yes, ma'am."

I was flustered, I hadn't seen this coming. "Oh…let me just put these in water. I'll be right back." I stopped before entering the kitchen. "I like this, well done."

Jensen crossed his arms and leaned against the doorframe. "I'll wait here."

Once the flowers were in a vase I met Jensen by the door. We walked shoulder to shoulder to his truck where he opened the door for me. "After you."

I hopped into the front seat and smoothed my dress down. Jensen ran to the drivers side and flew in. His face held no indication of where we would be going. A familiar aroma met me from the back seat. I turned to see a box of pizza from our favorite parlor in town. "Is that Joe's pizza?" I asked hopeful.

"Of course. Only the best."

"Where are we going?"

Jensen flicked on the radio. "Sit back and relax. We'll be there soon enough."

I grumbled and crossed my arms. Patience wasn't one of my strongest virtues. "You're not even going to give me a hint?"

Jensen sighed. "Well…it's somewhere we never spent as much time as we should have."

My lips twisted as I mulled over his response. I was stumped. "I don't like that answer. It tells me nothing."

Jensen laughed. "We'll be there in fifteen minutes or less. Hang in there. I know you can do it."

The sun began to set as dusk drew near. We drove passed the town strip and turned left at the stop sign. The truck rattled over the railroad tracks and the pavement turned to gravel. I sat up straighter as the field whirred by. I knew this road. I peeked at Jensen and he wore a half smile. Jensen turned into an empty parking lot and there in the darkness stood our old high school.

"A place we didn't spend as much time as we should have," I muttered. "Very clever, Jensen, very clever."

"I thought so. Come on."

We hopped out and Jensen balanced the pizza boxes in one hand, while holding mine in the other. I looked toward the old blue building. So many memories were etched in stone here. Years may have passed, but the school looked exactly as I remembered. We walked passed the building and made our way to the football field. Everything was still in the quiet of the evening. The crickets sang their night song and the smell of freshly cut grass wafted amongst the warm air.

We settled onto a pair of bleachers and Jensen set the pizza boxes down. "Dig in."

I grabbed a slice and stared back at Jensen. "This is perfect."

Jensen took a bite and swallowed. "Some of my happiest moments in life took place here." Jensen pointed to a tree in the distance. "Remember that tree?"

My eyes followed his finger and I laughed. "I sure do. A girl never forgets her first kiss."

Jensen leaned back against the bleacher. "Do you remember what you did after I kissed you?"

I tapped my fingers in thought. A smile grew as the memory began to replay. I looked back at Jensen with a sheepish expression upon my face. "I laughed at you. I believe I said 'What took you so long?'"

Jensen tossed his arm around me, bringing me closer. "You sure did." He glanced down at me. "I have never been able to predict your responses."

I smiled proudly. "I like to keep a man on his toes. It's good for you."

Jensen shifted beneath me. "Come with me." He held out his hand and brought me to my feet. Jensen towed me behind, and led me to his truck. He opened the front door and rummaged through the back seat. "This outta be fun." He stood back, holding a football.

I raised an eyebrow. "What do you expect me to do with that?"

"Go long."

I looked at him warily. "Are you serious? I was never one for this game."

Jensen rolled his eyes and walked to the field. "Come on," he waved a hand through the air.

I hesitated before following. I stepped into the open field and Jensen jogged easily away. "Ready?" he yelled.

I kicked off my shoes. "No!"

"Here it comes!"

I ran toward the ball and clumsily reached out. The football bounced out of my clutch. I bent down and picked it up. Jensen laughed from across the way. "That was terrible."

"I was no football player," I grumbled. I looked at the ball and rolled it uneasily in my hands. "How am I supposed to throw this thing?"

Jensen studied me and grinned. "I could tell you but I kinda want to see how you pull this together yourself."

I glared back at him and gripped the ball tightly in my right hand. I extended my arm back and launched it with all of my might. The football glided through the air and Jensen caught it with ease. He tucked the football underneath his arm and clapped his hands together. I ignored the gesture and held my hands open ready to catch his toss. Jensen threw the ball and I began to run, arms wide open. The ball hit my forearms and it bounced. My hands worked quickly this time and I gave one more desperate clutch and pulled the ball to my chest.

"Ah ha! I did it! I caught the ball!"

Jensen beamed and raised his arms in the air. "Ladies and gentleman, she caught the ball!"

I ignored his mocking tone and heaved the ball his way once more. I didn't aim high enough and the ball socked him in the gut. Jensen let out a surprised breath and hunched over. He looked at me with an accusation.

I jogged over to assess the damage and began giggling. "I'm so sorry. Are you okay?"

"Damn girl," he muttered. "That has got to be one of the worst aims I have ever seen."

I slapped him on the back. "What are you talking about? I am a superstar."

Jensen straightened and picked up the ball. He gave me a cautious look. "I think I'm going to hold on to this for awhile."

I linked my arm through his. "Fair enough."

We walked lazily through the field until I stopped to lie in the grass. Jensen settled beside me and we stared into the clear sky. The stars twinkled above and we did our best to name the constellations. Jensen's hand found mine amongst the grass and he slipped his fingers through. "It's moments like this that make me think everything will be okay."

I squeezed my hand in his. "Everything will be okay."

Jensen didn't say a word. I peeked at him; his eyes focused on the night sky. I shifted my eyes to the stars. They burned brightly against the blackness. Fear settled over my heart. Despite the beauty in the moment, I was very aware I still remained on the outside. I always knew when Jensen slipped into the dark confinements of his mind. It would do me no good to pry, he would only share if and when he was ready. A cold chill crept across my skin, and it had nothing to do with the temperature. It was forewarning.

Chapter 20

Jensen

The drive home was quiet. Something happened in the stillness of the night, a small divide had forged its way back. Jensen kept his grip on the steering wheel tight. He didn't know why these moments came and went, but Autumn always sensed when he grew distant. He could see it in her eyes. He wanted to share things with her, but it had become easier to leave certain things unsaid.

The monster he wanted to keep locked away was fighting its way to the surface. Jensen shut down when his mind turned against him. It was easier to stay closed off, safer. The last thing he ever wanted was to hurt Autumn, and he didn't trust himself in times like this. A wave of tiredness hit him. Battling his dark longings took a lot out of him and so quickly. It was in times like these he worried about his future, he wasn't sure how much more he had in him to resist.

Autumn shifted in the seat next to him and closed her hand around his. Jensen felt her worried eyes upon him so he kept his eyes on the road before him. He squeezed her hand back in quiet reassurance. Jensen pulled into the long driveway home. His headlights lit up the dark drive and a familiar vehicle was parked next to Autumn's. Autumn tensed beside him. Jensen put the truck in park and turned off the engine. They hopped out and Jensen glowered at the blue pickup.

Autumn let out a surprised gasp. "Logan? What are you doing here?"

Logan sat against the front door, his long legs sprawled out before him. Jensen clenched his hands into fists. *Son of a bitch.* Logan looked up as though

Autumn were the only one standing there. "I've been waiting here for awhile. I'm glad you're home. Can we talk?"

Autumn's voice went harsh. "Logan, are you drunk?" She sent a worried glance toward Jensen.

Jensen took a careful step to Logan. He recognized immediately the dazed look in his eyes and the clumsy way in which he carried himself. Jensen's stomach recoiled in jealousy. Logan had dipped into Jensen's craving. Jensen forced himself to swallow and his heart began to race. Autumn leaned over and helped Logan up. Logan draped his arm around her neck and his eyes burned at her with longing. Jensen stiffened and his back went up. Autumn's eyes shifted uneasily. It was clear she was out of her element. Her eyes glinted in anger when she turned them to Logan, but grew bright with worry when she looked toward Jensen.

"I'm so sorry," Autumn looked at Jensen. "I'll take him home."

Logan grabbed on to Autumn's arm. "No, I don't need to go home. I'm fine right here."

"No, you're not," Autumn snapped. "You have no right to be here."

Logan looked at Jensen and smirked. "Because of him? I have some beers in my truck, just give him one and he'll go."

Autumn wriggled out of Logan's grasp and he stumbled against the door. He reached out to steady himself.

Anger burned throughout Jensen. "Get into the truck," he directed at Logan quietly.

Logan raised his eyebrow. "What?"

"Get in your truck. You're going home. You don't belong here."

"Neither do you," Logan spat out.

"Enough," Autumn pleaded.

Jensen stepped forward. "You have two choices, either we take you home willingly, or I will drag you out of here myself."

The smile Logan wore faded. "My, how the tables have turned. Look who's acting like he has everything together now."

Logan shoved past and stumbled to his truck. He opened the door and pulled out a can of beer. He pulled back the tab and took a sip. Logan sidled to Autumn and smiled. "Let's see just how strong he is." He extended the can of beer towards Jensen. "Go on, take a sip. You know you want one."

Jensen's hands began to tremble, he quickly drew them into a ball. His mouth went dry and his eyes fell to the open can. God how he wanted a sip, just one sip. He closed his eyes tightly and begged himself not to waver. He knew he wouldn't be able to stop at one sip, it would lead to so many more. And he would not prove this clown right. A loud commotion appeared and Jensen opened his eyes. Logan yelped as Autumn pulled back her hand from the side of his face. She grabbed the can from his hand and tossed it.

Autumn stepped toward Logan threateningly and placed her hands against his chest, and shoved him backwards. "Get out!"

Jensen snapped into action and took hold of Logan, and dragged him to his truck. "Time for you to leave." His tone left no room for discussion. "Get in the truck."

Logan deflated, he seemed to know he wasn't going to get what he wanted. "Fine," he looked at Autumn. "You blew your chance." Logan slid into his passenger seat and closed the door.

Autumn ran over to Jensen. "I'm so sorry. Are you okay?"

"Fine," he said curtly. "Do you want me to drive him back?"

"No," Autumn said quickly. "I can manage."

"Fine. I'll follow you." Jensen turned abruptly and got into his truck.

Autumn stood in the driveway for a moment, she looked shaken. A surge of guilt overcame Jensen but he pushed it away. He watched Autumn slide into Logan's truck and he followed them to Logan's place. During the drive, he saw Autumn and Logan's heads move back and forth, it looked like they were having an argument. Jensen wanted nothing more than to slam him into the ground. As the drive progressed, Jensen grew uneasy and agitated. The smell of alcohol had lingered on Logan, and Jensen could almost taste it.

Autumn pulled into the drive and got out. She left Logan in the truck and found the spare key hidden in a plant. Jensen watched her and felt a stab of jealousy. He knew she had spent a lot of time in this place, and it bothered him. *But you left her. You have no right to feel this way. You let her go.* Jensen cursed softly and got out of his truck. He helped Autumn haul Logan out and put him in bed, he was already passed out.

Autumn locked the front door and hid the key. "Can we go home?"

"Yes."

Autumn hopped into the passenger seat but Jensen lingered. He stopped at Logan's truck and stared at the cans of beer scattered about. Temptation called out to him ever so sweetly. His hand moved for the door handle. *One sip. Just one sip.*

"Jensen?"

Jensen turned toward Autumn's voice. It was heavy with worry. She rubbed her hands across her bare arms and shivered in the cold. Jensen stepped back from the dark enticement and jumped in the driver seat. He held one hand haphazardly on the steering wheel, and stared at the floor. Autumn touched his arm and he met her upset gaze.

"I'm fine," he said quietly. "Let's go home."

Autumn fought back tears. "I'm so sorry," she whispered under her breath.

⌘

On the drive home Autumn was silent. Jensen heard her sniffle in the dark, he knew her tears fell. Jensen said nothing to ease them. He was too busy battling the raging beast that was slowly breaking free. He pulled up next to the porch and cut the engine. They walked into the house in silence. Lucy seemed to sense something wrong. She didn't greet them in her usual gusto.

Autumn threw on an old night shirt and sat on her side of the bed. Jensen tore his shirt off and kicked out of his jeans. He balled them into a tight bundle and threw them against the wall. He let out a yell in frustration. He pulled his hand into a fist and threw it against the wall in a harsh, single blow.

Autumn pressed her eyes shut and jumped slightly. She sniffled once and spoke in a near whisper. "I don't know how to help you." There was a long pause before she spoke again. "I don't know what to do."

Autumn leaned forward and flicked out the lamp. She lay with her back facing Jensen. He stared at her, not knowing what to say. He decided it was best to keep his mouth shut, his temper was short. He knew he would only hurt her if he chose to say something, which would most likely come out the wrong way. Jensen lay down and stared at the ceiling. The voices of temptation rang loud in his head. He shifted from his back, to his side, to his stomach. Nothing felt right. Jensen threw off the covers in frustration and went downstairs. He found a pair of sweatpants and a T-shirt folded on the couch. He pulled them on and his eyes locked on his trucks keys. Slow footsteps sounded behind. He remained where he was, and stared at the glimmering keys.

Autumn stepped in front of him, her face raw in emotion. She looked at him. "Jensen? What can I do to help? You're scaring me."

Jensen kept his eyes out the window. "Please don't take this wrong way, but I think it's best if you leave me alone tonight. Go back to bed, it's late."

Jensen forced himself to look at her. She looked hurt. He placed his palm against his forehead. He knew he was being an ass and she was only trying to help. But she didn't understand, she couldn't. Most of all, Jensen did not want Autumn to see him like this. He felt the wildness dwelling inside. It was all he could do to try to contain it. He would either rise above the choking force, or succumb. He didn't know which of the two would win out, and he did not want Autumn around if he chose the latter.

"Please just leave me alone," he choked out.

Autumn pulled her eyes from his and walked slowly up the stairs. He watched her go before grabbing his keys. He needed to get out of here, he needed to be on his own for a little while. Jensen started up his truck and drove mindlessly. He didn't know where he was going, he just needed to keep moving. His chest tightened, and his skin crawled. He glanced at the time, it was almost two in the morning. Nothing would be open to quench his thirst at this hour. An unsettling thought crept into his mind. Logan's truck. In the passenger seat of the blue pickup held the very thing he craved. It would be enough to satisfy the thirst that allured him.

Jensen's vision went hazy. He pulled over and stepped into the night air. He let out a yell and threw his fist against the side of his truck. Pain tore through him, momentarily shaking him. He let his feet slide out from underneath until he sat on the gravel, his back pressed firmly against the side of his truck. He placed his head in his hands and tried to take steady breaths.

He hated being here. He didn't want to feel this way anymore. Jensen lifted his head and stared into the night.

A part of him wondered if he would forever walk on a ledge, fighting the balance between staying sober or drowning himself in a bottle. Giving in to the alcohol was easy. Staying away from it was almost impossible. Why was doing the right thing so damn hard? He hadn't always been this way.

Jensen was eighteen years old when Jake passed. He hadn't turned to alcohol right away. At first Jensen got angry. He stayed that way for two years. He then lost himself in his projects, bringing old vehicles to life. It had been a wonderful distraction. As the years passed, the loneliness and anger turned to something he could no longer control: desperation. It was there he found alcohol. He avoided the substance for so long because it reminded him of that fateful day. He hated the taste. It was bitter, and guilt was heavily laced throughout the liquid. But the more he drank, the more comfort it provided. When he had no one, he could always count on alcohol. The potent potion would wrap him up like a long lost friend, gently erasing the hurt. But it also came with a price, one he couldn't afford to pay.

Jensen stood up stiffly feeling more alone than ever. He sat in his truck and started the engine. His thoughts turned to Autumn and what she must be feeling in this moment. He knew her mind would expect the worst and he hated himself for it. She had done nothing but bend over backward to help him, and this is how he repaid her? Jensen sighed heavily, lowering his head.

"You're an idiot, Jensen."

Jensen froze at the familiar voice. His blood ran cold. He hesitantly looked at his passenger seat. "This can't be possible," he breathed. Jensen blinked twice as he stared into the eyes of his long lost friend. Jake.

Jake smiled his boyish grin. "You look like hell man. What's going on?"

Jensen shook his head but Jake did not disappear. He would forever be eighteen years old with the same flyaway mussed brown hair. His brown eyes looked mischievous and his features were young and innocent. "This can't be happening," Jensen said. "Crap. It's happened, hasn't it? I've lost my mind."

Jake laughed his carefree laugh. "Naw, man, you're not crazy." Jake's brown eyes fell to his old friend. "You don't look so good."

Jensen couldn't tear his eyes away. "No…I'm not."

Jake's face fell. "I know. What about Autumn? Are you guys still close or did you screw that one up too?"

Jensen rubbed his head. He must be losing his mind, but this felt so real. "I lost her."

"What happened?" Jake encouraged.

"I left after you…you died." Jensen held his breath and looked over to his friend. Jake nodded encouragingly. Jensen continued. "I didn't even say goodbye. I just took off. As the years passed, I never once reached out to her until one day, boom. I came back."

Jake grinned. "How does she look?"

Jensen found himself laughing. "She's beautiful, like always. She's too good for me."

"She was a real looker. I still can't believe she chose you over me. I mean come on, look at me!" Jake held out his hands, motioning up and down. His voice grew serious. "It wasn't your fault. I remember bits and pieces from that day. You did everything you could."

Jensen grew pale. "I don't want to talk about it."

"Nobody ever does. But you need to. Go back, Jensen. Go back to where it started. You're never going to move forward if you don't look back. You need to make peace with it."

"I don't know if I can."

"Then you're going to be forever lost."

Jensen clenched his hands together. "Don't make me go back there."

"Nobody is making you do anything. You have a choice to make, Jensen. You have to fight. You will either fall flat on your face, or you will make it to the top. The choice is yours. But let me tell you, if you choose the easy road, the one that calls to you and tries to lure you in, there will come a day where you won't walk away. Ever. You will never come back." Jake paused and met Jensen with a fierce intensity. "You are living a fate that is worse than death."

Jensen felt as though he were socked in the stomach. He closed his eyes. "No." He looked to Jake, but he was alone once more.

⌘

Jensen stared at the reflection of the moon bouncing off the still surface of the lake. The sounds of water lapping against the shore caused Jensen to shiver. He remained in his truck, he could not move. Images he long repressed replayed before him. His eyes widened in horror as he heard Autumn screaming. That blood curdling scream plagued him.

Panic rose within Jensen, his breaths came out in short, rapid gasps. He clutched his chest and willed himself to relax. *Wake up, Jake! Come on, man, don't leave me! Get up! Jake!* Jensen placed his hands over his ears and willed for the voices to stop. He couldn't do this again. Jensen reached out for his phone with shaking hands. He dialed Autumn's number and prayed she would answer.

"Hello?" Autumn's voice was frantic on the other end.

"Autumn, I need you," Jensen choked out.

"Where are you?"

"The lake."

Silence fell heavy on the other end of the line. "The lake?" she whispered.

"Yes. Please don't leave me here. I can't do this."

"I'm on my way. Don't move."

Jensen let his phone drop to the floor. He couldn't move if he wanted to, his body remained frozen. After what felt like forever, a set of headlights cut through the night. Jensen heard a door shut and fast footsteps followed. Autumn ran toward him, concern etched in her pretty features. Jensen watched her approach him. Despite the urgency of the moment, he felt something that resembled a smile on his mouth. Autumn hadn't bothered to get dressed. Her hair was messy from tossing and turning in bed and she still wore the oversized T-shirt. He glanced down at her feet and noted she wore slippers.

Autumn hopped into the seat next to him. Her eyes carefully assessed Jensen. "What happened? Why are you here?"

Jensen closed his eyes and pinched the bridge of his nose. "I saw him, Autumn."

Autumn looked confused. "You saw who?"

"Jake," Jensen croaked. He opened his eyes to gage her reaction.

Autumn sat back and looked forward. "I don't know what I'm supposed to say to that." She bit her lip and looked at him hesitantly.

"I haven't been drinking. God knows I want too. Look at my hands. They won't stop shaking." Jensen held out his trembling hands in reluctance.

Autumn took his hands in hers. "What happened?"

"You don't think I'm crazy?"

"I think your repressed memories are no longer wanting to remain in the cobwebs. They're breaking free and they are going to do whatever they can to get you to notice. Tell me what happened."

Jensen took a shaky breath and filled her in on his conversation with Jake. Autumn's hand tightened around his but she said nothing. She let him finish his thoughts. Jensen closed his mouth tightly once done. He looked away and waited for her to leave him alone with the madness he faced. Autumn dropped his hand and stepped outside. She shut the door softly behind her. For a moment, she didn't move. Her eyes remained focused on the ground. Jensen looked away and squeezed his eyes shut. He didn't want to see her walk away.

A soft tap at his window caused him to look up. Autumn opened his door and led him outside. "You've made it this far, Jensen. It's time."

Jensen hesitated. "Time for what?"

"To face what happened that day. We're so close to where it all began."

Jensen tore his hand away. "I can't," he moaned.

"Look where you are. Look what's happening to you. I promise, I will be right here. I won't let you go." Autumn held out her hand and waited.

Jensen's eyes locked on the rocky shore. Images hit him like a thunderbolt. He staggered back and tore his eyes away. He gathered his breath, reached out and clasped onto Autumn's hand. This was it, Jensen was going to stare into the eyes of his tormentor.

Chapter 21

Autumn

Never in a million years would I have guessed to find Jensen here. When he took off into the night, I was sure I would never hear from him again. He had unraveled and there was nothing left holding him together. This was it. He would either walk away unscathed or this would forever break him. It was going to be up to him which road he would choose.

We now stood at the very spot it happened; the day our lives changed forever, and where one was lost. I swallowed the lump in my throat as our footsteps came to a halt. We stood at the edge of the dock. The water lapped against the rocks lying below. I squeezed Jensen's hands as my own began to shake.

"Are you ready?" I whispered.

"No."

"Me, either."

Jensen surprised me and took the first step onto the wooden surface. We walked to the end of the dock and stared at the dark water. I sat on the edge, Jensen followed suit. Neither of us spoke. The memory of that day broke through the clouds and replayed like an old film.

It was supposed to be the summer our lives began, not ended. For the guys, it was their last free summer, they were freshly graduated from high school. I was two years younger. I remember being green in envy at their newfound freedom. This had been our spot, we skipped many classes to sit under the old towering maples and float lazily on the water. It was on this lake that Jake and Jensen had made a plan to travel for the summer, driving the coast.

I had been offered an internship at the museum, even back then Anna had seen my passion for history. It was our last night together, just the three of us, before summer took us down different paths. It was also the first night we got drunk. Jake persuaded his older brother to buy us drinks. We toasted to the beginning of bigger and better things.

The day was hot, not a cloud above in the bright blue sky. The water was the perfect temperature; we floated easily in the light current. Laughter rang loud in the stillness of the woods around us. We had planned to stay the night, our last camping trip together for awhile. It was also the first summer Jensen and I announced ourselves as an official item. Jake was quite thrilled at the idea. He claimed he was the one who brought us together, bridging the gap between friends to young lovers.

We got to the lake at the crack of dawn. We had our first drink by ten that morning, justifying it was five o'clock somewhere. As the day grew hotter, the drinks came quicker. Food wasn't the first thing on our minds. I learned early that I was a light weight, I couldn't keep up to the guys. I had stopped drinking around noon. I remember the way the world began to spin, it left me feeling dizzy. I was never one who enjoyed feeling out of control.

I crawled into the bed of the truck to have a nap. A burning heat woke me; the sun had burnt the back of my legs. I blinked my eyes open sleepily and the guys tossed around the football, hooting and hollering away. Jensen noticed I was awake, and ran over to give me a kiss. Jake made a big production out of that, he always did. Jensen rolled his eyes and tossed the ball. I winced as I jumped off the tailgate, my legs hurt. I stepped into the lake and allowed the cool water to soothe my burns.

I floated lazily on my back, and watched the treetops above dance in a slight breeze. Bits of sunlight broke through the leaves and came down like a spotlight, sending the water afire like glittering diamonds. I closed my eyes and sighed in contentment. I snapped my eyes open as the guys thundered down the dock, running at full tilt. They smashed into each other in a mock fight. Their movements were clumsy and uncoordinated, their reflexes slow.

Jake had shoved into Jensen, and Jensen went down hard, shoulder first on the dock. Jake hollered in delight while Jensen dusted himself off. Jensen looked momentarily stunned and delicately investigated his shoulder. He winced in pain but a smirk quickly followed. Jensen ran and football tackled Jake. They both hit the water hard. I rolled my eyes at the commotion and closed my eyes once more. A pair of arms enclosed my waist, and before I had time to gasp, I was pulled under the water. I broke to the surface in surprise, coughing. Jensen popped up beside me and broke into a cheery laugh. I tossed water in his face and slugged him in the arm. He gave me his puppy dog eyes and I wrapped my arms around his neck. He pulled me close and spun me in slow motion. I tightened my legs around him and leaned my back in the water. Jensen continued to spin me softly, around and around.

Jensen released my grip and raised an eyebrow. "You better swim fast. I'm going to get you."

I let out a mock squeal in terror and swam as fast as I could. I glanced back and couldn't see Jensen anywhere. A ripple of urgency came over me, so I picked up my pace. If he found me, I would be dunked. My arms and legs moved at top speed through the water. I was getting closer to the dock. I stole one more glance behind me and saw nothing. My speed came to a halt as I hit something.

I stopped in surprise and looked in front of me. Jake floated face first in the water. Something about the way he bobbed about made my blood run cold. A pool of red floated near his head. I grabbed his torso and flipped him around. Jake's eyes were open, but they didn't look right. His gaze looked distant. Blood dripped down his face, a large gash ran along his hairline, spreading to behind his ear. I let out a blood curdling scream.

"Jake! My god, Jake! Wake up!" I shook him fiercely. Uncontrollable sobs escaped my lips, and I started to scream in a hysterical manner.

Jensen appeared out of nowhere, concern heavy in his face. "Autumn, what the hell kind of scream is that—" His eyes took in the scene before him and he went white. "Grab his legs. I'll take his torso. Get him to shore now!"

Jensen placed his arms underneath Jakes and lifted. I grabbed his legs and we carried him to the shore.

"He's too pale, Jensen. Is he dead?"

Urgency fueled Jensen. "He's still breathing. Jesus. Jake? Jake, can you hear me man?"

"Does he have a pulse?" I cried.

Jensen tilted Jake's head back and gave him CPR. He looked toward me, eyes wild. "Grab a towel, we need to stop the bleeding."

I ran as fast as my legs could carry me. That was the moment that made me take up running. The faster my legs went, I felt as though I could outrun the fear that gripped me cold. I had been running ever since. I reached the pick up and grabbed a towel. I tripped once, scratching my palms and knee, but jumped up in a matter of seconds. My feet moved swiftly and carried me to a vision I didn't want to see. I skidded to a stop and placed the towel against Jake's head. Tears began to blind my vision as I sobbed. "Don't leave us, Jake! Say something! Do you hear me! Say something!" I begged. I turned my gaze onto Jensen. "How long was he in the water?"

Jensen paled. "I don't know."

"Think, Jensen! Think!" I screamed. "Did he come up after you guys dove in?"

Jensen closed his eyes and opened them. He looked distraught. "I don't think so. Shit." Jensen looked at me. "I came up and I saw you floating in the distance. I went straight to you. I thought he was behind me."

"The rocks," I sobbed. "Did he hit a rock?"

Jensen curled over and threw up. His hands gripped the sandy surface. "I don't know. We hit the water so fast." Jensen's eyes took in Jake. "Run to the road, Autumn. Flag someone down, anyone."

I bent down and gave Jake a quick kiss. "Don't leave us," I sobbed. I pulled myself to my feet and took off running.

My feet screamed in pain as the rocks and shrubbery from the earth ripped at the tender skin. I broke free of the trail and stepped onto the burning asphalt in the road. I let out another scream, this one heavy in fear. A rusted old pickup rounded the corner ahead. It clicked along at a decent speed and headed my way. I ran blindly into the middle of the road, waving my arms frantically.

The truck skidded to a stop and two men hopped out. "What in the name of all that is—" The man snapped his mouth shut and took in my appearance.

I trembled from head to toe, tears streamed down my face and my teeth clacked together as my mouth chattered in an uncontrollable manner. Jake's blood had dried onto my hands and a smear ran down my torso.

"My god," said the other man. "What happened?"

"My friend," I sobbed. "I think he's dying."

The driver of the pick up nodded to his friend. "Call for help, now! I'll go with her." The man stepped forward and carefully touched my arm. "Where is your friend, honey? Show me."

I grabbed the man's hand and took off running, towing him along. We broke through the trees onto the shoreline. I let go of the man's hand and my heart caught in my throat. Jensen sat near Jake, his knees drawn to his chest, his hands in his hair. He kept his head down and he rocked gently back and forth. He looked up at the sound of footsteps, tears streamed down his face. I knew in that moment, Jake was gone. My eyes fell to Jake's lifeless body. The man bent down and gently examined him. He looked up sadly and shook his head. Another scream escaped my lips, one I hadn't felt coming. My legs gave out and I hit the hot sand heavily. Jensen ran to me, helping me to my feet.

"No," I sobbed. "No!"

Jensen fought back hysterics himself. He pulled me into a hug. "I'm so sorry, Autumn. He stopped breathing, I couldn't bring him back. I tried so hard." Jensen began sobbing.

I pressed my hands to his chest and shoved him away. "No! This cannot be happening. This isn't real. No, no, no! Today was supposed to be a good day!"

Jensen took a step closer and I held out my hands. "Don't you touch me. Stay away from me."

The passenger from the truck stepped into the clearing. He took in the scene before him and his eyes widened. "Oh, sweet Jesus," he breathed.

His friend knelt near Jake. "Is somebody coming?"

"The ambulance is on its way."

The man nodded. "Good, take the girl away from here. She shouldn't see this." The man looked at Jensen. "Go with her too, you don't need to be here."

I began to sob uncontrollably. "Jake! I told you not to leave us. Come back. Open your eyes dammit!"

Jensen came toward me, his face pale, his eyes swollen from tears. He extended a hand and I slapped it away. I ran for Jake when Jensen scooped me up by the waist. "We have to go, Autumn. Please."

"No," I screamed and tried to wriggle free. Jensen kept a firm grasp on me as I tried to slap him away. He began walking to the road, one of the men walked beside him quietly. Jensen kept his jaw tight, his eyes stared straight ahead. He put me down once we were near the old pick up. I tried to run past him, but he placed a firm hand against my chest. "No, Autumn. Stay here. You can hate me all you want, but I will not let you go back there."

I glared back at Jensen before crumpling to the ground. I sat with my head between my knees, fighting for breaths. Jensen sat a good distance away. He didn't say a word. He laced his fingers within each other, grasping until they turned white. His eyes grew dim and hazy. He stared into the distance, lost in his head. The ambulance pulled up minutes later and the paramedics ran for our lifeless friend.

Words and voices came from around me, but I couldn't make out what they said, everything was foggy. I turned my tear stained eyes to Jensen. "Is this really happening?"

Jensen's voice was tight. "Jake is dead. I saw it. I watched the life fade away and it's all my fault," he sobbed.

I leaned my head back against the rusted old truck. I didn't say a word. Realization struck me hard, our friend was gone, forever more.

⌘

My breath came out in a ragged gasp as images from that horrible day dissipated in mid air. Next to me Jensen's hand squeezed mine so hard, I could no longer feel it. I turned my damp eyes to his, knowing he had been reliving the same nightmare as I. Guilt ate at me, knowing why Jensen had chose to leave afterwards.

A part of me blamed him for what had happened. I knew in my heart it hadn't been his fault. It was an accident. It could have just as easily been Jensen who met the rock, but Jake had drawn the short end of the straw. I hadn't remembered how hard I had made things for Jensen, I blocked out the memory. Regret coursed through me once more, I knew he carried it with him every day.

I cleared my throat. "I am so sorry, Jensen. I never meant to blame you."

Jensen tightened his jaw. "You had every right to blame me."

"No, I didn't. I was young and scared. It felt better to take it out on someone, anyone. I'm so sorry," I whispered.

Jensen stood. "We should have never come back to this place. What good did it do?"

"I don't know," I mumbled.

Jensen held out his hand to help me up. "Let's go home. I'm tired."

He avoided my eyes as I gazed toward him. "Okay."

We got into our separate vehicles and drove home. I was emotionally and physically exhausted. The memories felt so real like I had relived it all over again. Jensen and I crawled into bed, the silence growing heavy. I caught his eyes a few times and he looked absent. Jensen reached out and pulled me close. I settled into his chest as he flicked out the lamp. Even though we were physically close, I had never felt so far away from him.

I awoke early the next morning. I sat up, and glanced at Jensen. He lay on his side, back facing me. I tiptoed out of the bedroom and laced up my running shoes and took to my favorite running route. Lucy had to run at full tilt to keep up with me. Today I was not running for enjoyment, I was trying to outrun the nightmares that had plagued my slumber. Jake's lifeless image had infected my dreams.

I pushed my legs to their breaking point. I left the memories behind once, I was determined to do it again. The sound of my scream echoed in my mind and Jensen's sobs. I pushed my legs to keep going, desperately trying to pick up speed. As the years passed, my speed had improved greatly. *If only I had run faster that day. Maybe then I would have been able to save him.* I came to a stop and bent over, and tried to regain my breath. It wasn't only Jake's image that had cursed me, it was the look on Jensen's face as I screamed at him to stay away from me. I squeezed my eyes tighter but it was no use, the tears fell thick. I limped over to a grassy ledge and sat. Lucy sat next to me and I grabbed her in a fierce hug. She sensed my sadness and did not struggle to get away.

I wiped the last of the tears away and walked home slowly. I came to an abrupt halt at the sight of Logan standing next to his truck. He looked up at the sound of my footsteps and walked over to me.

He held up his hands in a gesture of peace. "I'm so sorry for last night. I was a real ass." Logan dropped his playful smile as he studied me. "What's wrong?"

I held up my hands in a quick wave. "It was a long night."

"Was it because of me? I'm sorry if I caused any issues between you and Jensen."

"No, it's not that."

Logan placed his hand under my chin and tilted my head back. "What is it?"

I couldn't hold back the tears anymore. Logan wrapped me in a safe hug and held me. I sniffled through the tears. "Jensen and I went to the lake last night, where it happened. I remembered everything. It was awful. I was so cold to him. I drove him away."

Logan hushed me softly. "It wasn't your fault. You can't blame yourself. I can't even imagine what you went through."

I gripped onto Logan's shirt and he held me until the tears stopped falling.

Chapter 22
Jensen

Jensen woke to an empty bed. He lay in the quiet and thought of last night. He was surprised the memories didn't split him in two like he expected. They seemed to have more of an effect on Autumn. Jensen closed his eyes. He felt nothing, nothing but the old familiar numbness in his chest. Though he never thought he would go back to the lake, the memories from that day had always remained vivid for him. No amount of time had erased the images, it was something he carried with him everyday.

Jensen rose with a low groan, perhaps last night had more of an effect on him than he realized. He gently rolled his shoulder, it was stiff today. When Jake tackled him onto the deck, he tore the muscle. He never bothered to care for it properly, and now it flared up every now and then. A part of Jensen enjoyed the pain it brought. It let him know he still felt something. He was still alive, it hadn't all been a terrible dream. It was in fact, reality.

He stared at the empty bed and wondered how Autumn was doing. Last night she looked small and frail, like a frightened child. Jensen went downstairs and found the pack of cigarettes. He stepped onto the front porch and lit up his smoke. He scanned the driveway and pulled the cigarette to his mouth. His eyes fell onto Autumn in the arms of Logan. He blinked once to make sure he was seeing things correctly. He could tell by her body posture she was upset. Logan's hand ran soothingly up and down her back. Jensen felt a surge of jealousy course through him as he let out a puff of smoke.

Logan's arms fell away as Autumn took a step back. Logan gestured for her to turn around and she glanced over her shoulder. She sighed and walked toward the house, Logan followed. Jensen watched as Autumn wiped away a fallen tear. Her eyes were swollen and dark circles formed underneath. "Logan wants to talk to you," she said quietly. "I'm going to take a shower. You boys play nice. I'm exhausted." Autumn shut the screen door behind her.

Logan stepped to Jensen. He cleared his throat. "I want to apologize for last night. I took a cheap shot at you, I'm sorry."

Jensen flicked his cigarette. "We all have moments we regret."

Logan studied Jensen. "Yeah, we do." Logan rubbed the back of his neck. "Autumn told me what happened last night."

Jensen gazed at the fields. "Yeah, it was a rough night."

"I bet." Logan shifted uneasily.

Jensen looked his way. "Say it."

"Say what?"

"I know you have more to say. Let's hear it."

Logan looked confused. "I don't know what you're talking about."

Jensen lit another cigarette. "Then I'm going to ask you something." Jensen took a long puff. "You don't like me much, do you?"

Logan's eyes opened wider. "Uh," he stammered. "No. Not really."

"Figured as much. And Autumn?"

Logan said nothing and looked away. Jensen studied him and continued. "You let her walk away. She told me what happened between the two of you. You only saw her as a good time. You were never there for her when she really needed you."

Logan stood up straight. "I know. But you think you're so much better than me?"

Jensen looked at him. "What?"

"I know how much you mean to her, Jensen. I also see the way you look at her. I know you care about her. But ask yourself this, do you even know what you really want? You strike me as a man with a lot of unfinished business. Don't get her hopes up if you're just going to hurt her in the end. She's been through enough."

Logan paused and squared his shoulders. "I feel like an ass, but I needed to get that off my chest. No matter what you think of me, I do care about her.

There, that's all I'm going to say. Just think about it. Make sure you're here for the right reasons."

Jensen watched Logan walk away. His words echoed in his head and he realized that they held very real truths. Jensen finished his cigarette and went inside. He sat on the couch and looked up as Autumn came downstairs. Her hair was wet, leaving a wet spot down her shirt. Her eyes still looked raw as she stepped into the kitchen. With a sigh of resignation, Jensen followed her. Autumn stared at the kitchen counter, unmoving.

"Are you okay?" Jensen asked quietly.

"Fine."

He winced as her voice broke. He took her in his arms and rocked her gently. She fell limp, her hands dangled at her sides. Jensen felt a wave of uncertainty wash over him. The hug he witnessed this morning between her and Logan had been much different. She clung to him like a lifeline, and here she was in his arms, lifeless. He let her go and took a step back.

Autumn pulled her eyes to his and studied him. "I'm going to sleep. I'm not feeling very well."

"Oh, okay. Do you need anything?"

"Just sleep."

Jensen watched as she trudged up the stairs. Lucy sat next to him, and stared up with her chocolate eyes. He ruffled her ears and leaned against the counter. Something had changed in the way Autumn carried herself. To him, he sensed defeat. Her big eyes clouded over in sadness, and her ever smiling mouth was pulled into a frown. Her voice was flat and uninterested. He wondered if this was the girl she had once been right after he left. He hoped not. He felt another surge of remorse. It was his actions in a desperate hour that would be responsible for reviving the broken girl she had worked so hard to leave behind. Jensen studied the room around him. He couldn't just sit here. He had to do something.

Jensen stepped into the sunlight and strode to the shed. He pulled out his tools and busied himself with an oil change. He started with his truck and for the hell of it, he did Autumn's as well. He sat on the porch steps and wished he could celebrate with a cold beer. His thoughts quickly turned to Jake. He couldn't explain it, but he somehow felt a small sense of closure in revisiting the lake. He had never truly said goodbye to his old friend. In the long moment of silence he and Autumn had shared at the dock, he felt Jake's presence nearby. He chose to take comfort in the feeling instead of recoil at it.

Jensen placed his head in his hand. Autumn had walked him through his darkest hour. She stood by him and did as she promised, she never let him go. Jensen's eyes fell to her bedroom window and hoped he hadn't broke her in return. Jensen rose stiffly and went inside. He took the stairs two at a time and entered the bedroom. Autumn was on her side looking toward the door. She was awake. Her eyes followed him as he crawled next to her. Jensen settled on his side, facing her.

"Did I break you?" he asked quietly.

Autumn managed a small smile. "No, you didn't." She bit her lip and breathed heavy. "I forgot how awful I was to you. Was it me who drove you into the dark?"

Jensen opened his eyes in surprise. She blamed herself for his fall? "No, you didn't do this to me, Autumn. It was my own doing. I think it was a good thing I left. I was a miserable son of a bitch for a long time. I would have only pushed you away and hurt you."

Autumn smiled weakly. "I'll be better tomorrow. Last night took a toll on me."

"I know."

"How is that you're okay?" she asked.

"I hide it better. You always were one to wear your heart on your sleeve."

Autumn laughed dryly. "You don't hide things that well."

Jensen reached out and pulled Autumn close. He let his head fall back against the pillow. Jensen ran a hand through her hair and stroked the side of her face softly. He lifted his head and pressed his lips to hers.

Autumn sighed and let her head fall heavy against him. "Can you stay with me until I fall asleep?" she whispered.

He squeezed her tighter. "Of course."

⌘

Monday morning came quickly. Autumn seemed to have recovered from her momentary lapse. Autumn gave Jensen a quick kiss and they went their separate ways for the day. Jensen pulled into his parking spot and checked the board for today's duties. He felt at ease in the presence of work. His mind had begun to play games with him again.

On Sunday, he and Autumn had gone to a friends for a summer get-together. He had enjoyed himself for the most part, and Autumn looked down right thrilled by the outing. It wasn't until the drinks came out that Jensen stammered. He grew tense and irritable. He knew he had to learn to survive in the real world, he couldn't stay sheltered forever. The look of horror on Autumn's face was still fresh in his memory. She had tried her best to hide it, but those eyes of hers weren't designed for secrets. They cut the evening short and made their way for home. Jensen caught the look of disappointment in Autumn and he carried it with him through the night.

Jensen finished his work day without any slip ups. He was out the door quickly and decided stop at the grocery store on his way home. Jensen wandered the aisles, tossing things in the basket here and there. He waited in line, and stared over the heads in front of him. From across the parking lot he saw the brightly lit sign for the liquor store. He tore his eyes away and paid for his groceries. He kept his eyes down on the asphalt until he reached his truck. He put away his purchase, hopped inside and drove away, and kept his eyes forward on the road ahead. Thoughts of Autumn kept him moving.

Jensen pulled up the drive and clicked the truck in park. As he came through the front door, the soft strums of guitar filled his ears. Autumn sat on the floor, guitar in her hands. She still wore her work clothes; a button down silk blouse and pencil skirt. Her feet were bare and her hair was wind swept from the drive home. Jensen set his groceries down and came to listen. She looked up and smiled coyly. Her eyes quickly fell back to the strings as she played her favorite song.

Autumn set the guitar down, and stretched her arms overhead. She stood and held out her hands. "Dance with me." She wiggled her hips from side to side, grinning.

"How could I say no to that?"

They drew each other close and danced throughout the living room. Jensen led her out the front door onto the porch. He twirled her and the last of her hair came free of the clasp. Autumn laughed carelessly and pulled him closer. Jensen led her backwards until she was pinned between him and the house. He pressed his lips to her neck and she hummed a soft sigh in content. Jensen moved his hands to her blouse and began unbuttoning slowly. Jensen kept his eyes focused on her, they hadn't been close for quite some time now. He missed her, and right now in the moment, she wanted him. Autumn traced her fingertips down his bare arms before she grasped him tightly.

The crunching of gravel caused them to jump. Autumn quickly turned away, her hands worked quickly to button her shirt. "Who is that?" she hissed.

"I don't know."

Autumn peeked out from behind Jensen. "It's Greg," she said solemnly.

Jensen felt the air whoosh from his chest. Greg, Jake's older brother. He hadn't seen him since the day Jake had convinced him to buy them alcohol. Jensen felt uneasy as his eyes desperately clung to his truck. He could leave, so easily. Autumn reached out to grab his forearm. Her eyes told him to stay.

"What is he doing here?" Jensen asked.

"It's okay," Autumn soothed. "We've kept in touch over the years. He comes to visit every now and then while he's in town."

Jensen watched as Greg got out of his car. An ache tore through him that he hadn't expected. He forgot how much Jake and Greg looked alike. Greg looked at Autumn, and a warm smile came over him. Jensen watched as Greg and Autumn gave each other a welcoming hug.

Jensen studied Greg closely. He stood 5'11" and had an athletic build. He had the same dark hair and brown eyes Jake had, but where Jake wore his hair longer, Greg kept his short and tidy. When Greg smiled, Jensen had to look away, it was the spitting image of Jake's. It was like looking at a ghost. Jensen felt a sting of envy at how easily Autumn handled herself around Greg. The two of them laughed freely and spoke like old friends. She had kept ties close. Jensen knew that was a feat he would never overcome.

Autumn and Greg walked closely as they approached Jensen. Autumn whispered in Greg's ear who begun to study Jensen. He rubbed the back of his neck uneasily. Autumn shot him a reassuring smile and mouthed. "It's okay."

Greg stepped in front of Jensen and stopped. His eyes assessed him before he spoke. "Jensen. You've grown up. It's good to see you."

Jensen felt like a fish out of water. He spoke, but even to his own ears, his voice sounded small. "It's nice to see you. How have you been?"

Greg's smile faded. "Better now. I went through some rough years, but knock on wood life is good these days."

Jensen was taken aback by his honesty. Greg looked from Autumn to Jensen. "I'm sorry I can't stay long this time, Autumn. I wanted to pop in and see if the rumors were true that you got yourself a house." He studied the home and smiled. "It suits you."

Autumn smiled and stared dreamily at her home. "Thank you."

Greg gestured to Jensen. "Can we take a walk?" Greg gave Autumn a reassuring smile.

Jensen stiffened his spine in anticipation for the beating he would surely get. "Sure."

Jensen and Greg walked slowly to the field. For a moment, neither of them spoke. Greg stopped and leaned against the fence. "I heard you've been having a rough go."

Jensen cursed to himself. "A bit."

"We don't blame you for what happened." Greg looked at Jensen sadly. "I'm sorry if you ever felt that way. I went through a really rough time. I fell pretty hard. How do you think I felt? I was the one to buy the stupid booze in the first place."

Jensen looked at Greg in sympathy. In all the years, he had never thought of the ripple effect Jake's death would have. All Jensen could see was his own misery. "I'm sorry."

Greg straightened up. "It didn't happen overnight for me. It took time and a lot of stumbles along the way before I found my footing, but I made it through. You can too. I just wanted you to know that." Greg took a deep breath. "I have a family now, can you believe it? My life is a good one. I never thought I'd see the day."

Jensen stared into the tall grass. Jake's smiling image flashed through his mind once more. "I miss him."

"I know." Greg's voice went low. "We all do." Greg turned to Jensen. "What is it that you're looking for?"

"What do you mean?"

"Don't play coy with me. I know the look, I wore it once. You're not quite settled yet, something's still eating you."

Jensen clenched his jaw and looked away. "I don't know."

"I think you do. It's fine, you don't have to tell me." Greg glanced toward the house, and his voice went low. "I just want you to know from experience…you can never let someone else in until you have dealt with all your loose ends. It's not fair to them, or you. You will never move forward, or be at ease until whatever you're holding on to is let go." Greg looked at his watch. "I should go. I want to say a quick goodbye to Autumn before I leave. I'm really happy to see her doing so good."

"Yeah, me too."

Jensen and Greg walked to the house. Autumn waited on the porch. When she saw them coming she looked between their faces in anticipation. Jensen shot her a smile, letting her know all was okay. Greg and Autumn said a warm goodbye. Before Greg got into his car, he gave Jensen one last look before driving away. Jensen watched the car disappear in a haze of dust. He thought about what he said, wondering if Autumn sensed his uneasiness as well. Jensen stared out at the quiet beauty around him and knew change was on the horizon. Soon.

Chapter 23

Autumn

It had been three weeks since Greg's visit, and something had changed between Jensen and me. From the outside looking in, no one would notice anything. We appeared to be happy. We were attentive to one another's needs, we made each other laugh and we were affectionate. Yet something in my gut had been growing uneasy. I sensed a restlessness in Jensen's spirit. With each day that passed I was pushed towards the edge, waiting for things to break.

I didn't like the way Jensen had begun to look at me. The familiar sadness was back in his eyes. He also began to study me, and with every kiss we shared, it felt like our last. Sleep began to evade me, I was afraid I would wake up to find my world changed once again.

On Thursday, I called in sick. Once Jensen left for work, I laced up my running shoes and intended to take Lucy on a very long run. I didn't get very far, instead I sat under a large oak tree and cried. I didn't know what had brought on the surge of emotions, but I felt such a strong sense of loneliness. The man I had loved for so long faded before me. Though he was physically here, emotionally he was absent. His eyes took on a strange look. He was in a world only he could see. I didn't like the woman I was becoming. With each day I grew weaker, it was getting harder to find the bright spots. I felt like a race horse in the starting gate, ready to jump at the slightest sound.

I walked home slowly with Lucy, lost in thought. I grabbed my car keys and knew where I needed to go. I drove quickly and pulled down a paved drive, following the long curve in the road. I looked for my marker, a stooped over evergreen tree near the watering station. I pulled my car to the side, got out, and walked to the familiar gravestone. I lowered myself into a seated position and wiped away the brush that had fallen over Jake's resting place.

"I wish you were here, Jake. There's so many things I want to say to you." I stopped for a moment, hoping to hear his voice. I was met by silence. "I don't know what to do anymore about Jensen. I'm losing him."

I lowered my head into my hands and began to sob. "I told you not to leave us. I told you to come back." But Jake was never one to listen. He always had plans of his own.

"You know what the worst part is? I almost *want* Jensen to tell me he's leaving, just to put me out of my misery. I feel like I'm waiting for things to fall apart, but I don't know when it's going to happen. Not knowing, that is the hardest part."

I drew my knees to my chest. "I hope you're happy, Jake, wherever you are. God, I miss you so much." I wiped the last of my tears away and stood. "See you soon, old friend."

I walked down the rows of sites and knew who else I needed to see. My grandmother. I found her stone and sat next to it. "Hi, Grandma, I'm sorry it's been so long." I traced my fingers over the writing carved into stone and sighed. "I bought a house with the money you left me. It's beautiful. I wish you could see it." I smiled softly. "Even though you are no longer with me, you're still taking care of me. Thank you."

I brought my legs into a cross seated position and thought of the note she left me. *You will fly my girl.* I stifled the doubt that had arisen in me. "But what if I fall?" I whispered. I focused my eyes once more onto her stone. "I love you, Grandma, miss you every day."

I slowly ambled toward my vehicle and slid into the front seat. I stared out the front window. I didn't want to go home, not yet. I wanted an answer. I was tired of waiting. I needed to know if I was about to take a hit. I turned the key and headed for the garage. I found an empty parking stall and bypassed the office. I walked to the back of the building and entered the shop. I wandered through until I found Jensen's bay. He leaned under the hood of an expensive looking car, his hands were busy.

Before I lost my nerve I spoke. "If you have no intention of staying, why did you come back? Why did you have to find me and make me fall in love with you all over again?"

Jensen jumped up, startled. His face wore a mixture of surprise and confusion. "Autumn, what are you doing here?" His eyes narrowed as he took in my appearance. "Are you okay?"

My voice rose. "Does it look like I'm okay? Just tell me, are you leaving?"

Jensen looked around unnerved at the attention I drew. "How about we talk outside?"

He took a step forward and placed a hand on my shoulder. I shook it off. "After you." I gestured my arm.

Jensen pressed his lips together and strode away. I followed him outside, and he marched to his truck. "What is this all about?"

"You tell me."

Jensen opened his mouth and tossed his hands in the air. "You gotta give me more to go on than that."

"You're pulling away from me. It's like you're not even here anymore. A girl can sense when something isn't right, and something is off. You don't even look at me the same way anymore."

Jensen smacked the hood of his truck. "Dammit, Autumn, what do you want me to say? I'm not drinking, isn't that enough?" He let out a frustrated breath. "What do you mean I look at you differently?"

I fought back a sob. "It's like you're trying to memorize my face. It's like you're saying goodbye." I sniffled. "I'm glad you're not drinking, I'm so proud of you. But tell me this, are you happy? Are you happy here, with me? If you're going to leave, just tell me. Put me out of my misery."

"Jesus, Autumn." Jensen rubbed his face. "Is that what you think? That I'm going to up and leave you?"

"Are you?" I challenged. "What is it you're not telling me?"

Jensen closed his eyes and hung his head. "I don't know."

"You don't *know?* That's it? That's my answer?"

Jensen stepped forward and placed his hands on my waist. "Look at me." I did. "I'm sorry if I scare you. I'm…I don't have everything figured out, not yet."

"What does that mean?"

Jensen looked at me softly. "I promise you, I will not up and leave you. I just get stuck in my head sometimes. I have pushed people away for so long, I don't even realize when I'm doing it."

I bit my lip to keep it from trembling. "So I won't wake up to find you've disappeared?"

"I promise you. I'm right here." Jensen leaned forward and pressed his lips to mine. "Are we okay?"

I lifted my gaze to his. Jensen's face was soft, his eyes alert. "I'm sorry I came here and made a scene."

Jensen kissed the top of my head. "I'll see you at home."

"Okay."

⌘

I took another detour on my way home. I stopped at the restaurant where I used to work, I knew Kendra would be on shift today. I slid into a booth in her section and waited.

"Autumn?"

I looked up at the sound of her voice. "Hey."

Kendra raised an eyebrow. "Shouldn't you be at work?" She studied me closer and began to walk away. "I'll be right back, don't move," she tossed over her shoulder.

I watched as Kendra disappeared to the backroom. A moment later she appeared with her purse. "Come on, I took my break early, let's go."

I followed her out to her car. She unlocked the doors and I slid inside. I pressed my head against the cool glass of the window and sighed. Exhaustion enveloped me from head to toe. Kendra tapped my arm. "What's wrong, Autumn?"

"I don't know."

"Yes, you do. Tell me."

I forced my eyes open to look at Kendra. She waited patiently, and gave me a smile of encouragement. I took a deep breath and filled her in on my gut feeling and the little observations I had picked up along the way. I ended things with my grand display of going to Jensen's work.

Kendra pulled her brows together in a thoughtful expression. "You can't live your life walking on eggshells and always worrying about what he will do, or won't. That's going to do nothing but tear you down. You need to live your life and focus on what's ahead. Think about what you have accomplished lately, Autumn. You bought a run down old house and you brought it back to life. It's *your* home. And to top it off, you landed an amazing job. You didn't seek it out, it found *you.* That's not something you just shrug off."

Kendra lowered her voice. "Jensen will either make it, or he won't. You have done everything in your power for him. Like they say, sink or swim, and I don't want to see you dragged down in the process."

Kendra and I talked for awhile. I made a mental note to make more of an effort to see her. I had forgotten how bright of a person she was. I silently scolded myself. I had let myself get so wrapped up in personal worries, that I forgot how good of a life I had and friends. I felt so alone, when in all reality, I was far from it.

Kendra's break came to an end and I decided it was time for me to head home. My head throbbed, and my stomach flopped around uneasily. A shiver tore through me, even though I was burning hot. By the time I got home and out of the car, I nearly had to crawl up the porch stairs into the house. Once I was inside, I groaned as I judged the staircase that would lead me to my bed; my wonderful, cozy bed. My legs felt useless and heavy, I wouldn't make it that far. My eyes fell to the couch and with a sigh of defeat, I plopped down and closed my eyes. The last thing I thought of before falling asleep was Jensen. I wondered how he was going to break my heart.

⌘

"Autumn? How are you feeling?"

The voice sounded like a dream. I blinked my eyes open and found myself staring into a pair of familiar brown eyes. "Jensen?" I croaked. "What time is it?"

Jensen placed a cool hand to my warm forehead. "A little after seven. You were out cold by the time I came home. I thought I'd let you sleep a bit longer before I woke you."

"I'm sick," I moaned. "Everything hurts."

"Take it easy and rest."

"Can we blame the fever on my outburst earlier today?" I asked meekly.

Jensen chuckled. "Sure, let's blame the fever."

"Okay," I sighed and let my head fall heavy against the pillow.

Jensen spoke with a smile in his voice. "You don't look comfortable at all. Do you want to go to bed?"

"I can't." I waved my hand in the air. "Too many stairs. Too much effort."

"I can take you upstairs if you'd like."

I propped myself to my elbows and patted the couch. "Do you want to watch a movie with me first? I'm starting to feel awake."

Jensen chuckled. "Sure thing." He scooted next to me and I placed my head in his lap, legs outstretched behind me. He flicked on the TV and I settled my eyes to the screen. Jensen stroked his fingers through my hair gently. "Do you need anything?" he asked quietly.

"Mmm, no. Just you." I settled back into his lap, growing heavier by the minute. In the moment, I felt safe, he felt solid. Halfway through the movie my eyes began to grow heavy.

Jensen pushed the hair out of my face, and peeked down. "Okay, time for bed."

"Mmph." Was all I could get out.

Jensen scooped me up and took me to the bedroom. I crawled under the covers and my head fell to the pillow. I let out a sigh of pleasure. Jensen crouched down at the side of my bed. He gazed at me softly. "Autumn?"

"Mm."

"I love you."

I opened my eyes slowly. "I love you, too."

Jensen's eyes grew sad. "I'm sorry if that's not enough."

My head began to swim. I was not in the right state of mind for this. "It's enough for right now." I closed my eyes and welcomed the blackness.

Chapter 24
Jensen

Autumn was down for a week with the flu. Jensen had been lucky in the sense that he escaped it. The first day Autumn felt human again, she awoke with a bounce and skipped out the door to go to work. While she was sick, she spent most of her time complaining, she hated to sit still. Jensen had found the whole thing rather amusing, it kept his mind occupied in the here and now.

Kendra came over quite often to check on her and keep her company. Jensen sensed the distinct shift in his and Autumn's relationship over the past week. Her eyes read him closely, searching for hidden meanings behind his words. She always seemed surprised to see him whenever he walked through the door. What he couldn't tell was whether it was a happy surprise or a disappointed one.

Jensen knew he was to blame for their shift. He had backed off and chose his words carefully. He began to pull away. He caught the looks of sadness in Autumn's eyes and the never ending worry. Even her friends had begun to notice and commented on the fact. Autumn smiled and brushed it off like it meant nothing. But Kendra knew. Jensen could not miss the looks Kendra shot his way. They held accusations that he was responsible. Jensen loved Autumn with everything he had in him, but he was beginning to realize he wasn't ready to jump into something, not yet. He was just starting the process in trying to fix himself, and he had a long ways to go. He knew he couldn't give Autumn what she needed, or deserved, not right now.

He had seen the changes in Autumn develop quickly. When he first came back into her life, she was so strong, full of hope and fight. These days she seemed small. She grew quiet and sullen. Her words lacked conviction, her actions robotic. Jensen had done a lot of things in his life he was ashamed of, but he would not be responsible for dragging another life down. For once, he would force himself to do the right thing.

⌘

As Autumn got ready to leave for work, she didn't run out the door like she usually did. She stopped in front of Jensen and gave him a long, slow kiss. When she pulled back, she didn't say a word. The look in her eyes told him more than words could ever say, she gave him permission to leave. Never had Jensen met anyone who could read him so well. That was going to make what he had to do so much harder.

Jensen watched her drive away and then he called in sick. He took his time walking around the house, memorizing every detail. He loved this place, it was one of the few places he felt safe. He hoped the road he was about to embark on would lead him back here, back home. Whether or not he would be welcomed back, that would remain in Autumn's hands.

Jensen called Lucy to come, and the two of them walked side by side to the barn. He slid open the large door and stepped inside. Jensen's stride took him to one of Autumn's favorite places, the tire swing. His heart ached at the memory of this room. This was where Autumn had finally let him in. Jensen's eyes grew hazy as he remembered her slip out of her dress, eyes locked on him the entire time. She walked the balance between strong and fragile all at once. Jensen sat on the tire and let the rope sway side to side. Jensen needed to take this journey. He had put it off for so many years. For the first time in his life, he felt in control of his actions. The dark desires still tempted him from the depths of his mind, but he was growing stronger, and he was about to put his strength to the ultimate test.

Jensen had unfinished business to attend too. For once, he was going to follow through with a promise he had made to himself. He was going to take the road trip down the coast he and Jake had planned so many years ago. Jensen was going to throw himself in the midst of the outside world and find out if he would be able to walk away unscathed. His weakness would either get the best of him, or he would rise above, leaving it behind once and for all. The only thing left to do now was say goodbye to Autumn, and that seemed to be an impossible feat.

⌘

Jensen drove to work and had a private conversation with Derik. He was finally able to look someone in the eyes and admit he had a problem. Derik looked at him with something close to admiration and wished him good luck. Jensen bent the truth a little, he said that he was getting help, and in a sense he was. Derik didn't need to know he was going it alone, fulfilling an old promise.

"I need you to promise me one thing," Jensen said.

"Anything." Derik waited expectantly.

"Watch out for Autumn, please."

Derik's gaze softened. "Of course, we will. Jensen?"

"Yeah?"

"Try to come back to her, if you can."

Jensen said nothing. *I hope I can.* He handed in his keys, and he walked away without a glance back. There. That was one thing he could cross off his checklist, the other wasn't going to be so easy. Jensen drove through town and pulled into the liquor store. He was playing with fire, but he wanted to see how far he could push himself. He needed to know a glimmer of hope lay deep inside. He hoped to start his journey with a small amount of confidence restored in his self control. Jensen stepped into the store and wandered the aisles. His eyes lazily read the bottles as he passed. Wine. Never been his thing. Rum. Went down so easy. Vodka. Nice kick. Beer. Helped him sleep. Tequila. It often led to company for the night. Whiskey. Jensen stopped.

Whiskey was his biggest vice of all. Whiskey numbed his wounds and offered him comfort when he had none. It provided him with a wonderful escape, one that he would have loved to get lost in permanently. But it was a two sided serpent. It altered the man he was, and more often than not, he couldn't remember what happened under its influence. Once the effects wore off, it damn near killed him.

A cold chill went down his spine, and he forced himself to keep walking. Jensen pulled open a glass door and reached into the fridge. He pulled out a six pack and paid for the purchase. Jensen walked to his truck and set the refreshments on the seat next to him. He didn't look at them once. He turned his key and drove home for the last time.

Jensen sat in the living room, the case of beer on the table before him. He sat, staring, while his leg bounced uncontrollably. Jensen wiped his hands on his legs and licked his lips. His mouth went bone dry and his mind screamed in protest. The ticking of the clock made him uneasy; it was deafening in the silence of the house. His heart thumped loudly in his ears. Jensen shifted uncomfortably; his skin crawled with anticipation. Jensen rubbed his hands over his face and quickly broke a single beer from the plastic. His fingers worked quickly as he popped the tab. In a single *click* he caught the scent of one form of his temptress. Jensen froze and stared down at the open beverage.

He took a deep breath and slowly raised the can to his lips. He took a small sip. Jensen closed his eyes as the smooth liquid went down his throat. He took another sip. Jensen opened his eyes and set the can on the table. Something didn't taste right. The beverage used to quench his undesired thirst. Once he took a sip, he couldn't stop. Every nerve in his body would plead for more. As the alcohol spread through his system, it erased all his struggles and worries. It quieted his mind. But his mind didn't want to be quiet any longer. He wanted to remember the past two months. He wanted to remember each and every time he fell and how he had someone to help him up, not just anyone, but *her*, Autumn.

Her kindness and strength forced him to take a good hard look at himself, and Jensen didn't care for what stared back in the mirror. For the man who looked back was weak and miserable. Autumn had given him a glimpse of someone he could be. He wanted to hold on to that more than anything. Jensen leaned back on the couch and stared at the ceiling. A part of him, a rather large part, didn't want to go. He didn't want to leave Autumn behind. But he also couldn't stay. This was something he needed to do on his own. The final test needed to be challenged. He needed to know if he could finally close the book on a part of him he wanted to bury.

If he didn't get lost along the way, he hoped the end of his trek would lead him back here, to her. Jensen made a promise to himself in that very moment. If he got swallowed up along the way, he would never come back to her. He would let her live her life in peace. He had caused enough hurt during his return, and he didn't want to be responsible for taking her life down with his. There comes a point in everyone's life where they need to find out where they belong, or in some cases, where they no longer belong, and Jensen was ready to find out.

"Jensen?"

Jensen froze as Autumn's voice cut through the quiet. He heard the horror in her voice. Jensen turned and waved her over. "Come here."

Autumn hesitated before taking cautious steps to him, her blue eyes wide. Jensen nodded at the beer can. "Pick it up."

Confusion flitted over her face but she leaned over and picked up the can. "It's full," she exclaimed in surprise.

Jensen smiled. "It wasn't what I remembered it to be. I didn't really want it after all."

A mixture of emotions over came Autumn. She let out a sigh and sat at his feet. She rested her head on his lap. "I'm so proud of you," she paused. "This is it, isn't it?"

"This is what?" he whispered.

Autumn pulled her head back and looked up at him, her eyes dangerously close to tears. "The end. You're leaving."

Jensen pulled Autumn into his lap. She rested her head against his shoulder, focusing her eyes on the wall. She kept her voice level. "I've been watching you. You haven't been here for awhile. You're in two places at once."

"This is something I need to do. I can't stay here and hide forever. It's not fair to you or to me." Jensen guided her face to his. "Please look at me."

Autumn lifted her eyes. "I see you."

Jensen smiled sadly. "I know what I'm doing to you. I'm not an idiot. I see the way you look at me, like you're waiting for me to fall apart. And I don't blame you. After everything I have put you through. *I* need to know I can make it on my own, Autumn. I can't drag you along on this ride. I don't want to wake up and find I've broken you too."

Autumn said nothing. As she blinked, tears fell. Jensen wiped them away. "I never want to see you look at me as though you hate me. You don't look at me that way now, but I fear one day you will if I can't figure this out. I don't want you to wake up only to find I have taken the very life out of you."

Jensen paused and took a shaky breath. This was it, the moment he never wanted to face. He was going to have to force himself to say goodbye. "If I stay here, that's going to be our fate and I won't be able to come back from that. You are my best friend. You have been able to pick me up and carry me forward more times than I can count. I can never thank you for what you have done. This is the only way."

Jensen let out a deep sigh. "I need to know if I can make it on my own. I need to know whether or not I will finally be able to walk away."

Autumn pressed her lips to his. She cradled his head between her hands. "And if you don't come back?"

Jensen closed his eyes. "Then I got lost. I wasn't strong enough."

Autumn let out a loud breath. "Don't let go, Jensen. Do whatever you have to too hang on. Please, do not let go."

Jensen pressed his forehead to hers. "I'll do my best."

"Please come back," Autumn whispered.

"Let's get out of here," Jensen whispered.

"To where?"

"I'm not sure yet. Let's see where we end up."

Jensen rose from the couch, towing Autumn with him. He took his keys and jangled them. "Ready?"

Autumn smiled. "Always."

They hopped into the truck and Jensen drove slowly, savoring every moment he had with her. Autumn settled into the seat, and looked at him like she was seeing him for the last time. Jensen ignored the stab that jolted his heart. He did his best to keep his voice light, and his smile carefree. If only she knew how much this killed him, how much he loved her. Love was a double edged sword, sometimes the kindest thing for another is the hardest sacrifice of all.

Jensen took safety in her presence. She was a bright light amongst all the haze. If his path didn't lead back to her, he hoped she could find happiness. He wanted her life to be a good one, a fulfilled one. And if her life no longer included him, he would take the smallest comfort in knowing that for a time, she had been his and he had experienced what it was to truly love another.

Jensen drove out of town and pulled off the main road. As soon as his tires hit the dirt, he knew where he was going. Autumn looked around at their surroundings and she beamed. "This is the perfect spot."

Jensen smiled. "I think so too." Jensen drove through the tall grass, the truck swayed from left to right over the uneven terrain. He drove to the middle of the field and killed the engine. Jensen turned to Autumn slowly. He smiled sadly and his hand turned the key until the radio came on. Jensen popped open his front door and ran to Autumn's side. He opened her door and helped her down. "Dance with me."

Autumn smiled past the tears and clung to him tightly. "Where are you going to go?" she whispered.

"Drive down the coast. I don't know where after that, or how far it'll take me."

"I hope your road leads you back home. With me." Autumn sighed. "If it doesn't, I will always wish for your happiness, Jensen. Always. For what it's worth, I'm glad you found me."

"You were the one who found me."

Autumn squeezed him tighter. "We found each other, together."

Jensen wrapped her closer. "When the world knocked me down, you built me up. You were always the one to build me up."

"You exist in two places, Jensen. The darkness and the light. I hope one will finally outweigh the other."

Jensen said nothing. She was right, she was always right. Despite the sadness this moment held for them, he was able to find a small glimmer of happiness. For he knew saying goodbye to her was one of the hardest things he would ever have to face, but he also considered himself lucky that he held something that proved so hard to leave. What they had was real. Time had never been able to take that away. They danced until the sun burned out of the sky. Darkness fell over the land and the creatures of the night awoke. For while their day would be beginning, others were ending. Jensen and Autumn held each other close until there was nothing left to say.

"I won't say goodbye to you. I don't believe in goodbyes," Autumn stated.

Jensen kissed her lips slowly. He wanted to remember how she tasted, how soft she felt against him. He pulled away with resignation. "Are you afraid you'll never get a chance to say hello again?"

"Sometimes saying goodbye is just another way of saying I love you, only it hurts. It's not supposed to hurt."

Jensen brushed the hair from her face. "I've always loved you, Autumn."

Autumn traced the edge of Jensen's jaw. "And I've never stopped."

Jensen pulled her into the tall grass. He held Autumn close, feeling her heart beat against him. He savored every moment, every touch, every smile. He didn't know what he had done to be so lucky to find someone like her. He was grateful for that fateful day in which he returned to the place he once ran from.

The image of Autumn having a breakdown in the parking lot while she beat her car in a milkshake stained uniform played through his mind. It brought a smile to his face. Who knew that would be the start of it all. In that moment, he fell in love with her all over again. Jensen stared up at the stars. Tomorrow morning he would rise with the sun and leave all the comforts he had ever known. He was going to separate himself from the world and see where he landed. He hoped the broken parts of him would finally be laid to rest. He wasn't sure what he would gain by all of this, but he knew what he didn't want to become, and that would have to be enough for now.

Jensen had been forced to face things he had long ago buried, and to his surprise, he still stood. Whether or not he continued to grow was entirely up to him and what he would face. He found it shocking that his mind could be the very thing that betrayed him, or be responsible for saving him. Jensen's gaze fell to Autumn and he was determined this would not be goodbye forever. He would create another opportunity to say hello.

Jensen leaned himself carefully on top of Autumn. Her hands traced down his sides and tugged at the corner of his shirt. She smiled softly. "We shouldn't waste a minute of our time."

Jensen smiled and brought her into his lap. He stroked the hair out of her face and traced his lips down her neck, and across her collarbone. He placed her gently amongst the grass, and he was determined to give her a goodbye to remember.

Chapter 25

Autumn

I awoke in the darkness of my bedroom. Jensen had his truck packed and I refused to say goodbye just to watch him leave. The sound of his engine filled the empty house and I listened to the tires crunch down the gravel drive. Loneliness instantly swept over my followed by regret. How could I not say goodbye? I sprang out of my bed and hit the ground running. I swung open the front door and let my feet take me down the drive at warp speed. Jensen's truck was up ahead. I waved my arms frantically and called out to him. "Jensen!"

The truck kept moving forward. I dug in for another burst as my feet cut into the gravel. "Jensen! Please stop! Wait!"

The truck halted to a stop and Jensen stepped out into the early morning light. His face broke into a mixture of sadness and relief to see me one more time. I jumped into his arms. "I'm so sorry," I breathed. "But I'm not here to tell you goodbye." I placed my hands on the side of his face, forcing him to look at me. "I want to say hello. Make you sure you give me that chance again."

Jensen forced a smile. "Take care of yourself, Autumn."

My heart fell at his response. His eyes remained a careful mask. "Jensen?"

"I need you to make me a promise." His voice remained solemn. "Please."

"Okay."

"If you find you have a chance for happiness, even if it doesn't include me, promise me you will take it."

"Oh," I groaned and unraveled my legs from his waist. My bare feet screamed in protest from the ground below. "No."

"Autumn, please." His voice sounded tired.

I studied the man before me, he barely held himself together. Every last ounce of his strength was being tested. I was making this harder than it had to be. I raised my chin. "Okay, I promise. But you have to make me one too."

Jensen sighed and looked wary. "What is it?"

"Don't let go." I stepped into his chest and pressed my lips to his.

I pulled away but his hand wound in my hair, holding me in place. His lips met mine with a force that knocked the very breath out me. Jensen stepped back and I kept my eyes lowered to the ground. I dared not look at him for I was afraid I would break and beg him to stay. I couldn't do that to him. He needed to go and I knew it. I held out my hand, gesturing him to remain quiet. I turned on my heel and walked back to the house. I held a hand over my mouth, and tried to contain the sobs. At the sound of Jensen's truck, I stopped. I stared up toward the open sky until I could no longer hear the sound of his tires. The moment had finally come. Jensen was gone.

⌘

I was once so proud of this house. I remember the moment I crawled through the window and wandered its dust covered halls. It felt like home. Now, here I sat in the middle of the entrance hall staring at my bloody feet. It no longer felt welcoming, but empty and hollow. I wiggled my toes to assess the damage, nothing seemed broken. The gravel had tore at my tender flesh and left it exposed. I grimaced as I thought that's how my heart must look right now.

With a sigh I hobbled to the washroom and sat on the edge of the tub. I cleaned out the wounds and swore softly as the ointment stung. I was going to pay for this for awhile. I let out a grunt of anger knowing I wouldn't be able to run for a bit, and just when I needed a mini escape from my head. I stood slowly and went to the bedroom. I drew the curtains shut and crawled back into bed. I had no intention of getting out anytime soon.

⌘

A knock at my door sounded two days later. I tossed the covers off angrily and slammed my feet into slippers. I grabbed my robe and threw it over my pajamas. Lucy paced by the door and I opened it up. Logan stood on the other side, his eyes quickly judged my appearance.

I opened my eyes in surprise. "What are you doing here?"

"Rumors travel fast in this town. Can I come in?"

"No," I snapped.

"Too bad, I'm coming in anyway." Logan pushed back the door. "I have reinforcements."

"What?" I squawked and peeked past him.

Kendra and Derik followed behind. Kendra's eyes widened. "Autumn, I've been calling you for days. I was getting worried so…" she gestured to the men beside her.

"Sorry," I mumbled. "I've been busy."

Logan cleared his throat. "I think you should shower. It might help wake you up."

"I am awake," I said dryly.

"Maybe so, but you look like hell."

"Gee, thanks."

"I can drag you in there myself if you want."

I let out a heavy sigh. "I can do it myself, thank you very much."

I gathered clean clothes and stepped into the warm water. I hated to admit that it was a good suggestion. The fresh scent of soap and shampoo revived my spirit somewhat. I slipped into clean clothes and made my way to the kitchen. The aroma of coffee and French toast lured me in. My friends sat at the table, all eyes on me.

I felt exposed in the moment and forced a small smile. "It smells delicious."

"Sit. Eat."

I sat amongst my friends and we ate together. The food tasted so good on my tongue, and my body rejoiced from the fuel. I thought back to the past few days and couldn't remember eating much of anything. I tore my eyes away from the plate before me and looked to my friends in embarrassment. "I'm okay, really, I am. I'm just…moping."

Kendra cleared her throat. "Hey guys, can you give us a minute?"

Derik and Logan left the room quickly. They gave me a reassuring squeeze on the shoulder before disappearing outside. I focused on Kendra. "Out of all the people, you brought Logan?"

"Despite everything, he does care about you. He heard what happened and was going to check on you. If you had answered the phone I could have told you that earlier."

"Sorry," I mumbled.

Kendra softened her voice. "How are you doing?"

I sighed heavily. "I'm a ray of sunshine." I bowed my head. "I miss him. I'm so worried about him."

"He did the right thing, in leaving. I know it's hard for you to wrap your head around it but he needed to be on his own for awhile to figure things out. Was he planning on coming back?"

I closed my eyes. *No.* "Maybe. He wasn't ready to be close to someone else, he was so afraid he was going to slip up and drag me down with him. He needs to figure out if he can stand on his own two feet before he lets someone else in."

Kendra squeezed my hand. "The fact that he realized that himself speaks volumes. I think he'll come back."

"I hope so." Even as I spoke the words, it sounded like a lie. There was a large part of me which feared he would never come back, and I would have to say yet another goodbye to a friend.

⌘

A month had passed and I heard nothing from Jensen. I had hoped he would have contacted me, just to let me know he was okay. I broke down one night and tried to call his cell, but his number had been disconnected. I hung up the phone as disappointment hit me, he really had cut off all ties. I suppose he needed to, he couldn't have anything enticing him back to what he left behind.

Summer was now over. Fall was well on its way. The days were still sunny but the air now held a crisp cold, and the leaves were beginning to change. I filled my days with work, running, and spending quality time with my friends, something I had been missing for awhile. I had even taken up a new hobby; baking. So far it wasn't going well, nothing turned out quite like the stupid recipes promised. On the bright side, I learnt my smoke detectors worked.

As the days went on, the void grew smaller. My life had been pretty full before Jensen had come back into the picture. In order for me to move on, I had to move forward. I couldn't lock myself in a box forever. I had to let him go, completely. I could spend minutes, hours, driving myself crazy wondering where he was and if he was okay. But what was the point? He wanted to disappear and I had to let him. The more I held on, the smaller I felt. Once I made up my mind to let go, a burden lifted. His absence did not break me the way I thought it would. A weight had been freed from my chest. I was able to breathe easier. I was no longer holding my breath waiting for things to crumble before me. Looking back now, I hadn't realized just how much of myself I had lost while trying to find him. It was Jensen who saw it. I couldn't forget him completely; that was an impossible feat. His memory often came to me like a passing rain cloud. It hit fast and hard but before I knew it, it dissipated.

Midweek was finally here. I lied awake in bed, growing more restless by the hour. I glanced at the clock and groaned. Two in the morning, and I was wide awake. I grumbled as I sat up and decided to go through a yoga sequence. Twenty minutes later, I finished my last round of sun salutations when the phone rang. I stood and ran to the phone, this was not the hour for happy phone calls. As I picked up the phone, I knew bad news would greet me on the other end of the line.

I placed the phone to my ear gingerly. "Hello?"

"Autumn." The female voice broke on the other end.

"Kendra? Oh god, what's wrong."

Muffled sounds came from the other line. Derik's voice replaced hers. "I'm coming over. I'll be there in ten minutes. Be ready to go."

The phone fell out of my hand. It had to be about Jensen. Horrible thoughts filled my head. I would be burying another friend. I paced wildly back and forth in the living room waiting for headlights to appear. I had told him not to let go. Why couldn't he listen? He had worked to hard to go out this way. A burst of light lit the dim house. Derik was here. I ran to the front door and met him on the front porch.

"Is it Jensen?" I held my breath.

Derik was in a pair of sweats and a T-shirt. His hair was tousled and he looked shaken. "No, it's not Jensen. It's Logan."

Surprise hit me. I let out a whoosh of air and mulled over Derik's response. Logan? Nothing was supposed to happen to Logan, he was settled. A wave of uncertainty followed. "What happened? Where is he?"

"There was an accident. He was coming home from work and someone ran a red light. He was taken to the hospital."

I closed my eyes processing what I heard. Logan was on night shifts for the month. Instead of being safe and sound in his bed, he was awake while the world was asleep. "How bad is he?"

Derik paled. "I'll take you to him."

Derik grabbed my hand but I planted my feet. "Derik, I-"

Derik stopped and looked at me, bewildered. "What?"

"I can't lose another person. I just can't."

"Hey," Derik softened his tone. "Let's go see him. He shouldn't be alone. I'll be right by your side."

I nodded and fought back tears. I scrambled into the passenger seat and pressed my forehead to the window. Neither of us said a word, I watched in silence as the world sped by. Lights came into view as we pulled into the hospital. Derik clasped onto my hand and led me into the bright building. Nothing made sense to me, the images blurred together. The white walls, fluorescent lights, and nurses scrubs all molded into one hazy image. My teeth clacked together as a force grabbed me by the shoulders and shook me. The images before me went clear like someone had flicked on a switch.

"Autumn. He's in here." My eyes followed Derik's pointed finger. "We can see him."

Derik opened Logan's door and I hesitantly peeked inside. Logan lay in the bed and looked small. A bandage wound around his head. My world came to a crashing halt. I was taken to the day we lost Jake. I saw him lying lifelessly on the shore, a towel wrapped around his head as I tried to stop the bleeding. *Oh God, Jensen, is he dead? Wake up, Jake! Please, open your eyes!* Panic tore through me and my breaths came out in hysterics.

Derik grabbed me, trying to quiet me. I desperately clawed at him until I broke free from his grasp. I flew out of Logan's room and slammed my back against the wall in the hallway. My knees trembled until they gave out. I slid to the ground and hugged my knees against my chest begging the image to go away. *This isn't happening. It's not real.*

I opened my eyes and screamed out in horror. Jake stared back at me, head cracked and broken. His skin was pale and cold, his face pulled into a frown. He dripped wet, water began to pool around him. Jake studied me quietly, unmoving. He tilted his head slowly to the left, then to the right. I couldn't move. In an instant, he opened his mouth wide and let out a scream.

I covered my ears, trying to block out the eerie sound. It didn't sound human. Like a bolt of lightning, Jake grabbed me by the hair and smacked my head into the concrete wall. Searing pain tore through me as I heard the sickening crack. Jake raised my head once more and I let out one last scream before everything went dim.

⌘

I fell to the floor with a thud, tangled in my bedsheets. I fought the blankets off in a panic until I realized where I was. I was in my bedroom. My hands flew to my head, investigating if it was still in one piece. I wiped at a bead of sweat and realized it had been a nightmare. I fell back to the floor, and waited for my heart to stop racing before I could move. It had all felt so real. Logan, Jake. *Jake.* What a terrible way to visit my friend in a dream. After Jake had passed, I suffered from nightmares for weeks. He was the star in all of them. It had been so long since they haunted me. I wondered what had awakened them.

Lucy sat up and watched me from the corner of the room. I called her over and gave her a hug. Uneasiness settled over me followed by a chill. I swallowed a lump in my throat and felt like a small child; I was scared. *Logan.* I glanced at the time, 3:30 a.m. There was some truth to my dream, Logan was on the graveyard shift, and would be on his way home shortly. I stood and called to Lucy. "Come on, pups, we're getting out of here."

I ran down the stairs, trying not to look around the house too much. I felt jumpy and on edge. I was scared I would come face to face with something that shouldn't be here. I tossed my jacket on and grabbed my keys. I was almost at my car when an owl flew from a nearby tree. I screamed to high heaven and nearly fell. I clutched at my heart in terror. I recovered quickly and jumped inside, Lucy right behind me. I fumbled with my keys, and my hands shook slightly. I fired up the engine and drove to Logan's.

I pulled into his driveway and called Lucy out. We stood at his door and I knocked loudly. Footsteps sounded from the other side and the door flew open. Logan's caution turned to surprise when he saw us. "Autumn? Is everything okay?"

"Can we come in?"

Logan stepped back. "Of course."

Lucy and I stepped inside. I turned to him and explained my night terror. I swatted my hands against my legs. "And so, I ran out of my house as fast as I could. Silly, I know." I bit my lip. "Can we stay here for the night?"

Logan stifled a yawn and smiled. "Of course, you can."

"Thank you."

"I can sleep on the couch if you'd like. I'll let you have the bed."

I reached out to stop Logan from walking away. "Please don't leave. Can you stay with me, just for tonight? I…well, I don't want to be alone." I smiled sheepishly.

Logan looked taken aback. "Of course, I can stay with you."

I followed Logan to his bedroom and Lucy followed. We spent a lot of time in this house back in the day, and Lucy hadn't forgotten her spot. She flopped in the corner of his bedroom and drifted off to sleep. I watched her in envy, I wish sleep could come that easily for me.

Logan fell to his bed groaning loudly. I laughed, he was always vocal when it came time for bed. "Some things never change," I mumbled.

Logan smiled sleepily. "No, some things never do."

I lay beside him quietly. He kept to his side of the bed. "Goodnight, Autumn."

"Night, Logan."

Once he flicked out the light and the room went dark, I tensed. The nightmares images were still fresh in my mind. I drew myself closer to Logan until my arms enclosed him. He let his fall over me, and he held me until the morning light. I had a dreamless sleep. It was a wonderful relief.

⌘

My work day was coming to an end, and for once, I was glad. I was overtired from last nights episode. I had never expected myself to be the type of girl to run back to her ex, but last night, I did not want to be alone. The morning came quickly, and I left Logan a thank you note. He was on a very different sleeping schedule than I, and I saw no reason to wake him.

The clock struck four, my work duties were done for the day. I said a quiet goodbye to my coworkers and drove home. I dreamt of a bubble bath, a glass of wine, and an early night. I stopped at the mailbox on the way and stuck the mail on the passenger seat. I made it home and kicked off my heels as soon as I was in the house. I poured myself a glass of wine and sat on a kitchen stool, glancing through the stack of mail. I picked up an envelope with familiar writing. My heart came to a halt. I looked on the back of the envelope for a return address, there was none. I quickly tore open the letter and unfolded the contents inside. My eyes read the script quickly.

Autumn,

You did not come into my world quietly, you tossed it upside down. You made me question the right from the wrong. There is a distinct mark from the moment you entered my life and the moment I left you behind. You helped me up when things went sideways and I will be forever thankful. You were able to do the impossible; to love the unlovable. I don't know what you saw in me, but I will forever be grateful. When the skies grow dark I find myself looking for you in the stars. I will hold your memory close to my heart.

My days are not easy. I have done things I regret, but your voice rings loud in my head. Your memory drives me forward. There is not much I can say or do to change what I have done in the past. All I can do now is keep my promise: I will hold on, I will not let go. Regrets are useless but just know, if there is one thing I could change, I would have come back to you sooner. I could have loved you for so much longer.

You once told me there is always light within the darkness but some people are too damaged to decipher where one ends and the other begins. They are simply stuck. You were right. But please know this, no matter what happens or where time may take us, not a day goes by that I don't love you.

Jensen.

I clutched the letter to my chest. Jensen broke through the locked confinements of my mind that I had shoved him into. My heart began to ache in longing, and fear. It sounded like he was saying goodbye.

Chapter 26

Jensen

The day Jensen left Autumn standing alone in her driveway damn near killed him. He had almost turned around at multiple points, but a small voice whispered for him to keep moving forward. He was an idiot. Why in the hell would he leave something, someone he had been missing for so long? Jensen knew how fragile life was. It could change in the blink of an eye. He should be holding on to those he treasured, not leave them behind. *You were growing restless. You have unfinished business. It's time to find out if you will sink, or swim.*

Jensen gripped his steering wheel tighter and pressed on the gas pedal. His truck surged forward and Jensen took the exit leading him out of town before he had time to turn back. This was it. Before Jensen could let someone else enter his life completely, he had to dance with the devil. He needed to know if his old allurements found him, he would be able to say no. Jensen was also fulfilling an age old promise, one he and Jake made so long ago. The summer before college, he and Jake were supposed to take a trip down the coast. They wanted to experience one last hurrah of freedom before life and all its restrictions tied them down. It was now or never. Jensen turned up the radio. He welcomed the noise, it drowned out the voices in his head. He wasn't ready to face them, not just yet.

Days turned into weeks. Jensen never stayed in one place for very long. He picked up odd jobs along the way, but he never looked under the hood of a vehicle. He didn't want to get lost in a project. He didn't want to have a reason to stay. The weather remained fair, the sky a lazy blue. The temperature had begun to drop, the air turned chilly, erasing the last remnants of summer.

Jensen pulled off the highway to fill up his tank. He bought a pack of cigarettes and tossed them in his truck. It was one habit he was no longer willing to give up. Jensen drove through an unfamiliar town and unconsciously pulled into a nearly empty parking lot. He stared at the building and its glowing sign. Jensen got out and strode inside. The bell jingled as he opened the door. He gruffly nodded at the clerk who greeted him.

His eyes remained focused on the back wall, he knew what he was after. Jensen grabbed a bottle of his seductress, whiskey. He paid for his poison and carefully stuck it under the front seat of his truck. He had a plan. He wouldn't touch it until he reached his destination, if he could make it that far. He would soon find out.

⌘

Jensen pulled off the road and parked his truck along the beach. The sun began to set; the world was being put to rest. He was restless tonight. he had been gone for close to a month now. Jensen cut the engine, grabbed his cigarettes and hopped into the back of his truck. He lit the smoke and lay in the bed of the truck, and zipped his jacket up tighter. The air had a bite near the water.

Jensen took a long drag and slowly released the cloud of smoke. He watched the white puff dance amongst the breeze, only to be taken by the sea. Jensen stared at the night sky and he listened as the waves lapped the shore. The air was salty and damp; it clung to his skin and caused him to shiver. He did not care. It was nice to feel something, anything. This trip wasn't what he thought it would be. He had hoped the farther he traveled, he would have some sort of epiphany. He wanted to feel the weight fall from his shoulders. He wanted all the broken pieces to come together and heal.

As Jensen gazed at the lights in the sky, his thoughts turned to Autumn. He hoped she knew how much he loved her. She was the only bright spot in his memory. She had done so much more for him than she could possibly know. With the touch of her hand, she had given him hope. No one dared to walk beside him, but she did. It was such a simple act of kindness and blind faith. It had opened his eyes and forced him to look at the man he had become. And it was also the reason he left.

Jensen still clung to the past and he needed to let go. He could not stay with her, he did not want to suffocate her. Her kind eyes and warm smile floated in his head. Jensen managed a grin as he thought of her. She was a powerful force. Like a hurricane, she came into his world and knocked down barriers without a second thought. She knew when to shove him forward and when it was time to gently guide him. Autumn had done something that no one could have seen coming. Not even himself. She had built him up while everyone else let him fall.

Loneliness fell heavy beside him. Jensen tossed his cigarette into the sand and sat up. He wanted to call her, to hear her voice. But he did not. He had his number disconnected, he couldn't risk any distractions. Still, he wanted to reach out to her in some way. He hopped out of the back of the truck and slid in his passenger seat. He opened the glove compartment and found a pen and paper. He wrote Autumn a letter, the first and the final. He folded it up carefully and set it aside, he would send it tomorrow. Jensen stared out at the ocean. The constant sound of the waves against the shoreline soothed him. He shifted his legs and something hit the bottom of his heel. He bent down to investigate. The familiar dread spread to his soul. It was the bottle of whiskey.

Jensen bent down and picked up the liquid. He stared at it in defiance. "Not yet. You will have to wait." Jensen shoved the bottle deeper behind the seat. He kicked off his boots and pulled at the blanket he stored in his truck. Jensen used his jacket as a pillow and closed his eyes. The sound of the water lulled him to sleep.

The next morning Jensen woke to a light drizzle. The sky was gray and dark. It suited his mood just fine. The ocean was choppy, white caps formed as the waves crashed together. Jensen stretched clumsily before he started the engine. He made a quick stop for coffee and breakfast. He took it to go. Jensen found a post office and mailed the letter to Autumn. As Jensen pulled back onto the highway he noticed his mind was quiet today. Nothing toyed with him, nothing hurt. Jensen kept his eyes forward and studied the wet road ahead of him. He took it as a sign he was heading down the right direction.

"It's beautiful out here, isn't it?"

Jensen turned to his passenger seat. Uncertainty hit him as Jake stared back at him. He was in his swim shorts and an old T-shirt. Jensen pulled his eyes back to the road. He was going crazy.

Jake let out a deep sigh and pressed his forehead to the window. "It's just as I imagined it would be. Thank you."

Jensen fidgeted, but answered this time. "We're not there yet."

"No, but you're going the right way, for once."

Jensen kept his gaze ahead. He knew there was hidden meaning in his words. Jake spoke again. "Do you mind if I stay here for awhile? I'd like to see the sunrise."

Jensen looked his way for a split second. "Stay as long as you want."

Jake nodded. "I just want to see the sun. I miss it. I'll be back when you get to the end."

Jensen glanced at the sky. "I'm not sure the sun will be out today."

Jake sat back. "It's coming. I feel it." Jake looked at Jensen. "If you wait long enough, the light will always break through the clouds." Jake looked toward the sky in anticipation.

Jensen continued driving. They drove in silence for half an hour. Jensen's eyes darted between the road and Jake. It was strange that he took comfort in the presence of the dead. But he was glad for Jake's company, whether it was real or not. Jake was supposed to be sitting beside him on this drive. It was meant to mark the beginning of their futures, and the ending of childhood. In many ways, this drive still marked a beginning and an end. The dark clouds above began to lighten. The rain came to a halt and the sun broke free. The damp road glinted like diamonds as the light teased it.

Jake grinned. "See. I told you."

"Was it worth the wait?"

"It sure was. The good things in life are always worth the wait." Jensen turned to him but he was gone. He was alone, once again in the confines of his truck.

⌘

In the still of the night Jensen awoke in a cold sweat. He sat upright and quickly opened his door. Jensen stepped in the chill of the night air. He was parked on yet another beach. During his trip, he didn't want to bother checking in and out of motels, his truck was good enough for what he needed, a place to rest his head before he went on his way. Tonight, however, he did not feel safe. The whiskey called out to him, and he wasn't ready for it. Not yet. He was so close, within an arms reach. Jensen ambled through the sand and sat on a washed up log. He let his breath come out in white puffs, and he clasped his hands together tightly. *Give me strength. Do not let me fall. I can't let go. Don't make me let go.*

"You're going to be okay."

Jensen looked over as Jake sat beside him. "I don't feel okay. I'm on the verge of falling, Jake."

"It only feels that way for now. You're so close, you will make it."

"I have too," Jensen whispered.

Jake nodded. "Take a deep breath, let the air burn your lungs. It will help you see things clearer. For tonight, put some distance between you and the bottle. Focus on the cold."

Jensen turned to Jake but he was gone. Jensen rose slowly and walked to his truck. Moonlight bounced on its dark frame, it was easy to spot in the blackness. Jensen wearily reached into his truck and pulled out the blanket. He slammed the door shut and stretched out in the back. He wrapped the blanket around him tightly, and focused on keeping the cold out. *Focus on the cold. Focus.* Jensen shifted onto his side and rolled himself into a ball. He took deep breaths and let the ocean air burn into his lungs. *Don't let go. I will not let go. I'm so close.* Jensen felt his eyes grow heavy and he was welcomed by a dreamless slumber.

⌘

Another week had passed and Jake did not return. Today, Jensen hoped he would. He was coming to the end of his trip and he hadn't given in, not yet. As the days began to pass, the only place Jensen wanted to be was next to Autumn. He wanted to go home. He was ready. Jensen pulled over to the side of the road and stepped out. He needed to stretch his legs, he had a long drive ahead of him but today, he would reach the final point where the coast broke free and the road climbed towards the mountains. Jensen took a final drag on his cigarette and crushed it into the earth.

A voice beside him caused him to jump. "Today's really the day, isn't it?" It was Jake.

"Yes. Are you ready?"

"I've been ready for awhile. Let's go."

They climbed into the truck and Jensen pulled back onto the quiet roads. He held his foot heavy over the gas, he wanted to get there as soon as he could. Jensen tapped at his wheel impatiently, the whiskey was on his mind. *It's almost time. We're almost there.* Jake remained quiet, his eyes focused on the greenery outside. The road began to climb, Jensen adjusted his speed to the winding roads. The trees were tall, they nearly blocked the sunlight with their turning leaves. Jensen slowed as he turned the truck off the main road. He drove carefully over the rough terrain that led to the bluff of the cliff. Jensen cut the engine. They were finally here.

Jensen turned to Jake slowly. "Ready?"

Jake looked at Jensen's feet and pulled out the bottle. "Take it."

Jensen stared at the glistening bottle. It was such an insignificant item. How could it have so much power over someone? Jensen found the last of his courage and swiped the bottle out of Jake's hands and stepped outside. Jake followed. They sat side by side on a large boulder, staring at the deep blue waters before them. The world was quiet and untouched. The wild things were left to grow and flourish. Down below, the waves crashed loudly against the rock bluff.

Jake cleared his throat. "So this is how it feels."

Jensen pulled his brows together in confusion. "How what feels?"

"To see the end."

Jensen felt his stomach dip. "Does it hurt?"

"No," Jake breathed. "It feels complete." Jake looked at Jensen and smiled sadly. "It's your turn."

Jensen nodded and his hands rolled the bottle of whiskey back and forth.

He took a shaky breath and slowly untwisted the cap. Jensen's hands began to tremble as the scent of his companion filled his lungs. Jensen closed his eyes, letting the aroma wrap him. Jensen rose on unsteady legs and strode to the edge of the bluff. He felt so small, but he was also caught up in the beauty around him. He focused on the water and watched the waves lap below. While it was beautiful, it was also dangerous. If you weren't strong enough, you could be swallowed alive, never to be found again.

Jensen's hand twitched, his mouth went dry. He lowered his eyes to the bottle. *Just like you. I could drown. Everything I know would be lost.* Jensen raised the bottle inches from his mouth and closed his eyes. He knew what would happen if the liquid met his lips, everything would be over, and he wouldn't care. He would retreat back into his shell and hide from the world.

The alcohol altered who he was, it transformed him into a self loathing individual. The hatred and guilt he tried to hide from found him when he was vulnerable. They tore him apart, piece by piece, and it was his own undoing. Jensen opened his eyes and in a quick motion, he tossed the bottle with a yell and watched as it fell into the depths of the ocean. Jensen crumbled to the ground and the chains he had long been carrying fell away. He almost heard them fall.

Jake sat next to him, smiling bright. "Do you see it now?"

Jensen nodded. "At first it felt so good, all the time. But then something changed."

"What changed?"

"It no longer felt good. Everything I hoped it would provide disappeared. It started to hurt, all the time. I no longer reached out to it to feel good. I *had* to reach out just to keep the pain away. It was a constant battle. One day I knew I wouldn't be able to stop. I wanted to lose myself completely. I wanted it to kill me."

Jake spoke softly. "The scars we wear don't mean we are broken. They show we got knocked down, but chose to get back up." Jake reached out and grasped Jensen's forearm. "You need to go home. You don't belong here."

Jensen let out a shaky laugh. "I don't, do I?"

"No," Jake smiled.

Jensen stood. "I'm going home." Jensen turned to his old friend. "I miss you."

Jake grinned. "I miss you, too. Just promise me one thing?"

"Anything."

"When I cross your mind, think of only the good times we had. I don't want to be remembered as the kid who had his life cut short. I want to be remembered as someone who really lived. Think of me and laugh. It's the last favor I will ask of you. Keep me alive in your own way. I don't want to be forgotten. My body may no longer walk this earth, but I'm still here."

Jensen nodded solemnly. "I promise. Take care, Jake."

Jake smiled and then he was gone. Jensen stood in the silence for quite some time. If this was all a dream, he would still hold Jake's words close to his heart. He wouldn't forget them. A chill cut through the air. It was time to go, he no longer felt welcome. It was time for him to go back to Autumn. It was time to go home.

⌘

As Jensen began his journey home, he felt light. He did the very thing he was sure he would never be able to do; he had looked his weakness dead in the eye and walked away. He never thought he would see the day, but it was here. He made it. A small part of him thought he should call Autumn to let her know he was coming back. He had been gone for close to two months, his only form of contact was a single letter. At the last minute, he decided not to call her, he wanted it to be a surprise.

Jensen was aware she could have moved on, and if that was the case, if she was happy, he would walk away. He knew the risks in leaving, and he would let her go if necessary. Jensen kept his eyes on the road and drove faster. He hoped that wouldn't be the case. He wanted to see her. He missed her and he made her a promise; he would not say goodbye. He would give her another opportunity to say hello.

Jensen had been on the road for almost three weeks and he was slowly getting closer. He decided to stick to the less scenic route, it would cut his travel time in half. His eyes were dry and heavy. He didn't set aside much time for sleep anymore, he wanted to get home as soon as he could.

He wasn't sure of the reaction he would receive from Autumn, but he chose to keep his thoughts positive. A large part of this journey was because of her. She led him into the depths of his fears and helped guide him through. While so many others would have left him there, she took him by the hand and walked with him. Coffee and energy drinks became his best friend, he would need all the help he could get in keeping him awake.

Jensen pulled into a gas station and filled up his tank. He made a mental calculation in his head, if he kept up to the rate he was going now, he should make it home within four days. Jensen screwed on the gas cap and jumped in his truck. He drove through the town, trying to find his way back to the highway. A red light stopped Jensen. He put his brakes on and grumbled, he wanted to get a move on.

The light turned green and up ahead, Jensen saw a sign guiding back to the highway. He took the corner, he had one more set of lights to go through before he was at his marker. The light stayed green. Jensen smiled and pressed on the gas a little harder. Jensen's truck began to soar. Out of the corner of his eye, something didn't look right. A large red force came at him. It shouldn't be there, the red thing should have waited, it wasn't its turn. Jensen had the green light. His brain worked slowly, still lazy from lack of sleep. And then it hit him. A cold fear fell over him, there was nothing he could do but wait. The world around him seemed to freeze, everything moved in slow motion.

Jake appeared next to him, his face twisted in agony. "No!" he screamed. "It's not your time, not like this!"

Jensen slammed on the gas and desperately hoped he could outrun the blow. The sound of brakes squealing came from all directions. Jake let out a scream and covered his ears. Jensen held his breath and waited for the impact. The large red truck came barreling toward him, his last burst of speed wasn't going to be enough to outrun the blow.

The crunching of metal and shattering of glass was sickening. Jensen was thrown forward, his chest slammed into the steering wheel and his head hit the dash with a crack. Pain enveloped him. Jensen blinked his eyes open once, but everything around him was unfocused and the world began to spin. Jensen closed his eyes and let out ragged breaths. He welcomed the darkness, but he wasn't alone. An image came to focus, and he took comfort in it. The last thing Jensen Owens saw was Autumn.

Chapter 27

Autumn

"Autumn?"

I blinked my eyes open sleepily and stared at the bed. I let out a breath of surprise as Jensen lay next to me. I scrambled up. "Jensen? Is that you?"

Jensen smiled. "I made it home."

Tears welled in my eyes as I sat up and threw my arms around him. "I've missed you so much."

Jensen tightened his grip around me and planted a kiss against my lips. "I promised you I wouldn't let go."

I pulled back and studied his face. He looked so tired, but a small smile played across his mouth. I brushed a lock of hair from his eyes and pressed my lips to his. He got out of bed slowly and took me by the hand. "We can't stay here."

Confusion swept across my face. "Why not?"

"Come with me."

Jensen led me to the bedroom door and pushed it open. He stared at me with a solemn expression. I stared in wonder at the other side of the door. I was no longer standing in my house. I stepped forward onto the wooden dock. I looked over my shoulder and Jensen was no longer standing beside me. I turned around to step back into my bedroom but the door had disappeared.

I was now alone at the lake. I hugged my arms around myself, it was cold. A heavy fog hovered over the water, and I shivered in fear. I did not want to be here. Something grabbed my arm from behind. I let out a scream and turned. As much as I wanted to close my eyes, I couldn't. They remained wide open.

Jake met my gaze. "Autumn, we don't have much time. This wasn't supposed to happen. He's not supposed to be here."

"Who?"

Jake shook his head sadly and pointed. I followed his finger and my feet began running toward the lone figure sitting at the edge of the dock. My feet came to a halt.

Jensen looked up and smiled. He patted the seat next to him. "Sit with me."

I shivered as the fog crept closer. "This doesn't feel right, Jensen. What's happening?"

Jensen frowned and looked around. He waved his hands and the fog faded. The sun broke through the trees and a summer warmth filled the air. "C'mon, sit with me. You don't know how hard it was to find you."

I sat next to him, our feet dangled in the water below. I sighed and leaned my head against his shoulder. "What happened, Jensen?"

"I made it."

I watched his face. He looked content, at peace. "I knew you would." I kissed his shoulder. Jensen drew a smile and lied back, taking me with him. We stared as the white puffy clouds drifted lazily amongst the breeze. Jensen reached out and slipped his fingers in mine. I squeezed him tightly. I had missed his touch so much.

Jensen turned his face to mine. "I forgot to tell you something."

"Oh? And what's that?" I teased.

"Hello."

I started to laugh. "Hi."

From behind us, laughter filtered through the air. I sat up quickly and looked behind me. My jaw dropped as Jensen and Jake ran toward us. Only they were teenagers. From behind me, I heard another voice coming from the water. I turned and saw myself as a young girl. I floated in the lake and yelled teasingly at the boys.

"Jensen? What's happening?"

Jensen said nothing. He continued to look up at the sky. The boys ran for me and I scrambled to get out of the way. They soared off the edge of the dock and cannon balled into the water. I stared out, and watched in wonder and fear before the vision faded before me.

I sat down next to Jensen and he leaned closer. "Autumn?"

"Yes?"

Jensen's face fell. "It hurts."

Concern swept over me. "What hurts?"

"Everything," he whispered. "I don't think I can stay here much longer." Jensen looked at me in an urgent manner. "I don't know if I can come back. I don't know how to find you."

I stared, eyes wide. I was flustered. I didn't understand what was happening. This dream wasn't making any sense.

"Tell him how you feel, Autumn." Jake's voice came from behind. "He doesn't have much time left."

I focused my eyes on Jensen and rested my hands against his face. "Jensen?"

"Yes."

"Not a day goes by that I don't love you."

Jensen placed his hands over mine and he sighed. "Thank you." He looked at Jake who watched from a distance. "How do I show her?"

Jake lowered his voice. "Are you sure you want too?"

Jensen looked at me sadly. "I think she should know. I don't want her waiting forever." He leaned over to give me another kiss. His eyes slowly swept over my face, memorizing every small detail. "I hung on for as long as I could. You were the last thing I saw."

Fear clawed at my heart. Jensen was beginning to fade away before me. "Jensen!" I screamed. "Don't go. Don't you dare leave me, not here, not like this! What were you going to show me?"

A vacant look filled Jensen's eyes. "I can't, it's happening."

I reached out to him, but he was no longer there. The sun disappeared and fog quickly overtook the land. Jake walked to me and brought me to my feet.

"What happened?" I cried.

"Wake up, Autumn."

"I don't know how."

"Wake up. Find him."

"How?!"

"Open your eyes! Find him!" Jake stepped forward and shoved me over the edge. I fell into the murky water below.

⌘

I woke with a start. I was safe in my room, in my house. I looked at my bed, it was empty. I was the only one here. I sprang out of bed and ran downstairs, hoping to see Jensen had come home. There was no sign of him anywhere. I looked outside, my truck was the only one in the drive. I sat on the couch and replayed the dream. What was that? It felt so real and it carried with it a strong sense of urgency.

"You need to find him. He can't be there."

I jumped to my feet with a squeal. I stared wide eyed at Jake. I pinched myself to see if I was dreaming. It hurt. "No. This is not real," I whispered.

"You're awake. This is very real."

"No," I stomped my foot.

Jake grew angry and he jumped in front of me. "Look!"

"I don't know where," I said meekly.

Jake shook his head. "He was almost home." I looked up and he was gone.

⌘

I told no one of the dream. The sense of urgency it had left behind stayed with me in the days that followed. I scoured the Internet looking for anything that would lead me to him. I came up empty. His parents weren't listed and I hadn't kept in touch with them over the years. After Jake's death they cut ties from this town. I grew frustrated with each day that passed. I was out of moves, I wasn't sure what to do next.

After work I came home and took Lucy for a long run. Once we got home, I went straight to the barn to my tire swing. I didn't bother to turn on any lights. The last of the daylight broke through the cracks in the boards and streamed inside. The rope creaked from above and my mind began to wander. If something had happened to Jensen, I hope somebody would have the decency to tell me. I didn't want to wonder where he was for the rest of my life.

"I don't know where to find you. I don't know where to look." I spoke to no one in particular. Secretly, I hoped for a response, but none came.

I rose stiffly and headed for the house to have a warm shower. I turned off the last of the water and stepped out of the tub. The windows were fogged from the heat of the shower. I ran my hand over the mirror and wiped away the steam. I stared at my reflection hoping to see Jake or Jensen appear. If horror movies had taught me anything, ghosts always found you in the washroom. I waited and searched. Nothing came. I slammed my hand against the sink in frustration. I was going crazy. I pulled on an old nightshirt and crawled into bed and shut my eyes.

I shifted onto my side and felt as though someone watched me. I opened my eyes and Jensen knelt by my head. He looked sad. "I don't know where to find you," I whispered. I blinked my eyes and he was gone. It all happened so fast, I wasn't sure if he had really been there. I flopped onto my back and kept my eyes tightly shut. I didn't want to see anything that made me question my sanity.

⌘

I knew I was dreaming. Everything was so still and the color was off. I willed myself to wake up before anything happened. I didn't want to see anything else. I was done. But I remained trapped in the dream. I sat in my truck with the engine running but I had nowhere to go. I felt like I had already reached my destination. Something hit the side of my window and I turned to see Jensen standing there. His palms pressed against the glass and fear marred his face as he screamed at me to get out of the car. He sounded so far away, like he was in another world all together.

"Autumn, get out of the car! Now!" Jensen reached for the door handle but the door wouldn't budge. I looked out the passenger window and saw it coming. A large truck sped my way. I knew it was too late to do anything. I was about to be hit. I glued my eyes to Jensen before the impact tossed me sideways. It didn't last long, I felt nothing. A second later, I stood in the driveway face to face with Jensen.

Jensen smiled sadly. "I can't come back anymore. You wanted to know what happened. I can show you." Jensen hesitated for a moment. "This might hurt."

Before I could say anything he pressed his hands against my face. I gasped in shock as images sped through my vision at warp speed. I was inside Jensen's truck, the sound of brakes squealed, glass shattered and a red truck sped my way. It all happened so fast yet nothing seemed to move. The impact took my breath away and Jensen released me.

"No," I breathed. "No."

Then I woke up.

I lay awake and felt cold. It couldn't be, surely somebody would have told me. But who would know about me? After everything we had been through, I refused to accept this is how things would end. I flopped around in bed, trying to find a comfortable position. It was no use, I didn't want to sleep. I didn't want to dream. I got out of bed and headed downstairs. I plucked up my guitar and sat on the porch steps. My fingers worked quickly as I picked the strings, the music floated through the still night. I played until my fingers hurt. I set the guitar down and sighed. I pressed my back into the beam and stared out into the shadows, wondering what lied within them. Tiredness finally found me. I went inside and curled up on the couch, hugging myself into a ball. I went to sleep praying tomorrow would make some sense.

The shrill ring from my phone woke me with a jolt. I jumped up in forewarning. I knew this was going to be about Jensen. "Hello?" I said frantically.

"H-hello. Is this Autumn Miller?"

"Yes. Who is this?"

"Judy Owens."

I collapsed against the kitchen counter. It was Jensen's mother. "Is he dead?" I squeaked.

"No."

Relief shot through me and I began to laugh. "Thank god. Is he okay?"

Judy cleared her throat. "He was in an accident. He's here with us now. He…he kept calling out your name and there is only one Autumn I know of. I figured it was you."

I felt a little short tempered with Judy. She hadn't answered my question. "Is he okay?"

"He will be. He has some healing to do, but overall he's lucky to be alive."

"Go on, Judy, spit it out!" I winced as the words were out. I hadn't meant to be so brash.

"His chest is badly bruised, he broke some ribs and…He was unconscious for a few days. He took a good smack to the head. He has a nasty gash down the left side of his face. It's going to leave a scar."

"Can I see him? Please."

"I hoped you would say that. Do you have a pen?"

I looked around and hopped stomach first on the counter, reaching for a pad of paper. "Yes."

Judy read out her address and I scribbled furiously. I hung up the phone and ran upstairs to gather my things. "Come on, Lucy," I hollered. "Let's go!"

I ran for the Bronco and let Lucy in first. I slid in after her and pressed my foot to the gas. I found Jensen after all.

Chapter 28

Jensen

Jensen didn't remember much from the accident. Autumn's image stayed with him until he opened his eyes. By then, he was in the hospital. Once he awoke, he had learned he had been unconscious for four days, his head had taken a good beating. There was no brain damage, for that he was grateful. The left side of his ribs were shot to hell, how he didn't break an arm or a leg, he'll never know. They monitored him for internal injuries and bleeding, and he was given the green light. When Jensen had regained consciousness, he had given the hospital his parents contact information. They were there within hours. Jensen had learned the man who drove the other truck was drunk.

Jensen couldn't help but see the irony in the situation. The other guy wasn't so lucky. He hadn't been wearing a seat belt and was thrown from the vehicle. He didn't make it. Jensen asked his dad to arrange for his truck to be towed to his parents house. He wanted to assess the damage himself and if there was a chance, he would piece her back together. His mother had been the one to break the news about his face.

Judy pushed his hair back and smiled sadly. "When they found you, a large piece of glass was lodged against your cheek. They removed it and stitched you back together. They say it's healing very well but there will be a scar."

Jensen stared ahead blankly. His face had been bugging him, it ached and burned. "How big?"

Judy squeezed his hand. "Pretty large."

Jensen pulled himself out of bed and went to the washroom despite her protests. He peered into the mirror hesitantly and stared at his reflection. "Jesus." The stitches started at the left corner of his lips and ended near his ear. "Shit." He placed his hand over his reflection in disgust. To Jensen, it looked like he was a project from the Texas Chainsaw Massacre. Any hope of ever seeing Autumn again faded before his eyes.

His parents took him home. Jensen hadn't said much. The doctor recommended a counselor for him to talk too. He crumpled the card and threw it away when he wasn't looking. There was no need for it. His parents pulled into their driveway and his eyes fell to his truck, his poor truck. He got out of the car before it came to a complete halt and walked over to his beast. The passenger side was severely crushed. Chips of red paint from the other truck marred with the black. His front tire needed to be replaced, no saving that. Jensen ran his hands over the frame slowly, calculating the work he would need to put in to it. With a few new sheets of metal, paint, wheel bearings, he could save her, he knew he could.

Jensen shook his head sadly. "Poor girl. We're quite the pair, aren't we?" *At least I can fix her.*

Jensen ignored the doctors request to take it easy and rest. If he stayed still he would drink, he could feel it. Jensen got to work by dismantling the broken parts of the truck and tossing them away. He made a few calls to old contacts for parts he needed. He asked his dad if he could pick them up, he didn't want to be seen in public. Jensen ignored the stabs of pain that tore through him as he cranked the equipment. He worked in a blind daze for three days. He didn't speak to anyone if he could help it. He had nothing to say. His world had been turned upside down on him…again. It was hard to believe a few days ago he felt as though he had a home, and someone to call his own.

Judy watched her son work on the only thing he seemed to love these days. She was worried about him, she knew how much he had been through, and the demons that haunted him. She approached Jensen carefully. "Son?"

Jensen froze for a moment then continued working. "Yeah?"

"Who is Autumn? Is it Autumn Miller by any chance?"

Jensen let his wrench fall to the ground. He turned to face his mom. "What did you say?"

Judy winced at his harsh tone. "You were calling out her name at the hospital."

Jensen's face crumpled. "I was?" He closed his eyes and once again he could see her beautiful face, her flawless unmarred face. Jensen opened his eyes and turned his attention back to his truck.

Judy marched into the house. She was a woman on a mission. She would not let her son fall into another hole. She failed him the first time. She would not do it again. Judy ran a name search through the phone database. She dialed the number she found and prayed it would be her. The voice on the other end confirmed her hopes. Judy hung up the phone and looked out the window at her son. She decided not to tell him Autumn was coming. She had a feeling he would put up a fight.

⌘

Judy sipped on a cup of tea when she saw Autumn pull in. She watched from the window carefully. She studied the girl from a distance. She had grown up to be a beautiful young woman. Autumn tucked a long strand of hair behind her ear and marched to the door. Judy tsked as she saw a dog, a rather large dog, followed her. Judy glanced at her clean house and was willing to make the sacrifice for her son. For the first time, she would allow a dog in her home. Judy opened the door before Autumn could knock. Autumn glanced up at her with startling blue eyes. Judy's eyes fell to her sidekick who sat next to her, tail wagging.

"I'm sorry," Autumn began. "Lucy goes everywhere with me and I left in a hurry. I wasn't thinking," she apologized.

Judy took a deep breath and pulled her shoulders back. "Nonsense. Come in, both of you."

Autumn stepped inside, her eyes taking everything in. She set down her bag and took a shaky breath. "I saw his truck."

Judy watched as the poor girl broke. Her motherly instinct took over and she wrapped her up in a tight hug. "He's going to be okay."

Autumn pulled back and watched her with tear filled eyes. "How is he?"

Judy knew what she was referring too. "He hasn't had a drink. He's being pig headed and refusing his pain medication. I promised him I wouldn't let him get addicted to anything else. I was going to keep an eye on them," Judy shook her head. "Emotionally he's having a hard time. His face…it won't be as bad as he thinks. Once the swelling goes down and the stitches are out, it won't be terrible at all. He's still so handsome."

Autumn smiled weakly. "Does he know I'm here?"

"No."

"Where is he?"

"His room. If he's not with that truck, he hides in there."

"Can I see him?"

"Of course." Judy pointed to the room. "Good luck."

Autumn took a deep gulp and smiled meekly. "Thanks."

⌘

Jensen sat in the dark. His mind went to very lonely places, he felt as though a part of him was forever gone. Jensen raised a finger and lightly touched his cheek. He flinched as it stung. His scar would forever be a reminder he almost made it, he was so close. A knock at his door made him look up. He said nothing, he knew it was his mom checking in on him. The door creaked open and light from the hall spilled inside.

Jensen raised his eyes slowly and his heart faltered. He couldn't be seeing what he thought he saw. "Autumn?" he nearly whispered.

"Can I come in?"

Jensen wanted to say yes with every ounce of his being. He wanted to touch her, smell her, feel her pressed against him. But he couldn't let her see him, not like this. He wasn't the same person she kept in her memory. "I don't think that's a good idea."

Autumn hesitated. "I'm sorry, but I wasn't really asking your permission. I came here to see you." Autumn stepped inside and flicked on the lamp. She closed the door behind her.

Jensen turned his good side to her and kept his eyes on the wall. "Please don't come any closer." Jensen winced as she ignored him. "Please," he begged. "Don't look at me."

But she did. Autumn knelt in front of him and placed her hands on his legs. She leaned forward and studied him softly. Jensen grew weak from her touch, he was glad he was sitting down. He closed his eyes and waited for her to revolt.

"Open your eyes, Jensen. Look at me."

He did. He found himself staring into those wonderfully kind, big blue eyes. She wore no mask of horror, no disgust. He released the breath he had been holding. Autumn moved in closer, watching him cautiously. She pressed her lips to the top of his head and gently traced her finger over his jaw.

Jensen turned his head away before she could move to his broken side. "Autumn…"

Autumn let her hand fall. "You're still my Jensen. Broken parts and all."

Jensen stood and let out a dry laugh. "No, I'm not." He met her eyes. "Who would want this? I can't even look at myself!"

Autumn stood and raised her hands to his face. She pulled them back once she realized what she was doing. "I thought you were dead," she strained.

Jensen slumped against the wall. "I made it you know. I went to the spot Jake and I talked about. I drove most of the way with a bottle of whiskey under the front of my seat." He raised his eyes to hers. "I didn't touch it. I didn't take a sip. When I got to the lookout, I finally opened the bottle. I wanted to take a sip so badly, you have no idea, but I didn't. I threw it over the edge and walked away."

Autumn placed her hands over her heart. "Jensen, that's huge. I'm so proud of you."

Jensen barked out a laugh and raised his hands, wincing as his ribs screamed. "Yeah, things worked out so well, didn't they?" He turned around and threw a punch at the wall. "I was so close goddamnit! I was coming home…to you."

Autumn caught her breath. "I'm not going anywhere, nothing has changed for me." Autumn closed the gap between them. "Do you still want to be with me?"

Jensen leaned his head back. "Yes," he croaked. "But nothing is the same anymore."

"How? You still have working limbs, don't you? You still have a functioning brain," she held her hand carefully over his chest. "You still have a strong heartbeat. Everything else will heal in time."

Autumn ran her hands down his sides ever so lightly. She clasped the bottom of his shirt and gently lifted it. She raised it higher and higher until she pulled it over Jensen's head. She ran her hands carefully over his bruises and kissed his chest softly.

Autumn studied his mouth with careful caution. "I don't want to hurt you."

"You won't."

Autumn stared at his stitches, they looked raw. She pressed her lips against his neck and on the corner of his mouth that wasn't close to the wound. Jensen felt himself go limp and he pressed her against him, taking her in a tight hug. The broken parts of him protested but he did not care, for this was a moment he was certain would never come.

"How did you know I was here?"

"Your mother called me. Lucy and I got here as quickly as we could."

Jensen looked at her in surprise. "Lucy? She's here, in the house?"

"Yes, why?"

"Huh, my mom never lets animals inside."

"What? Oh," Autumn stared at the door and made a face. "Whoops."

Jensen chuckled even though it hurt his cheek. "I guess she must really love me." He reached for his shirt and pulled it on. "I'm sorry, I'm really tired. I'm not feeling too well."

"Okay. I can let you sleep then."

Jensen grabbed Autumn by the arm. "Get that dog of yours and bring her in here. Let's go to bed."

Autumn smiled. "I haven't had a good sleep in a long time. It sounds wonderful."

Autumn cracked open the door and whistled for Lucy. She bounded in the bedroom, wiggling in delight. Autumn made sure Lucy was gentle around Jensen. Lucy settled onto the floor quickly. Autumn crawled next to Jensen. He noted she was being very careful around him as not to jostle him about.

He held her close and breathed her in. He had underestimated her, again. He had expected her to look at him as if he were a monster; she did no such thing. Her touch had made him feel wanted. Her gaze made him feel loved. Jensen let his head fall heavy against her, perhaps there was hope after all.

⌘

Jensen awoke before Autumn. He had been scared to open his eyes in the morning, fearing she was a cruel dream. But once his eyes flitted open, there she was. Autumn was fast asleep sprawled out on her side. Her chest rose in slumber, her long hair spread over the pillow. Jensen leaned forward to give her a kiss on the back of her shoulder. He winced slightly, the stitches near the left corner of his mouth hurt.

He traced a fingertip over his soon to be scar, forcing himself to accept his mark. He would never be able to escape the memory now, he would carry it with him for the rest of his days. It would serve as a reminder to the day he finally chose to walk away from his dark side. It bothered him to know people would most likely stare, and inquire as to how he got the mark. It would force him to relive his past, and he did not yet feel any pride regarding the matter.

Jensen crawled over Autumn and called to Lucy. He stepped out of his bedroom and quietly shut the door. She needed to sleep, as soon as he saw her last night he could read the tiredness heavy in her features, and knew he played a rather large part in the fact. Autumn told him about the dreams that began to plague her. They sent a shiver down his spine. They sounded familiar, like he had been there too. Jensen let Lucy outside and went in to make coffee.

Judy sat at the kitchen table, her eyes hopeful. "Good morning, how did you sleep?"

Jensen sat across from his mother. "Best sleep I've had in awhile."

"Good," Judy beamed.

"That was a risky move, Mom."

"No, it wasn't. As soon as that girl showed up on my doorstep, I knew I had made the right decision in calling her. She cares about you."

"I know."

"You care about her too, a lot, don't you?"

"Yes."

Judy sat back and smiled triumphantly. "After all these years, you two still have it. Go figure." Judy looked at him teasingly. "A *thank you* would be nice." With that, Judy winked and left the room.

"Good morning," Autumn spoke sleepily behind him.

Jensen stood and walked over to her. "Mornin'. How did you sleep?"

Autumn yawned and wrapped her arms around his waist. "Like a baby. Oh!" she said in surprise, "I'm sorry, am I hurting you?"

"Not at all."

"Okay, good." Autumn looked around. "Where's Lucy?"

"Out in the yard, I can bring her inside now."

"Are you sure your mom won't kill me?"

Jensen managed to laugh. "No, no. You're safe."

"Good."

Jensen strode to the back door and called Lucy inside. Autumn found a bowl and filled it with water for her dog. She went through her bag and fed Lucy her breakfast. Jensen busied himself in the kitchen and made their coffee. He winced when his movements did not agree with his cracked parts. Autumn watched him and tsked. She forced him to sit while she made breakfast. After breakfast Jensen went out to work on his truck. His parents had come in to say hello before taking off for the day. Jensen invited Autumn to help him.

She watched him with a curious fascination and helped where she could. For such a tiny thing, she sure was pushy. Jensen was thoroughly amused as she demanded to take over most of the heavy lifting and pulling. He watched as her muscles strained to lift this and tear away that. She pushed her hair out of her eyes and smiled proudly when she completed a task. Jensen stood back and let her have her way, even though he could have done it ten times faster despite his condition.

Out on the street a group of boys played catch. One of them tossed the ball with a solid force and it landed close to where Autumn and Jensen were working. The ball rolled toward Jensen and he bent down to pick it up without a second thought.

The young boy ran to Jensen and stopped. His eyes widened and he began to stare, curiosity heavy in his eyes. "Whoa, what happened to you?"

Autumn dropped the wrench she had been holding. It landed with a heavy clank. Her eyes flew to Jensen in worry. Jensen felt his skin begin to crawl but he forced himself to smile. "Ran into a bear."

The young boy took the ball from Jensen and his jaw dropped. "No way! How cool is that?" The young boy's friends began to call impatiently. He turned and ran to them. "Thanks!" he yelled over his shoulder.

Autumn hesitantly stood next to Jensen. He looked at her from the corner of his eye. "I guess my face is going to be a good conversation piece from now on." His tone was thick in sarcasm.

"It won't be forever. Once the swelling and the stitches are gone it won't be as noticeable. Give it time."

"Oh c'mon, Autumn. A mark will always be there, people are going to stare, they're going to ask questions." Jensen winced as a pain tore against his side. He let out a frustrated breath. "I'm done for the day. I'm going to head inside."

"Okay," Autumn said quietly. "I'll clean up the tools."

Jensen forced himself to soften his voice. "Thanks."

Jensen went inside and sat alone in the kitchen. The boy had looked at him like he was a monster. Panic washed over Jensen, how was he ever going to leave the house? How was he ever going to face the world? Jensen lifted his tormented gaze to a cabinet in the living room. He walked to it with a purpose in his step. He bent down and opened the glass door. Jensen stared into his newly found prize. He had come so far, did he really want to give in, now? He mulled it over. Yes, yes he did. His life would never quite be the same anyways.

"You don't want it." Jake spoke with a fierceness in his voice.

Jensen shot back. "Yes, I do. Go away."

Jake stomped his foot impatiently. "I wish I could. I don't want to be here. I want to go home."

"Then go."

"I can't," Jake pleaded. "Not yet. Don't be an idiot. Walk away."

"Screw off, Jake. Please." Jensen reached in and pulled out a bottle of vodka. He walked into the kitchen and grabbed a glass. He twisted off the cap and poured himself a cup.

"Jensen, no." Autumn's voice dipped in horror.

Jensen cursed, he forgot she was there. "Please don't gripe about this."

"Are you kidding me?" she shouted. "After everything that you, *we*, have gone through, this is how you're going to go out? I can't do this anymore. I can't go down this road with you every time something gets hard. That's life, Jensen. It's not always going to be all roses and butterflies, sometimes you're going to have to go through crap. You need to learn to deal with it."

Autumn took a step toward him. "I love you, you idiot. But I will not, I cannot stand by and watch you destroy yourself. It's too hard." She took a deep breath and met his eyes. "You have to make a choice. It's either me, or the alcohol."

Jensen toyed with the cup in his hand, the clear liquid sloshed about. He spoke quietly. "You know where the door is."

Autumn recoiled as though slapped. "Well then, I guess this is goodbye." Autumn whistled for Lucy and grabbed her bags. She slammed the door behind her and took off.

Goodbye. Jensen slammed his fist against the table. Autumn never said goodbye, she hated that word. Remorse coursed through him. Now he had done it, he had pushed her away. That had never been his intention. His end goal was to go home to her. *What the hell just happened? What have I done?* It was a moment of weakness, of self-hatred and despair. And now it was too late, he couldn't take it back. Jensen's grip tightened around his glass. He looked at and stood quickly. He threw the glass against the wall and watched it shatter into a million pieces.

Jensen let his head fall into his hands. He ignored the aches and pains. "I didn't even want it," he whispered.

Jensen pushed the chair back and stepped outside. He stood in front of his broken truck. His eyes focused on the damaged pieces and his anger reached its peak. Why was he here? Why did he constantly sabotage himself? Why did he have to get hit by that stupid truck when he was so close to home? Jensen picked up a crowbar and began to smash his one and only prize, quickly undoing any progress he had made.

Chapter 29

Autumn

Tears blinded my vision. I couldn't believe Jensen had dismissed me so quickly. The question had always been in the back of my mind, if given the choice, me or alcohol, what would he choose? When it came down to it, I had always thought he would have chosen me. I was sorely mistaken. I drove home in complete silence. I had even turned the radio off. The only sounds to keep me occupied was the sound of tires speeding on the asphalt. I pulled into my driveway and sat in the truck for awhile, my engine still running. I felt beaten. Lucy whined next to me and it pulled me out my trance.

"Sorry, Luce," I mumbled. I turned the engine off and stepped outside.

I blindly grabbed my bags from the backseat and dragged my feet toward the house. I let the bags fall to the floor once I was inside. I leaned against the wall and looked around. Now what? I was emotionally exhausted and I had no moves left. I gave Jensen a choice and he had chosen all right. There was no room left for me in that world. I could not, would not, watch himself disappear before my eyes. I loved him too much to watch him go out like that. I kicked off my flats and replaced them with my running shoes. I laced them up tightly, tossed my hair into a ponytail and headed out the front door.

I didn't bother warming up with a slow jog, I went all out at once. I dug my feet into the ground and pushed as hard and as fast I could go. I watched the world blend into one blurry image. My lungs burned and my breaths came out short. I hadn't run this hard in a very long time, not since after Jake had died. Running became an escape. I tried to outrun all the things I could not change. I told myself the hurt could not find me if I kept moving. I used to wish I was a machine, built solid and strong, then I could run forever.

But I was no such thing. I was human, with brittle, and delicate joints, and limbs. Today however, I was here to push those limits. I ignored the tweaks of protest from my knees and ankles. I tossed away the fact my lungs were truly on fire now. *Keep going. Don't stop. Run the hurt away. Run the anger away. Keep going.* I sounded like a freight train, breathing became difficult, but I kept going. I would have kept going forever but as my body began to exhaust itself, and I grew clumsy.

My left toe hit the dirt at an odd angle. I went down hard and fast. I held out my hands as a reflex, trying to protect my face as I met the ground, stomach first. The breath whooshed out of me and sharp stabs of pain tore my palms and legs. I lied there, face down on the roadside for quite some time.

I rested my cheek against the gravel before it was time to investigate how badly hurt I was. I dug my torn palms into the ground and pushed myself into a seated position. I swore as my favorite leggings were now torn. My knee was bleeding and my left ankle throbbed. I got up slowly and tested out my ankle. It hurt and it was already beginning to swell.

"Fantastic. Just fan-freaking tastic," I grumbled.

I distributed my weight evenly on both feet but had to readjust quickly. My left ankle would have none of that. I grabbed at my hair in annoyance and let out a yell of frustration. It felt good, so I let out another. Everything that built up inside me had a momentary release. All the anger, fear, disappointment, hurt, even love echoed in the vast landscape before me. Up ahead, my yell had scattered a herd of cattle. They ran in confusion, wondering what hidden beast was after them. I let my hands fall against my legs and hobbled for home.

⌘

Time passed quickly. I forced myself to carry on with my life as though Jensen Owens had never been apart of it. I went out with friends, went to work and did my best to fill all the empty spaces in between. I kept myself moving, I was always, forever moving. I dreaded the night for that was when his images found me, once I remained still. I saw his face in my dreams. They came in many forms. Some images were of him as a boy. Other times his face was twisted in pain when he had first come back to me.

Lately, his face was how I recently remembered it, forever marked. His soon to be scar had not bothered me, if anything, it had made me love him even more. He would have always remained my Jensen. I often thought of him and how he was doing. I tried not to dwell on those thoughts for too long for I assumed the worst had happened. I never heard from his mother again. I still had her number in my phone but I chose not to call. I had dialed it a few times, but I could never find it in me to press send. What would be the point? I chose to focus on what lied ahead, not behind.

Chapter 30

Jensen

"Are you ready?

Jensen nodded. "Yep."

The doctor worked quickly and carefully. His hands moved in an expert manner as he pulled the stitches out. The doctor smiled. "It looks good. Healed up nicely."

Jensen's eyes watched as the doctor grabbed a small mirror. "Do you want to take a look?"

Jensen took the mirror hesitantly and moved his eyes to the reflection. The scar didn't reach as far as he thought it would have. A thin, white line ran from the corner of his left mouth towards the lower half of his cheek, the rest of him remained unmarked. Jensen widened his eyes in surprise and trailed his finger along the scar. "It's not that bad."

The doctor smiled and took back the mirror. "At first some things appear to be worse than what they really are."

Jensen looked at the doctor in an accusing manner, his words reminded him of Autumn. "Yeah," he said quietly and hopped off the exam table. "Thanks for everything, Doc."

"You're welcome. Take care."

Jensen grabbed his coat and tossed it on. He stepped outside into the cool air and walked over to a blue SUV. He hopped inside and started it up, immediately missing his truck. His truck had more damage than he initially thought. He had to replace all the panels from the passenger side, the wheel bearings and axles. His driveshaft had been damaged from the impact as well as his steering column. His passenger side also needed a fresh coat of paint. Jensen had put a lot of time and effort into his truck, he worked on it 24/7.

Working on his truck was the only thing that got him up in the morning. It kept him from thinking about her. For the meantime, Jensen had rented a vehicle. It wouldn't be for long. Today his truck went in for its paint job, its final process in healing. He would pick it up in the afternoon. Jensen drove through town with no place to go. Without the distraction his truck provided him, he was faced with a new set of challenges. What was he going to do now? Jensen stopped at a coffee shop and got himself a hot drink. He sat at an outside table and watched his breath float in the wintry air.

His cell rang and he pulled it out. "Hello?"

"Is this Jensen Owens?"

"The one and only."

"This is Rick from the automotive shop. Your truck's done."

"I'll be there in five minutes."

Jensen ended the call and hopped into his vehicle. A smile spread to his face. He would have his baby back once more. Jensen dropped off his rental and walked across the street to the auto body shop. Jensen paid for the damage and soon enough sat in his front seat. He let out a content sigh and savored the moment.

Jensen turned the key and once again, his best roared like the proud lion it once was. "That's more like it," he muttered.

Jensen took his time returning home. He drove his truck carefully and tried to detect if anything still needed tweaking. It drove like a dream. Jensen pulled into his parents drive and just for the hell of it, he popped open the hood. He inspected the truck's inner workings. Everything looked as it should. Jensen closed the hood in disappointment, he hoped for a distraction. Jensen sat on the front steps and lit a cigarette. His mind turned to Autumn. His thoughts always went to her, and the last thing he said to her. He hadn't meant it. He would give anything to take it back. The last image he had of her was the look of pain and betrayal upon her face, and that was on him.

Jensen flicked his cigarette. He had wanted to call her but he couldn't find it within himself to face her. After everything he had gone through, he was going to end up alone in the end. Jensen thought it was his punishment for all of his poor choices in the past. Jensen looked up at the graying sky. This didn't feel like home to him. He no longer felt the need for people to watch over him. It was time for him to move on and find out where he belonged…again. His heart still ached for the one place he used to consider home, but it was no longer an option for him. He would have to carry the regret with him every single day.

It all came down to choices in the end. One insignificant choice can take you down a road you could never see coming. In the moment, a simple decision can seem so straight forward, can even feel right, but you have no way of knowing where it will take you. You have to have faith and follow it through. It may not always work out in the end, but as they say, sometimes you have to travel the wrong road to find out where you don't want to be. Sometimes that's just as important as finding where you belong.

Jensen put out the cigarette and went inside. The house was empty and a stack of mail was on the kitchen table. He went through it for something to do and froze when he saw a letter addressed to him. He read the return address. It was from Autumn. Jensen slipped his thumb under the seal and tore it open. His eyes drank her words eagerly.

Jensen,

I can not escape your memory. I find myself often thinking about you and I worry. Running has become a big part of my world, even more so than it used to. But I cannot outrun you. I try, but my limbs cannot move fast enough. I still see you. This is a cruel fate, is it not? I was given a glimpse of something so kind and tender, yet in the blink of an eye you took that away from me. Why? Why do you keep coming back if you're not going to hold on? I tried so hard to help you, but you kept me on the outside.

Our finest hour was dancing in the dark. It was a kind touch, a gentle word. You started a fire in my heart that simply will not die. As time passes and the days drag on, you are still with me.

But you know what kills me? That fire you started serves as no promise we get to spend our lives together. It remains a cruel taunt of what could have been. You started the blaze and it may be forever left burning for you. How could you do that to me?

I think the hardest thing of all is knowing my love wasn't good enough for you. I lost myself trying to hold on to someone who clearly didn't care about losing me. I hope you find your happiness, Jensen. I do not wish bad things for you. It is with great regret that I release you into this world just as you have done too me. The things we leave unsaid holds more of a weight than any goodbye.

Autumn

"You don't belong here."

Jensen tore his eyes away from the letter. Jake stood before him. "I can't go back."

Jake shook his head. "I don't understand you. You spend your life running from the things that cause you pain. Why in the hell are you running away from the one place, the one person who makes you happy?"

Jensen had no answer. Nothing held him where he currently was. "I don't know. I don't know how to be happy."

"Yes, you do. Don't you realize what happened? You fought your beast Jensen and you won. Don't you get that? Even now, you still chose to walk away. You did not fall, you held on."

Jensen looked up at his old friend. "You're right." Jensen looked around the house. "I don't belong here. I'm going home."

Jake stopped him. "Can we make one stop first?"

Jensen looked surprised. "Oh…sure."

Jake looked at him pleadingly. "It's important."

"Are you okay, Jake?" Concern ran thick in his voice.

Jake smiled. "Yes. I'm ready to go now."

"Go?"

"Yes. I want to go home, too."

Chapter 31
Autumn

It was a cold night. Snow would be making an early appearance this year. I ambled home from a night walk with Lucy by my side. The ground beneath me was frozen, my boots crunched as the icy layers spread over the land like a disease. My breath came out in white puffs. I pulled the toque lower over my ears, trying to keep the frost from biting. The night was clear, the stars twinkled brightly in the sky above. I felt strangely at peace tonight. Memories I had locked away over the past few months broke free, one by one. They were of Jensen, but tonight they did not hurt. I found comfort in them and took that as a sign he was okay.

I stepped into the warm house and peeled my layers off. Lucy flopped on the area rug and drifted off into a happy slumber. I made myself a cup of cocoa and curled up on the couch with a good book. I read until the words began to blur. I shut the book and placed it on the end table. I walked to my bedroom, Lucy followed sleepily. I slipped into a pair of fleece pajama pants and a long sleeve shirt. I loosely braided my hair and crawled into bed. My eyes fell closed and I was asleep within minutes.

⌘

It was bright, the sun was shining and the heat ran heavy in the late sun. I dipped my toes into the water and leaned back, the sun warming my face. The dock no longer scared me. I felt close to those I loved here. Jake sat beside me, his body language told me he was peaceful.

Jake looked over and winked. "This is nice, isn't it?"

"Yes. I miss you, Jake."

"I know. I miss you too, but I'll always be around."

"I won't be able to see you soon though, will I?"

Jake turned in surprise. "No, not like this. How did you know?"

I pursed my lips. "I don't know, just a feeling I guess. You look happy."

"I am. Everything I needed to finish is now done. I can rest."

"I'm happy for you."

Jake looked upwards and smiled. "It's happening. We're almost at the end."

I looked confused. "The end of what?"

Jake pointed. "Just watch."

The sky dimmed and the seasons sped by in a matter of seconds. The leaves changed from yellow to orange in a fluid motion. The leaves bristled and fell until the limbs of the trees were bare with the coming of winter. A layer of ice covered the lake and it cracked from the cold. The sun set and it was night. The stars burned in the sky, all was still. All was quiet. I looked at Jake and he smiled. He glanced back at me and laughed at my expression, I had no idea what was going on. A set of headlights lit up the darkness and we both turned at the sound of closing doors.

"Who else could be here?" I whispered to Jake.

Jake looked back at me. "It's time for you to wake up."

I bit my lip knowing this was our goodbye. "I don't want to. I'm not ready."

Jake smiled. "Come find me."

"What?"

"When you wake up, come find me. It's my birthday wish." Jake clasped his hands around my shoulders and shoved me backwards. I let out a gasp in surprise and began to fall into the darkness.

I awoke with a start. I shot out of bed and looked at the time, it was midnight right on the nose. "November 25th," I whispered. Jake's birthday.

I jumped out of bed and ran downstairs. I bundled up and shoved on my boots. I grabbed my keys and slid in the Bronco. The engine started and I took off into the night. I drove carefully as the roads were icy. My headlights cut through the darkness and I turned off the main path in the road.

My vehicle bounced as I drove over the low lying brush. This was as far as my vehicle would take me. I grabbed a flashlight out of my glove box and stepped into the night. My boots snapped at the twigs scattered on the ground. I picked my way carefully until I walked the familiar shore of the lake. I approached the dock and stopped. Something moved ahead. My heart jumped into my throat, the silhouette looked big. I cursed at Jake, if he had led me to death, I would…well, I would kill him. A small flash of light came from the silhouette, whoever it was had a flashlight as well.

The small beacon of light moved forward. I stepped back and yelled. "Stay back. I swear if you come any closer I will drop you to the ground."

The light did not listen. I froze in fear and gripped my flashlight harder. I could use it as a weapon if I had too. The beam stopped inches away from me. I looked up and heart flip flopped.

The image before me smiled. "I didn't let go."

My eyes opened wide. "Jensen? Is that you?"

"I'm here. I found my way back."

I took a step back. "I'm dreaming, aren't I? Oh god, I've gone crazy."

Jensen let out a low lying chuckle. "No, this is very real," Jensen spoke quietly. "I got your letter." He let out a sigh. "I want to apologize, Autumn, for everything I have done. I just want you to know, the last thing I said to you, I never meant it. It was a moment of insecurity and I took it out on you. But you should know…I never had that drink."

I squinted my eyes and stepped toward him, and pressed my hands to his chest, at first hesitantly. I glanced up at him one more time before I lightly swatted him. "Just making sure you're real," I muttered. I paused and bit my lip. "Can you help me with something?"

"Anything."

"Can you lean forward so I can see your face? I mean really see it."

Jensen leaned forward. I kept my eyes glued to him and took his face between my hands. I noted his strong jaw, his laugh lines, and the small scar that marked his journey. I sighed. "It is you." I stepped back. "What are you doing here?"

Jensen spoke matter-of-factly. "Jake."

I nodded knowingly. "It's his birthday."

Jensen smiled and led my by the hand to the edge of the dock. He sat and dragged me with him. We lied down on the cold wood and let our feet dangle off of the edge. He kept my hand locked in his. I smiled as we turned our heads toward each other. "I once had a dream that slightly resembled this."

Jensen smiled softly. "You told me."

I nodded. "I remember." I looked at the sky and despite the cold, a warmth spread throughout my body. All the broken little pieces life had scattered about came together. All the wrong turns had led me, us, to this moment. The things that once hurt, had hurt for a reason and I needed to face them. We both did. Whether I had realized it or not, I was a little broken, and needed to accept that the broken pieces were not the end, they were a beginning. They served as a reminder that I had lived, and I had loved. I had also been forced to say goodbye.

Jensen squeezed my hand tearing me away from my thoughts. "Happy birthday, Jake," he whispered.

Though neither of us could see it, Jake stood behind us. He smiled softly. "Happy birthday to me." Jake let out a heavy sigh. "I can finally go home." Jake looked at us for one last time before he faded into the night, a smile on his lips.

Jensen turned to me. "There's something I need to tell you."

I shifted to him. "What is it?"

Jensen grinned. "This is long over due but here it is. Hello."

I smiled slowly. "I'm sorry I said goodbye." My eyes fell to the crystal sky. "Do you think Jake's up there?"

Jensen gazed upwards. "I think so."

I nodded and kept my voice to a whisper. "Black as night, the dark is the light, and I will forever mourn. I speak to you in the thousand winds that blow, your memory will forever grow. Though your time was short, you are always here, in our hearts." I sighed. "Happy birthday, Jake."

Jensen pulled me against his chest. His heart beat loudly in my ear. I smiled. He didn't lose himself along the way, he never let go. He never let me go. He was home.

⌘

Some people are meant to come into your life for a reason though it doesn't always mean they will stay forever. Everyone has a lesson to teach, everyone has a different story. Where one has an ending, some of us are only beginning.

There comes a time when you need to walk away from all the things that hurt you. What's left standing after you fall, well, that's entirely up to you. Jensen and I were damaged. We carried with us a tragedy neither of us wanted to remember. We challenged each other in so many ways; we pushed each other to the edge of our breaking points. We forced each other to face the things we didn't want to see in order for us to conquer the fears that paralyzed us. Good things don't come easy, but then again, anything worth fighting for will be well worth it in the end. We found the beauty within the broken.

Sometimes you need to be lost in order for you to find yourself. Jensen and I got lost along the way. We took our hits, our bumps and our bruises, but we made it to the other side. We climbed out from the rubble and we fought, we fought hard to find our way back home. Our story was far from over. In so many ways, we were just beginning. We didn't build it up to watch it fall. We built it up to last a lifetime.

Katt Rose

is an aspiring writer who has a love of music, animals, and writing. Katt worked in the health care field but she could not silence the stories inside her head. Once she began to write, she knew there would be no turning back. She was home.

A message to my Readers

If you enjoyed "Building It Up", please leave me a review on my Amazon page, the more reviews the easier it is for others to find me. You can also check out my other books there as well, or check out my website at

http://kat-rose-c1r1.squarespace.com/